The Jewels of Texas

From Ruth Langan

Diamond, Pearl, Jade and now Ruby

Ruby Jewel had never met the man
she could resist…

Quent Regan had never met the
woman he couldn't…

It looked as though the town of
Hanging Tree, Texas,
would never be the same

Dear Reader,

USA Today bestselling winning author Ruth Langan is back this month with *Ruby,* the next book in her ongoing series THE JEWELS OF TEXAS. This delightful tale of a flirtatious young woman and the formidable town marshal who falls under her spell is sure to please, whether you've been following the series all along or are discovering it for the first time. And keep an eye out for the story of the Jewel sisters' long-lost brother, *Malachite,* coming in early 1998.

The Forever Man is a new title from Carolyn Davidson, the author of *Gerrity's Bride.* It's the story of a spinster who has given up on love, yet discovers happiness when a widower and his two sons invade her quiet life. And Sharon Schulze, one of the authors in this year's March Madness Promotion, also returns this month with *To Tame a Warrior's Heart,* a stirring medieval tale about a former mercenary and a betrayed noblewoman who overcome their shadowed pasts with an unexpected love.

In *The Lieutenant's Lady,* her fourth book for Harlequin Historicals, author Rae Muir begins an exciting new Western series called THE WEDDING TRAIL. This month's story is about a hard-luck soldier who returns home determined to marry the town "princess," a woman who sees him as little more than a way out of an unwanted marriage.

Whatever your tastes in reading, we hope you enjoy all of our books, available wherever Harlequin Historicals are sold.

Sincerely,

Tracy Farrell
Senior Editor

Please address questions and book requests to:
Harlequin Reader Service
U.S.: 3010 Walden Ave., P.O. Box 1325, Buffalo, NY 14269
Canadian: P.O. Box 609, Fort Erie, Ont. L2A 5X3

Ruth Langan

Ruby

Harlequin Books

TORONTO • NEW YORK • LONDON
AMSTERDAM • PARIS • SYDNEY • HAMBURG
STOCKHOLM • ATHENS • TOKYO • MILAN
MADRID • WARSAW • BUDAPEST • AUCKLAND

ISBN 0-373-28984-7

RUBY

Copyright © 1997 by Ruth Ryan Langan

Printed in U.S.A.

Books by Ruth Langan

Harlequin Historicals

Mistress of the Seas #10
†*Texas Heart* #31
Highland Barbarian #41
Highland Heather #65
Highland Fire #91
Highland Heart #111
†*Texas Healer* #131
Christmas Miracle #147
†*Texas Hero* #180
Deception #196
*The Highlander #228
Angel #245
Highland Heaven #269
‡*Diamond* #305
Dulcie's Gift #324
‡*Pearl* #329
‡*Jade* #352
‡*Ruby* #384

†Texas Series
*The Highland Series
‡The Jewels of Texas

Harlequin Books

Harlequin Historicals Christmas Stories 1990
"Christmas at Bitter Creek"

RUTH LANGAN

traces her ancestry to Scotland and Ireland. It is no surprise, then, that she feels a kinship with the characters in her historical novels.

Married to her childhood sweetheart, she has raised five children and lives in Michigan, the state where she was born and raised.

To Patrick Jacob Langan,
the newest jewel in our family crown.
And to his proud parents,
Pat and Randi.
And, of course, to Tom,
patriarch of the dynasty,
and the love of my life.

Prologue

Bayou Rouge, Louisiana
1865

"I've missed you. Missed this." Onyx Jewel lay in the bed watching as Madeline St. Jacque began to brush the tangles from her hair. She had pulled on a silk wrapper and tied it carelessly at the waist, leaving more of her lush body exposed than covered.

He glanced around the room, which was like the woman who occupied it. A curious mixture of elegance and simplicity. The bed was large, the mattress down filled. Satin streamers in vibrant shades of crimson and violet hung at the four corners, and sheer netting draped the sides. The bed was mounded with dozens of pillows in rainbow hues. On the floor was the rug he'd had made just for her. Imported from Constantinople, it was woven with intricate flowers and butterflies in exotic colors. She had wept when she'd seen it, and had run barefoot over it, laughing like a child.

In many ways she was a child, he thought. Afraid to leave this hot, steamy little place she'd always called home. Afraid to take a chance on the life he offered her. And yet, he could never forget she was a woman. And what a woman. With one haughty look, one impish smile, she had captured his heart.

"When are we going to talk about Texas?"

Instead of turning, she studied his reflection in the looking glass. "I do not wish to speak of your little wilderness," she said with a pout.

"My...little wilderness is bigger than the whole territory of Louisiana," he said tiredly. They'd had this conversation before. And it always ended the same way.

"Why can you not come here to live in Bayou Rouge?" she demanded.

"Because I make my living in Texas, Madeline. And it's a very good living."

"I am a genteel woman," she said, setting down the brush with a clatter. "I would never survive that—" she wrinkled her pretty little nose "—primitive place you call home."

"It isn't primitive. I'll grant you, my ranch is miles from the nearest neighbor."

"You see?" she interrupted.

"But we have all the comforts a civilized person would crave."

"*Oui.* With savages and pestilence and wild beasts."

He grinned. He couldn't help it. He loved it when she got angry, and those brown eyes flashed, and her accent deepened. "Come here," he said in a growl.

She did turn then. Her little pout dissolved into a smile. "I have just fixed my hair. And you said you wanted to go to Ruby's school and visit her."

The school had been another battle he'd lost. He would have preferred tutors, instead of the rigid demands of the convent school. But Madeline, as always, had fought like a wildcat to have her daughter attend the same school that the St. Jacque women had attended for generations.

"We'll go. Soon." He held out his hand.

She crossed the room, disrobing as she walked.

His reaction was always the same. Just looking at the sway of her hips, the jut of her firm, lush breasts, he was lost. Madeline St. Jacque was the most sensual, desirable woman Onyx Jewel had ever known. And from their first meeting, he'd found himself bound to her. Despite the difficulty of spanning the miles between them, and the futility of ever hoping to coax her to make her home with him, he found himself unable to resist her charms.

"Sister Dominique." The Mother Superior of the Convent of Notre Dame du Bayou summoned the old nun to her office.

"*Oui*, Reverend Mother?" Considered unfit to teach, the elderly sister helped with domestic chores around the convent and, despite fingers swollen with arthritis, saw to all the sewing and mending.

"Go to Sister Clothilde and fetch young Ruby Jewel. Tell her that her mother and father are here."

Sister Dominique cast a sideways glance at the stranger seated beside Madeline St. Jacque. *Mon*

Dieu. He was the most dashing creature she had ever seen. No wonder the proud, headstrong Madeline, long considered the most beautiful woman in the bayou, had been persuaded to forsake her virtue. Her indiscretion had fueled the town gossips for years.

"At once, Reverend Mother."

The old nun made her way along the cool, darkened passageway that connected the convent with the classrooms. She paused a moment outside the door of Sister Clothilde's room, struggling to catch her breath. From inside she could hear the children chanting their answers in singsong fashion. Suddenly the chanting stopped, and their teacher's strident voice could be heard scolding one of her pupils.

Sister Dominique flinched, remembering her own moments of humiliation at the hands of such teachers. Sister Clothilde's methods of discipline were notorious. A first-time infraction meant a crack of the hands with a ruler. If a pupil was foolish enough to pull the hand away, the punishment would be doubled. For a second-time offense, it would be a willow switch, administered across the backside, often so firmly the receiver would be unable to sit for days. For any offense after that, it meant time in the box. That was what the students called the hot, airless closet in the back of the room in which Sister Clothilde stored her supplies. In this fierce bayou heat, a child could endure only a few minutes in the box before begging to be released. That would be followed by a public apology and a stern lecture to sin no more. The rest of the day would be spent scrubbing floors as an act of contrition. And woe to those who erred late in the day. It meant going without supper, to finish the penance.

Sister Dominique knocked, then opened the door to the classroom in time to see the recalcitrant pupil holding out her hand for her discipline. As the ruler cracked over her knuckles, the old sister had to look away. When she looked back, she had a glimpse of Sister Clothilde's face. It bore a chilling, satisfied smile.

"What is it, Sister Dominique?" the nun asked sharply. "Why do you interrupt my schedule?"

"Reverend Mother has sent me to fetch Ruby Jewel."

"Ruby?" She arched a suspicious brow. "Why?"

"Her mother and father are here."

The teacher's eyes narrowed. "Her father is here?"

"Oui." Though the old nun lowered her eyes, there was no mistaking the excitement in her voice. She had finally seen for herself the mysterious Onyx Jewel.

"Ruby cannot come right now," Sister Clothilde said sternly.

"But Reverend Mother—"

"Ruby is being punished."

The older nun cast a furtive glance at the back of the room. The closet door was closed. There was no sound from within. She waited the space of several heartbeats before asking, "Has she not been punished long enough?"

"For that one, it is never long enough. But this

time she will learn. She has been there over an hour.''

"An hour." The old woman stifled a gasp. Thinking quickly, she gathered her courage. She was not the only one unfit to teach the children. This time, Sister Clothilde's act of cruelty had gone too far. "The time she has already spent will have to serve as punishment. Reverend Mother has sent for her. I dare not go back without her. However, if you wish to explain to Reverend Mother yourself..."

Seeing the wisdom of avoiding such a discussion with Mother Superior, Sister Clothilde strode to the back of the classroom and opened the door.

There was no movement within.

"Ruby Jewel, you may come out now and confess your guilt," Sister Clothilde commanded in a shrill tone.

Around the classroom the children fidgeted. Though they were accustomed to their teacher's cruel taunts of this particular classmate, and often enjoyed them, it was plain that this time had been worse. They were highly agitated.

"I said, come out of there." The nun stepped inside, then took a quick step back.

It took her a moment to catch her breath. The enclosure was a steam bath. Leaning down, she dragged the still form of the child from the closet.

Twelve-year-old Ruby's auburn curls were plastered in wet tendrils to her neck and cheeks. Her skin was the color of chalk.

"She is dead!" Sister Dominique's tone was filled with accusation.

"She is nothing of the kind." Sister Clothilde touched a finger to her throat. Finding a pulse, she turned to the old nun. "Fetch some water."

When Sister Dominique returned with a brimming glass, Ruby Jewel was sitting on the floor, leaning weakly against the wall. As soon as the tumbler of water was held to her lips, she drank gratefully.

Sister Clothilde stood over her, showing no emotion. When the glass was empty she said, "Ruby Jewel, you will admit your guilt and repent."

Ruby lifted her head and met her angry look. But though her lips trembled, she refused to speak.

The nun's eyes narrowed with suppressed anger. "You are a foolish, headstrong child. But for now, you have earned a reprieve. You have been summoned by Mother Superior. I cannot keep her waiting. Go. But be warned. I have not finished with you."

Numbly the child stood and, on rubbery legs, followed Sister Dominique from the room.

As they made their way along the passageway, the old nun said, "You must have done something very sinful to have earned so much time in the box."

The child held her silence.

"What did you do?" Sister Dominique persisted gently.

"I called Sister Clothilde a liar." The voice was low, breathless. And defiant.

Sister Dominique stopped short, covering her mouth with her hand. "You didn't."

"I did." Ruby's voice was a fierce whisper.

"But why, child?"

"Because she called my mother a harlot."

Tears welled up in the old nun's eyes and she struggled for composure. "No one has the right to say such things about your mama, child. I will pray for Sister Clothilde, that God will soften her heart."

Alarmed at this unusual display of emotion, Ruby patted the old nun's thin shoulder. "Don't worry about me, Sister Dominique. I'll be just fine. Here." She reached into her pocket and withdrew a large brown rosary, pressing it into the gnarled hands. "When you pray tonight, think of me."

"But child. Wherever did you get this?"

A sly smile touched Ruby's lips. "I took it from Sister Clothilde's pocket when she wasn't looking."

"You stole?" The old nun was horrified.

"*Non.* Mama says that is not stealing. If someone is horrible, or cruel, or harms another, it is our petit vengeance."

"But Ruby," the old nun said, "no matter what you call it, you must not do it."

"And why musn't I?" the child demanded.

"Because it is one of God's commandments. Thou shalt not steal."

"And another of God's commandments is to honor thy father and mother," Ruby said logically. "That makes Sister Clothilde as guilty as I. She said I was just like my mother. She called me a spawn of the devil."

For once, Sister Dominique had no words. But she knew she had never met a more cruel, heartless person than Sister Clothilde, nor a more headstrong, defiant and courageous person than this child.

Courageous. That was what she needed to be now. Perhaps, she thought, this was why she had been spared death for so long. There was a task God was asking of her.

Sister Dominique stiffened her spine. She knew why Sister Clothilde had entered the convent. To escape an abusive father. But she hadn't escaped. She'd brought him with her. His cruelty lived inside her. And now she must be stopped, before she was allowed to do further damage to this child.

Sister Dominique still had some influence with Mother Superior. For Ruby's protection, she would beg to be given exclusive control over this child's tutoring. It could prove to be Ruby's only salvation.

"Come," she said. "Pinch some color into your cheeks and put on your best smile. You must put aside your troubles, for your papa is waiting."

"Perhaps he has come to take my mama and me back to Texas with him," Ruby whispered excitedly. "Oh, if only Mama and I could escape this place."

Beside her, the old nun echoed the same request in a prayer.

The reunion with her father had been, like all the others, far too brief. But Ruby had put on a brave face, and had absorbed all the pleasure she could from his visit.

But when he rode off—alone, as always—she could no longer hide her tears.

"What is this? Is my baby crying?" Madeline St. Jacque caught her daughter's chin as the girl tried to hide her tears. "Did you fall? Are you ill, child?"

Ruby pulled away, embarrassed at having been caught in a rare display of weakness. "It is nothing, Mama."

"Nothing?" Madeline watched as her daughter struggled to compose herself. "I think not. Now, tell me."

But Ruby couldn't tell her mother about the things that were said behind her back. To do so would be to break her poor mother's heart.

As if reading her mind, Madeline said, "Ignore what others say, Ruby. What do they know? Your papa and I love each other and we both love you. That is all that matters. And we are rich in love."

"If Papa loves us," Ruby persisted, "why does he live in Texas, while we remain here in the bayou?"

"Because," Madeline said patiently. She had said this hundreds of times, until she had almost convinced herself, if not her daughter. "Life here, simple as it is, seems better than living in some primitive wilderness." She wrinkled her pretty little nose. "As I have told your papa, I am a genteel woman, Ruby. I deserve better than that."

"But Papa—"

"Papa loves us. You will see. In time, he will come to his senses and make his home here with us."

"But he told you he must earn his livelihood in Texas, Mama. Why won't you believe him?"

Madeline merely smiled her mysterious woman's smile. "Onyx Jewel will come around in time, *chérie*. You will see. Remember this always. The wise woman does not bend. If someone bends, it must be your papa. He loves us too much to live without us. In the meantime, we will hold our heads high and ignore the taunts of others.'' She pursed her lips in distaste. ''What do those fools know?''

What, indeed? Ruby thought. But when her mother walked away, fanning herself in the heat, the cruel taunts of Sister Clothilde and her classmates crept back into her thoughts.

To escape the pain, Ruby concentrated on the image of her handsome father, and his life in that strange place called Texas. One day she would go there with him. And then everything would be different. Life in Texas would be perfect.

Chapter One

Hanging Tree, Texas
1870

"**Y**ou move a muscle, Marshal, and it'll be the last you'll ever move." The gunman holding a pistol to Marshal Quent Regan's temple motioned to his brother. "Get his gun, Ward."

"Why can't you do it, Boyd?"

The older brother swore loudly, fiercely. "Because it's my gun aimed at him, you coward. And my whip wrapped around him. The least you can do is take his gun."

"I'm afraid."

Boyd swore again. "The damned fool can't even move. How can you be afraid of him?"

"'Cause he's still got that gun at his hip, that's why. There's nobody faster in all of Texas than Marshal Regan. Just ask the Bruebaker brothers. They're both dead. And they both had their guns trained on him."

The gunman brandished his weapon. "I'm sick of your babbling. We're not the damned sniveling Bruebakers. We're the Barlows. And soon everybody's going to know about us. Now, get his gun."

Ward crept closer, all the while keeping a careful watch on the man with the badge. His hand snaked out and he slid the marshal's gun from its holster. As soon as he had it, he took several quick steps backward.

"Now what are you going to do, Marshal?" Boyd taunted.

Quent Regan's eyes narrowed. The sleeves of his coat were torn and blood soaked where the whip had bitten through the cushion of fabric to tear away his flesh. The ambush had been carefully planned, giving him no chance to escape. "This is your hand, Boyd. Go ahead and play it."

"Oh, I'll play it, all right." The gunman's weapon fairly shook with excitement. "I'm about to kill the meanest, toughest lawman in Texas. Maybe in all the West. You know how many men are going to look up to me when this is over?"

"You'll probably find a couple."

"More like hundreds, I'd say. Every outlaw from here to St. Louis is going to be looking to shake my hand."

Seeing the way the gunman was enjoying himself, the marshal said, "Oh, they'll congratulate you. Then they'll stalk you, just the way you stalked me. So they can brag about killing the man who killed Marshal Quent Regan. But, hell, Boyd, it'll be worth it, won't it? I mean, everybody will know your name.

At least for a few weeks, until the next slimy coward comes along to make a name for himself.''

"He's right," Ward muttered. He kept glancing over his shoulder, expecting a blaze of gunfire at any moment. "They'll be gunnin' for us, Boyd."

"You shut your mouth. He's just trying to spook us." Boyd cocked his pistol and reached out with his other hand to snatch the shiny badge pinned to the marshal's cowhide jacket. "You won't be needing this."

"And you will?" Quent Regan's voice was carefully controlled, betraying none of the emotion churning in his gut. In all the years he'd worn that badge, it had been hit with gunfire, sullied with the mud of battles and the blood of outlaws. But until today it had never left its place of honor over his heart.

"Always wanted one of these shiny tin badges." Boyd shoved it into his pocket. "How about you, Ward? What do you want?"

When the younger brother said nothing, Boyd taunted, "Come on. He's not going to have any use for his things." He glanced down. "How about his boots?"

"They're nice," Ward admitted. "I guess I could use 'em. And the jacket, too."

"See there, Marshal? Looks like you're going to die naked." Boyd jammed his gun hard against the marshal's temple. "We'll take the jacket first."

Quent glanced down. "I seem to be restrained at the moment. Would you mind removing your whip?"

"Don't do it," Ward called. "I don't trust him."

"You shut your mouth." Boyd uncoiled the barbed strips of rawhide that had become his trademark.

When he was free, Quent reached a hand to the buttons of his coat, and Boyd jolted back, bringing both hands to his weapon.

The marshal gave him a cool, appraising look. "Sorry. Didn't mean to scare you."

"I'm not scared. Not of you. Just cautious." The gunman swaggered a bit, to prove to his brother that he was still in control. "Now, take off the coat, nice and slow."

Quent did as he was told. When it dropped to the ground, Boyd picked it up and tossed it to his brother. "Sorry about the blood, Ward. But it'll still keep you warm. Now the boots, Marshal."

"Might take some doing." Quent motioned toward a nearby rock. "Mind if I sit?"

"Not at all. But make it quick." Boyd followed, keeping his pistol aimed at the marshal's head.

Quent sat and started working his foot out of the first boot. While he did, he assessed the situation. The younger brother, Ward, should be easy. As far as Quent knew, he hadn't killed anyone. That meant he'd be reluctant to start with a lawman. Besides, he was already distracted, trying on the jacket. But the older one, Boyd, was another matter. He'd already killed six people that Quent knew of. And maybe more that he hadn't heard of. That made this outlaw two things. Dangerous and desperate. What was worse, he was proud of his record as a killer, and was hoping to enhance it by adding a lawman to his list of victims. Boyd Barlow was a man who enjoyed killing.

As he reached into the second boot, Quent's fingers closed around the extra gun he always carried.

He needed to keep these two talking.

"You intend to wear that badge?" he asked.

"Damned right." Boyd withdrew the badge from his pocket and began to pin it over his chest. "Why, with this tin star I'll be able to ride right up to any ranch and get invited in for supper." He threw back his head and laughed. "They'll think they're feeding a damned lawman. And then, when they're relaxed, I'll just help myself to the rancher's wife, and maybe even his kids, before I kill 'em all."

"That's a good one, Boyd." Ward threw back his head and roared at the thought of his brother posing as a lawman.

The two brothers had identical high-pitched laughs that scraped over the nerves. Both were lean and lanky, with long blond hair and reddish mustaches that drooped over their mouths.

"Yeah. Real funny." Quent knew there wouldn't be time to aim. But he hoped to be able to take down one of them. At least that would even the odds.

Using his boot to shield the gun from view, he squeezed the trigger. The first shot slammed into Ward.

Startled, the gunman spun away, one arm still fumbling with the sleeve of the jacket. Then he dropped to his knees, holding his chest.

On the other side of the rock, Boyd dropped to the ground and took careful aim at the marshal.

Only his quick reflexes saved Quent's life. He flattened himself behind the rock and counted the shots as they ricocheted around him.

"Boyd. Help me, Boyd. I've been hit."

Ward's cries brought another hail of gunfire from his brother's gun, but from a different location.

Quent Regan gritted his teeth, waiting for the volley to end, wondering how much more ammunition the gunman carried, and where he'd head next.

He peered around the rock. Ward lay on the ground, an ever-widening pool of blood spilling from the wound in his chest.

"I'm dyin', Boyd. I'm..."

In the eerie silence that followed, Boyd's voice rang out. "Don't you touch him. Don't you touch my brother."

"You fool. You want him to die?" Quent waited, hoping his words would bring the older brother out of hiding.

"I swear to you," came Boyd's strangled voice, "if he's dead, so are you. Do you hear me, lawman? Any man who kills my brother, he has to pay the same price."

Quent gauged the location of Boyd's voice, then checked the bullets in his gun, before leaping to his feet and firing.

The spot where Boyd had taken cover was empty. The gunman had managed to slip away again.

Quent turned at the sound of hooves and watched in disgust as horse and rider disappeared into a line of trees. He'd already sprinted to his horse and vaulted into the saddle, prepared to give chase, when he heard Ward's voice.

"Water," Ward called in a trembling voice.

Quent Regan swore. There was no time to waste. If he didn't catch Boyd now, by this time tomorrow he could be anywhere, from Mexico to Indian Territory. Wearing a marshal's badge. Preying on innocent people.

With another vicious oath, he slid from the saddle and removed his canteen.

Hours later, when Ward Barlow had finally given up his life, Quent removed his jacket from the body and slipped it on. That done, he caught up the reins of the two horses and prepared to head for town.

As he rode, Marshal Quent Regan rubbed at the crusted blood of his wounds and thought about his pledge to keep this little section of Texas safe for all the people who called it home.

Sometimes it exacted a high price indeed.

"Oh, Papa." Ruby Jewel knelt beside her father's grave and crossed herself, then whispered a little prayer. "You know I'm happy to be here in Texas. But my heart is heavy because it was your death that brought me to your home."

She touched a hand to the mound of earth beside her father's grave. "I hope you'll forgive me in time, Mama, for having your remains brought here. I know you would have preferred an elegant marble crypt at your beloved cathedral in Bayou Rouge, where you would have heard the familiar strains of the choir lifted in hymns of praise. But here you can enjoy a different kind of choir, Mama. The sigh of the wind. The mournful cry of a coyote. The call of an eagle. Besides—'' Her voice caught in her throat and she had to swallow hard before she could go on. ''It comforts me to know that you and Papa are together at last. It's all I ever wanted, you see. The three of us together. A normal family, like the others in Bayou Rouge.''

To chase away her melancholy mood, she began chattering in a mixture of English, French and Cajun as she dug in to the pocket of her gown and began laying out an assortment of colorful beads. ''I've brought you something to cheer you, Mama. I know how much you always loved pretty things.'' A sly smile touched her lips. ''A peddler came to town offering the townspeople shabby wares. I saw him cheating a sweet old lady, the widow Purdy. Would you believe? He was selling vile-smelling bottles of creek water and dried weeds, and trying to pass them off as beauty creams and elixirs. But when I pointed out what they were, he denied it. And as he took her money he was most rude. So Mama—'' she wrinkled her nose, as her pretty mama always had ''—I had my petit vengeance.''

She held the beads up to the light, watching the way they glittered and gleamed. ''Which one do you like best?''

As if actually hearing her mother's voice, she chose a string of deep purple glass and laid it over Madeline's grave. ''You're right, of course. This one suits you. If you don't mind, I'll save the rest for Diamond, Pearl and Jade.''

At the mention of their names her smile deepened. ''Oh, Papa, I was so hurt at first when I discovered that you had other daughters. Hurt and disappointed. But now I am learning to care for them. Sisters.'' Her laughter was as fresh and lilting as a child's. *''Mon Dieu.* Who would have believed I would discover sisters? And because they now have husbands, I find myself with three brothers, as well.'' She clapped her hands together, as she often did when she was delighted. ''Adam, Cal and Dan are all so handsome. And kind. And they make my sisters so happy.''

A long sigh escaped her lips, though she wasn't aware of it. ''I am happy for them. But sad for myself. They are all so busy and active. Diamond and Adam have their ranch, which they work together. And, of course, the baby that will soon be born. Pearl has found so much love with Cal, and is teaching the town's children. And they are so pleased with Gil and Daniel, the two boys they have adopted. And Jade and her beloved reverend are so busy being an inspiration to everyone in Hanging Tree, they barely have time to eat or sleep.'' Ruby bit her lip. ''My life, compared with theirs, is rather meaningless. But what can I possibly do here in Texas? The only things I know are silly and frivolous. The good sisters despaired of ever teaching me much of anything. Except Sister Dominique, of course. It was she who took the time to teach me how to sew a fine seam.''

She stood and shook the dust from her elegant red

satin gown. "Oh, Mama, you must be ashamed of the way I look. But there are few frocks of beauty in Hanging Tree. I was so desperate for a new dress, I had to send for a bolt of fabric from St. Louis and make my own. Pity the poor women who cannot sew, or who have no time for such luxuries. They are at the mercy of Rufus Durfee, whose ready-made dresses are not even fit for working the fields."

The words she had just spoken struck her with the force of a lightning bolt. "*Dieu!* But of course!" The words tumbled from her lips in a torrent, as they always did when she was excited. "Here I have been wondering what I could do to fill my days in this strange place. Why not busy myself with the things I love? Oh, Papa. Oh, Mama. If I were to open a little dressmaking shop, I could not only have the lovely things I crave, but I could also fill a real need for the others in the town."

She lifted her skirts and twirled around and around. "I would no longer feel different. Like Diamond, Pearl and Jade, I would have something to offer the people of your town, Papa."

She blew a kiss toward the graves. "Forgive me, Mama and Papa. I must bid you adieu and hurry to make arrangements."

Leaving the purple beads on the grave, she stuffed the others into her pocket and climbed into the rig. With a flick of the reins, she headed toward the ranch in the distance, her mind already racing through details.

Ruby Jewel had never been noted for her reticence. And now, the very thought of beginning her new project had her energized. Thank heaven her papa had left a considerable estate. Of course, it was not hers for the taking. But if her sisters approved her project, she could begin at once.

She would need a building in town, where she could display her wares and attract customers. And she would have to send for exotic fabrics. Not the drab gingham and homespun found at Durfee's Mercantile. *Non.* She would offer the women of Hanging Tree silks and satins and feathered bonnets. As a new thought struck, she laughed aloud. Perhaps she would whip up some of Mama's balm, as well, and sell it in little vials. After all, her mother's smooth, unlined skin had been the envy of every woman in Bayou Rouge.

She touched a hand to her own skin, so like her mother's. Didn't the women of Hanging Tree deserve better? Especially since they were at the mercy of the unrelenting Texas sun?

Oh, her heart was racing as frantically as the horse and cart. For the first time since her arrival in this barren Texas wilderness, she was beginning to believe she had found a way to fit in. Not only with the people in the town, but with the strangers who had become her family. Her sisters and their husbands would be so proud of her.

Best of all, she would be doing something that gave her a sense of pride, as well. And there had been little enough of that in Ruby's young life.

Chapter Two

Marshal Quent Regan was feeling mean. Mean and ugly. In his left hand were the reins of the horse trailing his own, bearing Ward Barlow's body. He'd gone twenty-four hours without sleep. He rubbed his raw, bloody arm. It hurt like hell, adding to his temper. Worst of all, Boyd Barlow was out there somewhere, armed with a badge, endangering others.

Would the outlaw hightail it out of Texas? Or would he hide out, hoping to make good on his threat for revenge?

Quent's thoughts were as dark as the clouds scudding overhead.

Damned near thirty, and still living by his wits and his gun. It might have been exciting when he was a tough, ornery kid. Now it was just hard, grinding work. And every two-bit gunslinger, it seemed, was looking for bragging rights as the one who gunned down Marshal Quent Regan.

Right now the only thing that kept him going was the thought of a long, hot soak in a tub, a good cigar and a tumbler of whiskey before he hit the cot in his little room behind the jail.

Quent passed Neville Oakley's livery, Byron Conner's bank, Durfee's Mercantile and Barney Healey's barbershop, when he saw what looked like more trouble up ahead.

"Marshal Regan." Deputy Arlo Spitz came racing down the road, waving his hat for attention.

At the sight of his boss's steely-eyed glare, he skidded to a halt. Even though Arlo had worked for the marshal for more than four years, he was still in awe of the lawman. Arlo knew better than most that Quent Regan was a tough loner. If he got on the bad side of his boss, there'd be hell to pay. He hesitated a minute longer, then decided his news was too important to wait.

Quent fixed him with a scowl. His deputy was absolutely quivering with excitement. It could mean only one thing. The dark cloud on his day was about to get darker.

"What is it, Arlo?"

"You know that peddler that came to town a couple of days ago?"

Quent nodded. "The one selling snake oil from the back of a gaudy wagon?"

"That's the one. Well, Marshal, you won't believe it. He's been robbed."

Quent's eyes narrowed. "Couldn't you take care of it?"

"Well, sir, I would have. But the truth is, I just heard. And I saw you coming, and I thought—"

Quent cut him off. "Where is this peddler?"

Arlo pointed. "Over at the jail. I thought you'd want to ask him a few questions."

The marshal handed over the reins. "Take this one out back. Doc will want to look him over before we put him in the ground."

Arlo studied the body with a critical eye. Appeared to be only one shot. He wasn't surprised. The marshal was so quick and accurate with his gun, most times that's all he needed.

Arlo had tasted Quent Regan's temper a time or two. And he'd had occasion to watch the lawman in action. This wasn't a man who made idle threats, or enjoyed battering lawbreakers. He just did his job. And did it better than anyone he'd ever met.

"Who is it?"

"Ward Barlow."

"Mind telling me where?"

"Up on Widow's Peak. His brother got away. With my badge. Send a Wanted poster to all the lawmen in the territory. Tell them to be on the lookout for Boyd Barlow. Give a complete description. That one's dangerous." Quent nudged his horse into a trot.

His deputy watched him ride away. From the looks of the marshal's jacket, those two outlaws hadn't made it easy for him. But as usual, Quent was tight-lipped. And the townspeople would be left to speculate on just how much he'd had to endure before subduing this one.

Knowing the marshal as he did, Arlo was certain that Quent Regan wouldn't rest until the second outlaw was found. And Quent's badge recovered.

* * *

Weary beyond belief, Quent tied his horse and pulled open the door to the jail.

"Evening," he called.

Inside, the peddler stopped his pacing. "Marshal. My name's Vernon Mathis."

Quent accepted his handshake. "Mr. Mathis. I hear you were robbed."

"That's right."

"Why don't you tell me about it." The marshal crossed the room and settled himself at his desk, making a steeple of his fingers.

Vernon resumed his pacing. "Not much to tell. I had a pretty good day. I sold some skin balm and a youth elixir to an elderly woman. The widow Purdy, I believe she said. And a couple of bottles of tonic to a Mrs. Witherspoon. Then I got busy with a gentleman named Farley Duke who wanted to look at my collection of guns. I finally sold him a Remington six-shot."

Quent reminded himself to be patient. Sooner or later this peddler would get to the point.

"While you were busy with Mr. Duke, were there any other customers?"

The peddler shrugged. "Too many to count. But I'll never forget the thief."

"And why is that?"

Vernon's tone changed. "She thought she had me dazzled."

"She?" Quent sat up straighter.

The peddler nodded.

"Can you describe her?"

Vernon Mathis sighed. "I don't believe I've ever

seen a more beautiful creature. Eyes that flashed like fire. Hair the color of a chestnut stallion. And a body like a goddess, amply displayed, I might add, in a red satin gown that looked like it came from St. Louis. Or Paris, France. Know anyone in town who would fit that description, Marshal?''

Quent's frown deepened. He had it on the tip of his tongue to remind this peddler that there was a world of difference between St. Louis and Paris. But there was something far more important here. With every word out of the man's mouth, the marshal's mood had darkened. There was only one woman in all of Texas who fit that description. And she had the same effect on every man she met.

"How do you know the woman you saw is the thief?" Quent asked quietly.

"She accused me of selling shabby merchandise."

"And were you?"

The peddler flushed. "I'll match my goods with anyone's. But that's not the point. I was robbed. And I saw her do it."

"You saw her?"

His color deepened. "To be honest, Marshal, I couldn't take my eyes off her. That's why I'm so certain. She asked if she could look more closely at my collection of beads. I was still watching her when she slipped the trinkets into her pocket."

"Trinkets?" Quent Regan pounced on the word, shoving back his chair as he got to his feet. "You're here to report the theft of some...chcap trinkets?"

"Cheap?" The salesman stiffened his spine. "They may not be worth much, but I'll have you know the Cheyenne think very highly of my pretty baubles. It's the reason the chief allows me to trade with his people."

Fighting a wave of impatience, Quent dug into his pocket. "How much did they cost you, Mr. Mathis?"

"It isn't the money," Vernon protested. "I just don't like to be hornswoggled by some two-bit—"

Quent's hand was at the man's throat before he even realized what he was doing. His temper was reaching the boiling point. "How much?" he demanded.

"I paid two dollars for a tray of them in St. Louis."

"A tray? Would that be a dozen?"

"Six dozen."

"Two dollars for seventy-two cheap necklaces. And how many are missing?"

"A...couple." Vernon sucked in air and exhaled slowly as the marshal released him. His eyes widened as Quent peeled off a bill.

When Quent handed him the money, he added, "But they would have brought five times that much from the Cheyenne."

Quent peeled off another bill. "We'll split the difference and call it even, Mr. Mathis."

With a greedy little smile the peddler tucked the money away. "Now, about that thief..."

"I expect to see your wagon gone by morning, Mr. Mathis," the marshal said sternly.

"But I still have—"

"Before sunup. Any later, you'll find yourself a guest in my jail."

The peddler took one look at the marshal's stern face and swallowed. With a sullen nod of his head, he took his leave.

A few minutes later Arlo entered, looked around and scratched his head. "What happened to our peddler, marshal?"

"He told me what I needed to know."

"But doesn't he want to stay until you catch the thief?"

Quent shook his head. "I sent him on his way. Don't have much use for snake-oil salesmen. But I can't stop him from plying his trade in some other town."

Arlo watched as his boss picked up his hat and started toward the door. He knew, by the icy tone and dark scowl, that Marshal Quent Regan had just about reached the end of his patience. "You going to arrest the thief now?"

"You're damned right I am."

Outside, as Quent heaved himself into the saddle, he realized glumly that bed, bath and whiskey would have to wait.

Even the threat of rain couldn't dim Ruby's sense of elation. She lowered her shawl so the breeze could play through her hair. After a childhood in the steamy bayou, she was unaffected by the heat of late summer here in Texas.

Ruby was so caught up in her plans for the future, she didn't hear the pounding of a horse's hooves until the horse and rider were beside her. For a moment she was so startled, all she could do was stare. Then, seeing the marshal, she felt the lightning jolt she always felt whenever he came near. It was not the man, she told herself. It was that badge he wore. A badge of authority. All her life she'd resented those who wielded rigid authority. But she had learned, through experience, how to deal with them.

She drew in the reins until her horse and cart came to a stop.

"Why, Marshal Regan. *Enchantée.* I am, as you say, delighted to see you."

"Are you?" Quent's fury had grown with every mile. And now, looking at Ruby Jewel, he finally had a focus for all that pent-up anger.

"*Oui.* I am on my way to my father's ranch. Would you care to join me, Marshal?"

"I'd rather talk right here, if you don't mind."

"But of course." She gave him her most dazzling smile.

He saw right through her. He was already braced for that look she bestowed on men. Like rain on parched land. Like sunshine after a storm. But he was ready for it. Not today, Ruby Jewel, he thought. You're not going to dazzle this man with your charm.

In a bid to gain time and gather his thoughts, he took several moments to tie his horse to the back of her rig. Then he strolled up beside her.

"There was a theft today. From the wagon of that traveling salesman, Vernon Mathis. I thought I'd ask if you knew anything about it."

"I?" She placed a hand over her heart and saw the way the marshal's gaze followed the movement.

Pleased, she gave a delicate sigh. "How could I possibly know about this...theft?"

"Mr. Mathis told me you were there."

"But I am a stranger to this man. And he to me. How would he know my name?"

"He didn't. But he described you, and your gown, and your hair, and..." He'd almost slipped and said "body." He cleared his throat. "There's no other like you in Hanging Tree, Ruby." Or all of Texas, for that matter.

She gave a little laugh. "I think, Marshal, you are flattering me."

He bit back an oath. Damned if she wasn't trying to make him forget all his promises to himself. "I'm not here to flatter you, Ruby. I'm here to ask if you know about the theft."

"Perhaps if you would tell me what is missing," she prompted.

"Beads. Pretty trinkets."

"That is all?"

He nodded.

She closed her eyes a moment, deep in thought. That gave Quent time to study the way an errant curl had dipped provocatively over her forehead, brushing her brow. His gaze settled on the long, pale column of throat, then lowered to the swell of high, firm breasts, visible beneath the scoop of her neckline. That was where he was staring when her eyes snapped open.

He felt a new rush of fury and clenched his hand into a fist at his side.

"I have given this matter some thought, Marshal,

but I fear I can be of no assistance. I recall nothing suspicious.''

As she raised her hand to flick the reins, he spotted something dangling from the corner of her pocket. Something that caught and reflected the light.

His temper reached the boiling point.

It wasn't bad enough that Ruby Jewel, thanks to her father's generous will, was one of the richest women in Texas. He could understand a woman stealing, if she was driven to it by cruel circumstances. He'd seen plenty of frightened, hungry folks in his time. But this woman needed nothing. What made it worse was the fact that, confronted with the truth, she insisted upon lying. Quent Regan hated lying.

He was determined to give her one last chance. ''You don't know anything about the peddler's trinkets, ma'am?''

She shook her head, sending rich auburn curls dancing. It was imperative that she get away from this man. From his badge. From all that he stood for. ''Have I not said as much? Good day, Marshal.''

In that brief moment Marshal Quent Regan snapped. And did something he'd never done before.

Chapter Three

Without warning, Quent caught Ruby by the arm and hauled her out of her carriage. "Damned ornery female. I've reached the end of my patience with you. Now you're going to admit the truth."

His big hands clutched at her shoulders, as if to shake her. Or throttle her within an inch of her life. In all his years as a peace officer, he'd never had occasion to manhandle a woman. But this obstinate little liar had just pushed him over the edge.

That was before she bumped against his chest. Then he couldn't seem to recall just exactly what he'd had in mind. All he could think of was the shocking press of that perfect body against his. And the way her eyes, looking up into his, had gone all wide with surprise.

A man could get lost in those big green eyes, and happily drown in them. In fact, he was already going under for the first time, and fighting for air.

Ruby saw the dazed expression in his eyes. At least, she hoped that's what it was. She was feeling a bit dazed herself. But this was war. And she was already in the clutches of the enemy. She had to act quickly if she intended to get out of this mess. Hadn't Mama always said a woman must learn to use her wiles? The first defense, Mama had taught her, was plying the enemy with charm.

"You have made a terrible mistake, Marshal." She took in a deep breath, causing her chest to expand even farther against his. Then she fluttered her eyelashes as she had seen Mama do with Papa. "I am an innocent woman."

"Innocent?" He lifted his head and stared down at her. With that figure-hugging gown and that lovely display of flesh, this female was about as far from innocent as Lily, the madam at Buck's saloon. He ignored the rush of heat. "Sorry, ma'am. But there's no way in hell I can agree with that."

In the next instant her eyes grew stormy. And the words that issued from her pursed lips were unlike any he'd heard a lady use before. Ruby swore viciously in a mixture of French and Cajun. At least, Quent thought it must be swearing, by the way her already husky voice fell nearly an octave, and her eyes shot flames that practically singed his hair. When she had exhausted her vocabulary of obscenities, she pushed against him. Mama had always said that if charm and anger didn't work, the next step was righteous indignation.

"It would seem that in your quest for an admission of guilt, you are willing to overlook the truth, Marshal. Now, unhand me at once, do you hear? Or I'll…"

"You'll what?" His hands tightened and he heard her little gasp of outrage.

"I'll…" Threats. That's what Mama would have used. "I'll have your job."

"You'd better bring an army, ma'am."

His smug arrogance only inflamed her all the more. "I will not need an army. All I need is my family behind me."

In a way, they were an army, he had to admit. Her three very independent sisters and their husbands could probably sway half the town to side with them in any dispute. Not just because they were admired, but simply because so many of the townspeople owed their existence to the Jewel ranch.

"That's fine, Miss Ruby. You bring your family. And anyone else you'd like. Bring rifles. Bring knives. Bring a posse if you can summon one. But right now you're not leaving here until you admit the truth."

She lifted her chin in an infuriating fashion. She had always been able to bluff her way out of trouble. This time would be no exception. "Here is your truth, Marshal. If you wish to retrieve those pretty pink, purple and green beads, you will have to look elsewhere."

She shot him a look of triumph. And was surprised to see his eyes narrow and his lips curve into a dangerous smile.

"Thank you, ma'am. You've been a big help."

"I…have?"

"Yep. You see, I never mentioned the color of those beads."

A flush stole over her cheeks. "But you did. I distinctly remember."

"No, ma'am. I deliberately omitted that part. Which only proves that you did indeed see the peddler's beads."

She detested the thought of retreat. Still... "I may have seen them. Half the town probably saw them. But that doesn't prove that I took them."

"No, ma'am. It surely doesn't."

She blinked. This was too easy. "It doesn't?" As the meaning of his words sank in, her tone lightened. "Of course it doesn't. You see? You were mistaken, Marshal. But I will not demand vindication. This thing will be forgotten between us."

She relaxed. And let out a sigh of relief. Mama had been right. Men were so easy. Thank heavens she had not had to resort to tears. Though she had fully intended to, if need be.

She took a step back, expecting to be released. Instead, the marshal was staring at her in the strangest way. As though he couldn't decide whether to be angry or amused.

"You are—" she stared pointedly at the big hands crushing the delicate fabric of her sleeves "—wrinkling my gown, Marshal."

"Yes, ma'am, I am." There was that brief dangerous smile again, causing the strangest flutter around her heart.

Instead of releasing her, he ran his hands along her satin-clad arms. Heat pulsed through her veins, then spread all the way to her fingers and toes.

Mama had never explained to her how to react to

a situation such as this. In fact, all Mama's lessons had been on the art of flirting. Ruby had never gone beyond that. Had never needed to. Now, with Quent Regan's bold reaction, she felt completely out of her element. He was supposed to get all red in the face and flustered. He was supposed to back off. Instead, she was the one taking a step backward.

She didn't understand this heat. Where had it come from? How had it happened? Her breathing was quite erratic. And her heart was beating so wildly, she was certain the marshal could hear it.

The marshal was too busy with problems of his own. He wasn't certain just what had come over him. Maybe it was the fact that he'd gone too long without food or rest. Or the charms of a female. Whatever the reason, he was feeling downright frisky and light-headed.

"I must say, it's mighty fine fabric." He drew her close and ran one hand down her back, then up again. "We don't see too many soft, pretty things here in Hanging Tree. I don't believe I've felt anything this soft in a very long time. In fact, ma'am, if you don't mind, I'd like to feel more."

Tiny fires ignited all along her spine, heating her blood, heating even the air that backed up in her lungs. There was a strange tingling deep inside, leaving her weak and trembling. *Dieu,* was it possible to faint from a single touch?

"Um-hmm," he muttered against her temple. "I was right. Softer than a newborn foal."

"Marshal Regan." She pushed ineffectively against his chest, but he only tightened his grasp, pinning her hands between his body and hers, so that she was helpless to resist.

She started to wriggle and squirm. But as she turned her face, his mouth covered hers in a hard, punishing kiss. A kiss made more heated by anger, by frustration. A kiss so startling, so demanding, she couldn't move. All she could do was stand very still and absorb the shock.

His lips moved over hers with a thoroughness that left her drained. And still he continued moving his mouth on hers, drawing out every sweet, exotic flavor.

He hadn't meant to kiss her. In fact, even now, he didn't know how it had happened. He'd merely meant to intimidate her. But the minute his mouth was on hers, he realized his mistake. He'd been wanting to kiss her since the first time he'd seen her in Hanging Tree, all bold and sassy and done up in red satin. But one kiss and he was hurtling toward disaster, feeling things he hadn't expected, wanting things he had no right to.

Almost at once he lifted his head and stared down at her. God in heaven, he was reeling as if he'd just taken a blow to the midsection. His heart was racing as though he'd chased a gang of outlaws up one side of Widow's Peak and down the other.

What the hell was wrong with him? He'd kissed women before. Plenty of them. But he couldn't ever recall feeling like this. The taste of her was as smooth as Buck's best whiskey. And the sweet, earthy scent of her, like crushed roses, filled his lungs and clouded his mind.

What was worse, if he didn't know better, he'd think she'd never been kissed before. But that was impossible. It wasn't possible for a woman to look like that and still be innocent.

Damned if he wasn't going to have one more taste, just to make sure.

For a moment Ruby was certain he was as astonished as she. But then she caught sight of the slight curve of his lips. And the roguish glint of something in his eyes. Laughter? Was this big, rough Texan laughing at her?

With an oath she started to push away. But before she could break free he lowered his head and nuzzled her lips. It was the merest touch of mouth to mouth. A kiss so gentle, it felt like a dusting of butterfly wings. He held her as though she were a bunch of fragile wildflowers.

Her lips trembled under his, and she hesitated, unsure how to react. Her mind told her to back away. But her body betrayed her. Her hands crept up his chest and curled into the front of his shirt. A little sigh escaped her lips. And deep inside her, a warm liquid feeling pulsed.

Now she felt herself bound by something even stronger than his hands. A need. Strange and new. She stood rooted to the spot, unable to move. It was impossible to think. All she could do was feel. And oh, the feelings that rushed through her, overwhelming her with their intensity. Never, never had she known such a kiss.

There had been many who had tried to steal a kiss from Ruby's lips. And a few who had succeeded. But they had been clumsy boys, with eager, heated mouths and awkward, hesitant touches.

This was no boy. This was a man. A man who feasted on her lips as though they were the sweetest taste in the world. A man who drank from her lips as though dying of thirst. A man who knew just how to use his hands to soothe, to explore, to caress. Those same hands that held a gun, and subdued hardened criminals, were skimming her body with the greatest of care.

She swayed slightly. Just when she thought her legs would surely fail her, his hands tightened at her shoulders. He lifted his head and held her a little away, while he studied her with a strange, intense look.

"You..." She struggled for breath, all the while cursing the fact that, for the first time in her life, her clever, facile mind seemed to have deserted her. She could think of nothing to say that would cover this moment of awkwardness. "You are too bold, Marshal."

"Yes, ma'am." He took in a deep draft of air. Damned woman had a way of making him feel like a kid with his nose pressed to a candy jar. And a handful of pennies to spend on anything he wanted. And like a kid, he wanted it all.

"I will remind you, Marshal, that I am a lady."

"Yes, ma'am."

She swallowed, playing for time. "I expect an apology."

"An apology?"

She gave him what she hoped was her most challenging look. "For your rude behavior. As well as your ridiculous accusation." She sniffed. "As if I would resort to stealing cheap trinkets."

"You mean these, ma'am?" He held aloft the beads. "That I found in your pocket?"

She stared at the beads, then at his face. Her mouth dropped open, but no words came out. So that's what his hands had been doing. Not skimming her body. Searching her pockets.

With a knowing smile he offered his arm. "Allow me to assist you into your rig, Ruby."

She was nearly speechless. But she recovered quickly. "You mean I'm free to go?"

"Go? Why, yes, ma'am." He steeled himself against the heat of her touch as he helped her up. The taste of her was still warm on his lips. And the earthy scent of her still filled his lungs, making every breath the sweetest of tortures.

He surprised her by climbing up beside her and taking up the reins.

"Where do you think you're going, Marshal?"

As he caught up the reins, he realized his hands were none too steady. That knowledge only fueled his rapidly returning temper. "Why, with you, Ruby. To jail."

Chapter Four

"Here we are." Marshal Regan drove Ruby's rig around to the back of the jail, where he tied the horse, then offered a hand down.

She shot him a hateful look. She'd tried arguing, threatening, even tears, which had now dried on her lashes. Nothing would change his mind. He was determined to humiliate her in front of the entire town.

"I'll send Arlo out to notify your sisters," he said as he led her inside and opened the door to a cell.

"Why must you tell them about this?"

"Because," he replied patiently, "your house-keeper, Carmelita Alvarez, will be worried when you don't come home tonight. And she'll send her husband, Rosario, chasing after all your sisters, getting them all riled up. Besides, Ruby," he added with an extra bite of sarcasm, "you need a keeper. Maybe one of your sisters can talk some sense into you."

Now it wasn't just the town, she realized. He intended to embarrass her in front of her new family, as well.

He was rewarded by a string of oaths as he herded her into the cell.

"This way, Ruby."

With a last muttered curse she stepped inside and watched as he closed the cell door and turned the key.

While all this went on, Arlo stood gaping, unable to believe that one of the Jewel sisters was actually being held prisoner in the town jail.

In the cell next door to hers, Beau Baskin, the town drunk, was beginning to sober up in a hurry. His eyes were nearly popping out of his head at the sight of one of the Jewel ladies behind bars.

Quent turned to his deputy. "I'd like you to ride out to the Jewel ranch and tell the housekeeper that Ruby is here. I wouldn't want Carmelita to worry. Ask her to notify the other Jewel sisters that they can come and fetch Ruby in the morning."

"Yes, sir." Arlo was grinning, until he caught sight of Ruby. The smile was wiped from his face. Even with bars between them, he felt a rush of discomfort. This lady was definitely dangerous. Not the way Diamond was, with a gun. But those flashing eyes and sultry lips could flog a man at thirty paces.

He snatched up his hat and headed out the door.

When his deputy was gone, Quent walked to his desk and dropped the keys with a clatter. He was aware of Ruby still standing just inside the cell, her hands clenched at her sides, her eyes watching his every move.

"I am shocked and appalled, Marshal. Until today

I was not aware of this cruel side of your nature,'' she said.

"I'm sorry you see it that way, ma'am." He sat down and began sifting through the papers that littered his desktop. The stage had apparently been through, and Arlo had dutifully piled on his desk a stack of Wanted posters, along with a letter from a sheriff in Waco warning of a jail break by a couple of hardened prisoners. Quent put his feet up and leaned back in his rickety chair, trying to concentrate. But it wasn't easy, knowing Ruby Jewel was just a few feet away.

"I'm with you, Miss Ruby," Beau said between hiccups from the other cell. "Marshal Regan's the toughest lawman this side of the Rio Grande."

"I'll thank you not to interrupt," Ruby said, causing his jaw to drop. She turned to the marshal, who was doing his best to ignore her. "If it's your intention to humiliate me, Marshal, then you have succeeded. Once Arlo's wife has told her friends Lavinia Thurlong and Gladys Witherspoon, the whole town will be laughing at me."

"Now, that's the truth," Beau said, jumping right in. "Those two old biddies will spend the whole day running their legs off and flapping their jaws."

"Not another word, cowboy," Quent hollered. It galled him to know that Ruby and Beau were right. Effie Spitz couldn't be trusted to keep a secret if her life depended on it. That was the only reason why town gossips Lavinia and Gladys cultivated her friendship. As the deputy's wife, Effie could be counted on to know about every crime and scandal in the territory. Still, what was that to him?

"I think you ought to put the blame squarely where it belongs, Ruby. If you're so worried about your reputation, you shouldn't have stolen from that peddler."

"I did not steal." When Quent swiveled his head and fixed her with a look, she flushed. "Mama preferred to call it her *petit vengeance*. And it was only done to those who were found completely lacking in basic kindness."

At her admission, his feet hit the floor. He tossed down the posters and crossed the room until he was standing just outside Ruby's cell. "I don't care what you call it. Or how many of your ancestors chose to practice it. It's still against the law to help yourself to someone else's property. And it's my job to uphold the law."

Her hands gripped the bars. Her voice frosted over. "How nice for you that you find your work so enjoyable, Marshal."

Without thinking, he closed his hands over hers. "Do you think I liked arresting you?"

Her eyes flashed fire. "Liked it? No, Marshal. You loved it. On the way here you were positively gloating. It was apparent that you took great satisfaction in dominating me."

Once again, it would seem, he'd miscalculated. He'd allowed himself to get too close to the fire. He could feel the heat of her, could almost taste the exotic, earthy flavor of those pouting lips. Still, with the bars between them, he released her hands and caught her roughly by the shoulders. It wasn't the need to touch her, he told himself sternly. It was merely the best way to convey his anger.

"Woman, at this moment I'd take great satisfaction in hanging you. Now, give me some peace."

He saw the way her eyes widened, in that brief second before they slanted with fury. Oh, there was fire there. And great inner strength. But there was something else. Something as yet undefined. Something that had flickered just for a moment, before being swept away.

Fear? Could this tough little female actually harbor some deep-seated fear? If so, was it a fear of the law? Of anyone in authority? Or just a fear of him personally?

She backed away, wrenching free of his grasp, breaking contact. As she rubbed her hands she muttered, "If my papa were still alive, you would not be treating me with such disdain, Marshal."

"Yeah, well, your pa isn't here to protect you now, Miss Jewel." He shoved his hands into his pockets, relieved that he was no longer touching her. There was definitely something unsettling about getting too close to Ruby Jewel. He'd have to remember that in the future. "But if your pa was alive, he'd turn you over his knee and paddle your backside until you learned respect for the law." He sauntered back to his desk. "Just remember. The law will treat you no better than anybody else."

"I do not ask for better treatment. Only equal treatment." She wanted to sink onto the edge of the cot. She was so weary. The emotions of this day had taken their toll. But she would not give in. Instead she stood, her spine stiff, her head high, watching Quent Regan shuffling through papers. "But I suppose that is the price I must pay for bearing my father's name. Diamond said there will be many who will think they have something to prove to Onyx Jewel's descendants."

"I don't give a—" He caught himself. It wasn't his nature to swear in the presence of a lady. Even a lady like Ruby Jewel, whose vocabulary was as seasoned as a wrangler's. "I don't give a care about your last name." Annoyed, Quent opened a desk drawer and swept the posters inside, slamming it shut with more force than necessary.

But the thought nibbled at the edges of his mind. Had he treated her more harshly than he should have, because of her name? After all, he reasoned, he'd already settled the debt with the peddler for a couple of dollars. It would have been enough to give her a good tongue-lashing and send her on her way.

Why, then, was she sitting in jail? Because, he admitted, the crime had occurred at the worst possible time. Giving chase to a couple of deadly outlaws had heated his temper considerably. And there was just something about Ruby Jewel that raised the heat another notch. She was like an itch that he couldn't scratch.

"You sure do look beautiful, Miss Ruby," Beau Baskin said from the bunk where he lay. "Damned if you aren't the prettiest prisoner I've ever seen in a jail."

"You shut your mouth, cowboy," Quent snapped.

Ignoring Quent, Ruby bestowed a brilliant smile on the man in the next cell. "Thank you. At least there is one gentleman in this room."

Quent felt a stab of something in his gut. Jealousy? Ridiculous. He'd never felt such an alien emotion in his life. Just because she was flaunting herself in front of that drunken cowboy was no concern of his. What Ruby Jewel did was her own business, unless, of course, she flouted the law.

Passing a hand over his face, he gave a hiss of frustration.

"Tired, Marshal?" the cowboy asked.

"Yeah. It's been a hell of a day." Quent slumped back in his chair.

"The marshal's been up on Widow's Peak catching himself a killer," Beau explained to Ruby. "Arlo said he'd be burying the body first thing in the morning."

"Body?" Ruby looked startled. "You...killed him?"

Quent didn't bother to answer.

"It was probably the outlaw's life or his," Beau said matter-of-factly. "Most outlaws let their guns talk for them."

For the first time Ruby took a good look at the marshal. His jacket was crusted with blood. His chin was darkened with a growth of dark stubble. And his eyes were red rimmed and weary. She felt a tiny twinge of guilt. But only a tiny one, as she decided to use his weariness to her own advantage.

"I know what you need, Marshal. Whenever my papa came for a visit, Mama used to give him a back rub. He said he didn't care how difficult the journey to Louisiana was, as long as he had that to look forward to. It made all the miles disappear, and his troubles along with it.''

Quent glanced over at those long, graceful fingers, clenching and unclenching with nerves. The thought of them rubbing and kneading his tired muscles almost brought a sigh from his lips. But he caught himself in time and shot her a cold look. "Don't try to bribe me with back rubs, Miss Jewel. You'd better save them for yourself. That cot will prove to be none too comfortable."

She stomped a tiny foot, annoyed that he'd seen through her little ploy. "I cannot bear to stay here until morning." She wrinkled her nose and glanced toward the shabby cot. "On that."

Quent picked up the ring of keys and crossed to each cell, checking the locks. "I know it's not fit for a lady like you. But that's what happens when ladies help themselves to what's not theirs."

She watched in sullen silence while he lifted a lantern from a nail on the wall and made his way to a back room. He unlocked the door and it swung inward. Ruby had a quick impression of a simple bed and nightstand, upon which rested a pitcher and basin.

"You're taking away the lantern?" She swayed at the razor edge of fear that sliced into her.

"Yes, ma'am. You don't need light to sleep." He turned. The flickering flame of the lantern cast his face in light and shadow. It was a handsome, dangerous face that would put the devil himself to shame. "Make yourself comfortable, ma'am. There's a blanket at the foot of the cot. If you need anything else, just holler."

She looked as though at any moment she might break down and cry. But to her credit she kept her composure. Barely. "You have nothing here I need," she said through clenched teeth.

"That's fine. I'll say good-night, then, ma'am. Night, Beau."

He closed the door to his room, leaving the jail and its occupants in darkness.

For long minutes Ruby stood very still, fighting the sense of rising panic that threatened to choke her. The darkness was like a shroud, blotting out the light, the warmth. Cutting off her life. She was suffocating. She couldn't breathe. Couldn't stand the thought of being locked away in the darkness.

She clutched the bars of her cell as wave after wave of terror rose up like bile in her throat.

A sob was wrenched from her throat. Her voice came out in a strangled cry. "No. Please, Sister Clothilde. No more. I'll be good. I'll..."

They were the last words she uttered before she slipped bonelessly to the floor of her cell. Where she lay, still and pale and unmoving.

Quent pried off his boots and unfastened his gun belt. Setting his pistol beside his pillow, he blew out the lantern and flopped down on the bed.

After all the hours he'd put in, he should have fallen asleep instantly. But sleep eluded him. Instead, all he could think of was the woman in the next room. Lord deliver him from petty thieves and drunken cowboys. All Ward and Boyd Barlow had cost him was some blood. But Ruby Jewel was costing him sleep. And a whole lot more.

He didn't want to think about her lying on a cot in the jail. Didn't want to think about the way her lips had trembled while she held back her tears. Tears. It was a female trick. A ploy that twisted in a man's gut and made him feel guilty even when he'd done nothing wrong.

It occurred to Quent that the woman in his cell was a mystery. She dressed like a harlot, and certainly flirted with all the skill of a soiled dove. But it had seemed to him, when he'd kissed her, that Ruby Jewel had had little experience at kissing. And what a kiss. Just thinking about it made his heart pound like a man being chased by a gang of horse thieves.

If he was going to be honest with himself, he'd have to admit that part of Ruby's appeal was the fact that she was so damnably unpredictable. A wild woman one minute, a trembling milkmaid the next. Just who and what was she?

Why would an heir to Onyx Jewel's fortune resort to stealing worthless trinkets? But then, why did anyone steal? The answer came at once. To fill a need. What was the need in Ruby Jewel's life that needed filling? Here was a woman who seemed to have everything in the world. The face of a Madonna, the lush body of a temptress and the fearless nerves of a born villain.

It was obvious that the person she showed the world was a sham. There was a very private, secret Ruby hidden deep inside.

Quent had a sudden burning desire to know that other Ruby. A dangerous thing for a man in his position. After all, he was a man of the law. And she was, without a doubt, a thief. And not a very good one.

"Marshal. Marshal Regan."

He pressed an arm over his eyes and tried to ignore Beau's shouts. "Go to sleep, you fool," he growled.

"Marshal. Come quick," Beau called.

"Dammit man, I've had enough for one day. Now, stop that hollering." He rolled over, trying to make himself comfortable in the narrow bed.

"Marshal, it's Miss Ruby. I can't see in the dark, but I think something awful's happened to her. You'd better get in here."

Swearing under his breath, Quent rolled from the bed and lit the lantern. He strode barefoot into the jail, the lantern in one hand, his pistol in the other. The sight that greeted him had his heart stopping.

Ruby was lying as still as death on the floor of her cell.

After unlocking the door, Quent dropped to his knees and held the lantern aloft.

"Is she dead?" Beau asked.

Quent touched a hand to her throat. "She's alive. She must have fainted."

"Never saw a woman faint before," Beau said, grasping the bars of his cell. "She sure looks pale. What're you going to do, Marshal?"

Quent lifted her in his arms, cradling her to his chest. "I don't know yet."

"If you need me to go for Doc Prentice, just say the word."

"I doubt you'd get beyond the saloon, Beau," he snapped irritably. "Go on back to sleep now."

Quent carried Ruby to his room, where he laid her gently on his bed. He sat beside her and took her hands in his. They were cold as ice. He wrapped her in his blankets, then tossed a log on the hot coals in the stove. When the fire was blazing, he returned to her side and began to gently rub her hands.

She was so pale, it alarmed him. He touched a hand to her throat and felt a wild, erratic pulse. Wherever she had gone in her mind, it was a place that was so frightening, her only escape had been into unconsciousness.

"Ruby." He watched her lids. They didn't move.

He leaned close, shaking her gently. "Ruby."

Her lids fluttered, then opened. For a moment she seemed confused. Then, as the cobwebs cleared, she struggled to sit up.

"No." He pressed her back against the pillow. "Lie here awhile. I'd rather not have you faint again."

"Faint?" she said indignantly. "I do not faint. Ever."

"Whatever you call it, you were lying on the floor of your cell. Has this happened before?" he demanded.

She swallowed. "Of course not."

"Why do I think you're not telling me the truth, Ruby?"

She couldn't bear the intensity of that look. To avoid it, she closed her eyes a moment. But when she opened them, he was still there, watching her closely.

"I'd like you to drink this." From the table beside his bed he lifted a tumbler filled with amber liquid.

"What is it?" she asked suspiciously.

"Whiskey."

She started to shake her head, but he pressed it to her mouth and muttered, "Trust me. It'll help."

She had no chance to refuse. And though it burned a path of fire down her throat, causing her eyes to water, she managed to drink it.

He stood and crossed the room, to give her a chance to compose herself. With his arms across his chest he said, "Now maybe you can tell me what happened."

"It was nothing." She studied the way his dark pants hugged his hips and the flat planes of his stomach. Her gaze moved upward, to the sleeves of his shirt, straining against the muscles of his arms.

She was suddenly too tired to keep her eyes open. They closed against her will. She could hear Quent's voice, closer now. But she couldn't rouse herself enough to reply.

And then she felt his hand brushing the hair from her forehead. And his voice, close to her ear, whispering, "Go ahead, Ruby. Sleep now."

It seemed too much effort to sort things out. It was enough to know that here in Quent Regan's bed she felt safe. Safe and snug and warm.

She slept.

Chapter Five

Ruby awoke to sunlight streaming across the bed. She lay listening to the strange sound that had awakened her. Opening her eyes, she watched Quent scrape the razor across his cheek, over his jaw. With each movement the muscles of his back and shoulders bunched and tightened. She found herself staring at wide, muscled shoulders. He turned, giving her a glimpse of naked chest, covered by a mat of dark hair. And arms corded with muscles.

She'd never before thought of a man's body as beautiful. But Quent Regan's was. All muscle and sinew, the skin bronzed by the Texas sun.

When he finished shaving, he wiped the lather from his face. Ducking his head in the basin, he scrubbed his hair and scalp, then shook himself like a great shaggy dog before drying it with a square of linen. Afterward he dried his chest and shoulders before pulling on a clean shirt.

He was buttoning the shirt when he turned and realized that she was awake.

"Good morning."

Again she felt the intensity of that dark gaze. "Good morning."

"I'll be out of here in a minute so you can have some privacy." He sat on the foot of the bed and began pulling on his boots. It was an oddly intimate gesture that had her pulse pounding, though she didn't know why.

That done, he strapped on his holster and checked his pistol. The shiny new badge, which he'd salvaged from a desk drawer, winked in the sunlight as he pinned it on his shirt.

Seeing it, Ruby's mood darkened. She had forgotten, for a moment, that he was the enforcer of the rules. The one who meted out punishment to those who broke the rules.

He picked up the basin and pitcher, saying, "I'll fetch you some fresh water."

Within minutes he'd returned. He set down the basin and pitcher, then paused at the door. "Millie Potter always sends a breakfast tray over. It should be here any minute."

Then he was gone. And Ruby was left to stare around the room. It was sparsely furnished, with little more than a bed, a dresser and a bedside table on which rested the basin and pitcher of fresh water.

Why would a man settle for this life? Was he so wedded to that gun at his hip and badge at his chest that he would accept such puny rewards? A tiny, cramped room in the back of a jail?

She slipped from bed and stared down at herself with dismay. Her gown was wrinkled, her hair in disarray. She set about making herself presentable.

She washed her face and combed her fingers through her hair. There was nothing that could be done about her gown, but she smoothed the skirt and pulled on the fine kid slippers that had been set neatly beside the bed. She couldn't recall Quent removing them, but then there was much about the previous night that she couldn't recall. But she seemed to remember hands tucking the covers around her, and brushing her hair from her face. Hands that were rough and work worn. And surprisingly gentle.

As she made up the bed, she breathed in the lingering scents of horses and leather and tobacco. Scents she recalled from her father's infrequent visits. All through the night she'd found them somehow soothing.

How could this be? How could a man who earned his living with a gun be gentle and soothing? She shook her head, dispelling such foolish thoughts.

When she opened the door she saw Beau sitting on his bunk, enjoying coffee and biscuits. Quent was at his desk, frowning over some papers. A tray, covered by a linen towel, rested on his desktop.

"You're just in time," Quent said. "The coffee's hot, and Millie baked cinnamon biscuits."

"It's kind of Mrs. Potter to provide breakfast." Ruby accepted a cup from Quent's hand and began to sip strong, hot coffee.

"It's her job. The town pays her to provide meals for the prisoners."

Ruby almost burned her tongue. For a few minutes she'd managed to forget why she was here.

"Speaking of which…" Quent glanced up at the

sound of horses. "That's probably your sisters come to take you home."

At the chorus of female voices outside the door, Ruby braced herself for what was to come.

"Quent Regan, what have you done with Ruby?" Diamond, huge with child, dressed in her usual buckskins and dung-caked boots, strode into the jail, ready to pick a fight. At the sight of her sister calmly drinking coffee, she came to an abrupt halt.

"Oh, thank heavens you're all right." Pearl, trailing Diamond, pressed a hand to the bodice of her shell-pink gown and sniffed as she looked around the dingy room.

Jade, who strode in behind her sisters, shot the marshal an angry look. "You gave us quite a fright, sending that message with your deputy. We thought Ruby was actually in jail."

"She was. Is," he corrected.

"Make up your mind, Quent." Diamond made no effort to mask her impatience. "Is Ruby in jail? Or isn't she?"

"She is. But I'm releasing her to the three of you. And you'd better make sure she doesn't have reason to be back here."

"I think you'd better explain, Marshal." Pearl's tone was cool and polite. "Why did you arrest Ruby?"

"Because she helped herself to things that didn't belong to her."

"You stole?" Pearl turned to her sister, her brows lifted in stunned surprise.

"I didn't exactly steal." Ruby shot a furious look at the marshal.

"What did you do? Exactly?" Pearl demanded.

"I...was practicing Mama's petit vengeance." Embarrassed by her explanation, Ruby sloshed coffee over the rim of her cup.

Jade, looking cool and composed in green silk, took the cup from her sister's hand and placed it on the marshal's desk. "Perhaps," she said in her slightly accented voice, "we should discuss this back at the ranch." She glanced knowingly at Beau Baskin, who was looking from one to the other, hanging on every word. "I am certain we'll be more comfortable there. And it will certainly be more private."

Diamond turned to the marshal. "Is there a fine or anything, Quent?"

He was tempted. After all, he'd paid the peddler more than the trinkets had been worth. And the Jewel sisters could easily afford it. But, after seeing Ruby all pale and frightened last night, he just wanted her out of here and back home where she belonged.

"There's no fine, ladies. Just see that Ruby doesn't find herself in my jail again."

Ruby glanced at Quent's rugged profile. "Last night it was your intention to humiliate me. I am wondering why you had this sudden change of heart."

He shrugged. "I'm wondering the same thing. But your pa was a friend of mine. Maybe the first real friend I had in Texas. I owe him. Maybe I see this as a way to pay him back."

Ruby bristled. "You needn't bother on my account—"

"Thanks, Quent." Diamond dropped an arm around her sister and started to lead her toward the door, in an effort to keep her from saying more. Her hot-blooded sister and the marshal just seemed to rub sparks off each other.

"The horse and rig are out back," Quent called. "I had it brought over from Neville Oakley's livery, where it was kept for the night. You'll have to pay him for the oats and use of a stall."

"We'll take care of it," Diamond called as the three sisters escorted Ruby from the jail.

As they swept past his cell, Beau drew a deep breath. When the door closed behind them, he said, "Um-um, Marshal. Those Jewel ladies are like a bouquet of flowers. Every one of 'em prettier than the next."

Quent inhaled the sweet fragrance that trailed in Ruby's wake. Beau was right. A bouquet of flowers. And Ruby was a wild rose. With plenty of thorns.

"A seamstress." Diamond reached for a slice of corn bread. "You spent a night in jail because you decided to become a seamstress?"

Carmelita, housekeeper and ranch cook, rapped Diamond's knuckles with a wooden spoon and snatched the platter away. "Not until lunch is ready," she muttered.

The four sisters had ridden almost the entire distance from the town to their ranch in silence. Ruby had absolutely refused to discuss her "unsettling incident,'' as she referred to it, and the three sisters had finally given up the idea that they would ever break through that wall of silence she had built. The reason for her time spent in jail was a closed subject. But Diamond, as always, was giving it one last try.

Once inside the house, with hugs from Carmelita, surrounded by the wonderful fragrances of cooking, Ruby had surprised them by blurting out her plans for the future.

Now she shot a withering look at Diamond. ''That is not why the marshal arrested me.''

''Why, then?'' Diamond persisted. ''Quent said you helped yourself to somebody else's property.''

Ruby gave an exaggerated sigh. ''I do not wish to speak of that. I wish to tell you of my plans for my future. I have given this some thought. I can sew anything. I made this gown. Have you seen the stitches?'' She lifted the hem of her gown and insisted they examine it. ''These stitches would make Sister Dominique proud.''

''Sister Dominique?'' Jade looked puzzled. ''You have another sister?''

''*Non.*'' Ruby was becoming flustered. ''Sister Dominique was the nun, the teacher,'' she corrected, for Jade's benefit, ''who befriended me while I was a student. I cannot tell you how many times I was punished because Sister Clothilde accused me of some infraction.''

''Punished?'' Jade arched a brow. ''In what way?''

For a moment Ruby froze. Then she said softly,

"There were many punishments. One was to scrub the refectory floor on my hands and knees."

"What were the other punishments?" Jade persisted.

Ruby merely shrugged. "I have forgotten. But Sister Dominique was my friend. My only true friend at Notre Dame du Bayou. And so, to please her, I learned to sew as she did."

"I, too, had demanding tutors," Jade said. "They insisted that I learn all the erotic mysteries of the Orient."

Ruby gave a sigh of resignation. All of their lives had been so different. "I fear the nuns would have punished me day and night if I had even mentioned the word *erotic*."

"Speaking of erotic," Pearl said gently. "Sister Dominique might approve of your stitches now, Ruby, but I'm not sure she'd approve of your gown. There isn't much call for that kind of dress here in Hanging Tree. The women here are...of a practical nature."

"Practical," Diamond's eyes flashed back. "If they were practical, they'd wear what I'm wearing."

Pearl struggled with a grin. "Diamond, I love you. You know I do. But there isn't another woman in the whole territory of Texas who'd be caught wearing cowhide chaps and a gun belt."

The sisters smiled. As always, when they came together, they felt as if they'd never been apart. It was a source of wonder for all of them that, though they hadn't even met until after the death of their father, they had become a family.

Carmelita was in her glory. She had made all their favorite dishes. For Diamond there was the spicy mix of Mexican and Texas chilis. Pearl preferred the slowly simmered roast beef that her mother had made in Boston. Jade's exotic taste reflected her mother's homeland in China. And Ruby constantly lived up to her fiery reputation by insisting on the mouth-burning, eye-watering food of the bayou.

Jade looked up from the tea she was brewing. "I think a dress shop is a fine idea."

"Would you buy one of those?" Diamond pointed to the gown Ruby was wearing.

"What's wrong with my gown?" Ruby demanded.

"Oh, nothing." Diamond drank a glass of buttermilk and wiped her mouth on her sleeve. "Except the neck is so low it displays half your bosom. And the back end is so tight your rump sways like an old mare I once had."

Carmelita, choking back a laugh, began placing platters on the wooden kitchen table, in the hope of fending off a fight. "Lunch is ready," she said, shooting a sideways glance at Diamond. "You should eat and not talk."

But Diamond, never one for subtlety, continued as if she hadn't been interrupted. "And that color. If Adam's new bull saw you clear across the pasture, he'd come running."

"Are you finished?" Ruby demanded.

"I've just started." Diamond took her seat at the table and helped herself to several slices of corn bread before passing the platter to Pearl. "What's worse, Ruby, if the bull did spot you, you wouldn't be able to get out of the way. Look at that skirt. Why, you can hardly walk, let alone run. Can you picture Lavinia Thurlong or Gladys Witherspoon trying to waddle through town wearing one of your gowns?''

The image she suggested had the others giggling.

"Are you quite through?" Ruby asked through gritted teeth.

"Yep. I guess I am." Diamond sprinkled chilis over her beef and dug in to her lunch.

"I am not *l'imbécile*." As always, whenever she was agitated, Ruby's tones slipped into a French-English mix that only added to her haughtiness.

"No one is accusing you of being a fool." Pearl shot a look at Diamond, while trying to soothe Ruby's ruffled feathers. "But I think Diamond has a good point. Though your gowns look...enchanting on you, Ruby, I can't quite picture the women of Hanging Tree in them."

"They'd look like a damned pack of soiled doves hoping to get work at Buck's saloon," Diamond said, choosing to ignore Pearl's pointed looks.

"I'm not trying to force my taste on others." Ruby's food was forgotten. If she couldn't persuade her own family, how could she ever hope to persuade the townspeople?

Jade's words—calm, refined, with a hint of the Orient—broke through their thoughts. "From my earliest days I was instructed that even simple people have a need for beauty and elegance in their lives. It was the reason why the Golden Dragon was so successful."

"Is that why the Golden Dragon is now a church named the Golden Rule?" Diamond asked sarcastically over a mouthful of food.

"Oh, Diamond." Pearl laid a hand over her sister's sun-reddened arm. "Must you use every opportunity to pick a fight?"

Diamond shrugged. "It's just my nature. Pa taught me to be sensible."

"Maybe too sensible." Pearl forced her loveliest smile to her lips before turning to Ruby. "The town scoffed at my idea for a school here in Hanging Tree. But in scant months they've come to accept it. As they've accepted me. I think it's wonderful that you have a dream, Ruby. And I, for one, urge you to do all you can to fulfill that dream."

"I agree," Jade said softly. "You will add beauty and glamour to our little town. Not to mention a touch of fashion."

"*Merci.*" Ruby turned to Diamond. "But I desire your approval, as well, *chérie.* This is, after all, your town. These are your people. If my own sister does not approve, how can I expect it from strangers?"

Diamond glanced around the table and realized that the others had stopped eating and were staring at her. She shoved aside her plate. "I don't disapprove, Ruby. I think it's fine that you want to use your talents. Just don't expect the women of Hanging Tree to beat down your door. They work all day in the blazing sun, turning the soil or tending the herds. Every dollar they have goes to buy seed or tools or other necessities. There isn't room in their lives for fancy dresses and feathered bonnets."

"There is room in every woman's life for something soft and pretty," Ruby said fiercely. "If I make it attractive enough, and reasonable enough, they will buy."

"I hope so." Diamond shoved back her chair. "I've got to go. I promised Adam I'd help him clear some more brush today." She pressed a kiss to the housekeeper's cheek. "Thanks for the vittles, Carmelita. I sure do miss your cooking."

"Then you must come back one night this week," Carmelita pleaded. "I will make you and Señor Adam a special supper."

"How about tomorrow?" Diamond snatched at the opportunity to avoid cooking. "That'll give me a chance to hear more of Ruby's plans." She strolled around the table and brushed a kiss over each of her sister's cheeks. When she reached Ruby she kissed her, then added, "I don't mean to discourage you. Pearl is right. You have to follow your dream."

"Do you mean it?" Ruby's eyes were alight with surprise.

"Of course I do. Pa said that's what made Texas so special. It's a land of dreamers, who followed their hearts."

"Oh, *chérie*. You have made me so happy. I needed your approval."

"Then you have it." Diamond strolled to the door, then turned and added, "Just don't ask me to be your first customer."

Chapter Six

"Marshal." Deputy Arlo Spitz leaned on his broom, trying to look important. "Millie Potter sent Birdie Bidwell over to see if you're planning on coming to her boardinghouse for lunch, or if you want a tray."

Quent looked up from his paperwork, rubbing the back of his neck. He disliked this part of his job almost as much as he disliked looking down the barrel of an outlaw's gun. But it went with the territory.

"I'm not very hungry." He shuffled through the Wanted posters a final time, committing the names and faces to memory, before filing them away in a drawer.

"She said to tell you she's making chicken and dumplings."

Quent grinned. "Guess I could force myself. Tell Birdie I'll be along shortly."

He shoved back from his desk and crossed the room to pluck his hat from a peg by the door. "After lunch I'm planning to ride out to Widow's Peak. See if there's any fresh sign of Boyd Barlow. I should be back well before dark.''

"Don't worry about a thing, Marshal. I can handle the job.''

Quent strode down the dusty main street, knowing that his deputy was already sprawled in the chair, feet on the desk, hat over his eyes. It would take a dozen outlaws, guns blazing, to budge Arlo from that chair for the next hour or more.

As Quent strolled past the bank and the mercantile, he saw a crowd forming up ahead. Men and boys mostly, though a few women craned their necks, as well. When he got closer he saw the reason for the crowd.

Ruby Jewel was standing between Farley Duke, owner of the sawmill, and the handsome young banker, Byron Conner, staring at a spot of vacant land.

Quent shook his head. He should have expected that it was Ruby. No other woman in town could attract so many men. Like bees to honey.

As he drew near he could hear that smooth drawl. "Oh, no. It must have several steps up, so that the dirt of the road is not tramped inside on shoes. And windows, so that I can display my wares.''

Wares? That brought Quent up short. Lunch was forgotten as he veered off the path to join the others.

Farley finished his measurements. "I can start cutting the logs tomorrow, Miss Ruby. Soon as I finish up work on the Tates' barn.''

"That would be fine, Mr. Duke.'' Ruby pressed a fine silk handkerchief to her forehead, then touched it lightly to her throat. Both Farley and Byron Conner watched wide-eyed as her hand moved lower, to tuck the bit of silk into the cleft between her breasts.

"Morning, gentlemen." Quent stepped between them, then tipped his hat. "Ruby."

He saw the sudden narrowing of her eyes. It was the only indication that she hadn't forgotten. Or forgiven. "Planning on building something, are you?"

When Ruby didn't respond, Farley Duke nodded. "Miss Ruby is opening a new shop."

Quent couldn't hide his surprise. "That so? What for?"

"Miss Ruby is going to be making ladies' gowns and such," the banker said.

Quent knew his mouth was hanging open. But he couldn't help it. Somehow, he'd never imagined Ruby Jewel as a seamstress. In fact, it had never occurred to Quent that she knew how to do anything except flit around town like a colorful butterfly.

"It's just what this town needs," the banker went on. "The women of Hanging Tree will be delighted."

Quent felt a ripple of annoyance. If Ruby had been looking for a loan, this same banker would have laughed her out of town. But because the Jewel family kept all their money in his bank, he was positively fawning over her.

"Mr. Duke, my sister Jade said you might be willing to oversee the workers, as well. She said she couldn't have built the Golden Rule without your help." Ruby gave the owner of the sawmill a smile so warm it would have melted glaciers.

"Why, yes, ma'am. I'd be pleased to take care of that for you."

"Thank you, Mr. Duke. And thank you, Mr. Conner." She offered her hand and the banker accepted as though he were holding a banknote worth a king's ransom. "I value your opinion. For a woman alone, it is so comforting to know I have friends I can trust."

"And I value your...friendship, Miss Jewel."

Quent gave a hiss of disgust. Ruby Jewel knew exactly what she was doing. She had these two fools practically drooling over the chance to help her in any way they could.

"When do you think I can settle in?" Ruby asked.

Farley scratched his head, mentally calculating. "If the weather holds, ma'am, we can have the building up in a couple of weeks. After that, it'll be easy to finish the inside. I'd say a month. Maybe a little longer."

"Oh, that is wonderful news, Mr. Duke." She clapped her hands in delight and danced around, causing the hem of her gown to swirl. The display of shapely ankles caused both men to smile their appreciation.

Quent's frown deepened. These two were worse than fools. They were behaving like a couple of lechers.

"Well, ma'am." Farley glanced at Quent, then rubbed his hand on his pants and offered it to Ruby. "I'll be here tomorrow with a crew."

"That's fine, Mr. Duke. I'll be here, too." Ruby accepted his handshake, then turned to lay a hand on the banker's arm. "You will keep me informed of the cost?"

"Yes, ma'am." He closed a hand over hers. "I'll personally see to it that your money is well spent. You can count on me being here every day."

As would every man in town, Quent thought irritably.

When they walked away, Ruby remained, staring at the patch of dusty earth as though it were a palace.

Quent cleared his throat.

She turned her head and fixed him with a cold look. "Are you still here, Marshal? I thought by now you'd be busy arresting some terrible outlaw."

"There don't seem to be any outlaws around at the moment."

"Then perhaps you should arrest some poor helpless lady."

He threw back his head and laughed. He couldn't help himself. The fire in her eyes was positively scorching. "Ruby, you're neither poor nor helpless. And in fact, after that little charade, I'm not even certain you're a lady."

"Charade?" She turned on him, hands on her hips. "Whatever are you talking about?"

"Don't use that innocent act on me. Those fluttery lashes. The heaving bosom. That breathless little voice. And that smile when you thanked Farley and Byron. Ruby, you may be just about the best actress this town has ever seen."

"Oh, what a terrible thing to say. I was just being myself." She stomped her foot and turned her back on him. "You are a mean, miserable, spiteful man."

"And arrogant," he said, trying not to laugh. "Don't forget arrogant."

"Oh, you are that," she called over her shoulder before walking away.

A few steps later he caught up with her.

"Now what do you want?" she demanded.

"Nothing. I just noticed we're headed in the same direction." He was struggling hard not to laugh again, knowing it would only add fuel to the fire burning in those eyes.

As they passed Durfee's Mercantile, he caught sight of Lavinia Thurlong and Gladys Witherspoon huddling in the doorway with Effie Spitz. The three women fell silent and stared hard at Ruby as she approached.

Seeing them, she lifted her head and stared straight ahead.

"Is it true, Miss Jewel," Lavinia began, "that you spent the night in jail with Beau Baskin?"

Quent's head came up sharply, but before he could utter a word Ruby said, in her most charming French accent, "I do not believe I could have heard correctly. Is it your suggestion, Mrs. Thurlong, that Beau and I spent the night together?"

Lavinia's face turned several shades of scarlet, while Rufus Durfee and several men inside the store could be heard choking on their laughter.

"If that is what you are suggesting, then you must also think Marshal Regan would not only permit such a thing, but, in fact, demand it. Is that what you are implying? That your fine marshal is competing with Buck Coffee and his saloon?"

"You know perfectly well what I mean—" Lavinia began.

But Ruby cut her off with a tart "I would think your meaning is very clear, Mrs. Thurlong."

She swept along the walkway, her head high, her eyes straight ahead.

Beside her, Quent was silently cheering. This time, Lavinia had met her match.

When they reached Millie Potter's boardinghouse, and Quent climbed the steps behind her, Ruby gave a little groan of disgust. "I should have known there was no escaping you, Marshal. I suppose you're having lunch here, too?"

"Yes, ma'am."

"I hope you're satisfied," she muttered. "The idle gossip of your deputy's wife has made me an object of scorn."

"Only among those three fools," Quent said.

"Then you do not understand the nature of people," she said softly. "The tale will be repeated until I am made to sound like the most wicked creature ever born."

He didn't know about the most wicked. But looking down into those fiery eyes, he would have to call her the most beautiful ever born.

He reached around her and opened the door. As she brushed past, he inhaled the exotic fragrance of her perfume and felt the rush of heat. At once he realized his mistake. If he had half a brain, he'd skip lunch and head right out to Widow's Peak, where the only trouble he'd have to face would be an outlaw's bullets.

"Well, Ruby. What a nice surprise." Millie Potter looked up with a smile. In her hand was a pitcher of buttermilk, which she was pouring into several glasses. "I didn't know you'd be favoring us with a visit today."

"I was in town and thought I'd stay for lunch."

"I'm so glad." When Millie caught sight of the marshal directly behind Ruby, her smile grew considerably brighter. "Hello, Quent. I was hoping you hadn't forgotten."

"Now, how could I forget chicken and dumplings?"

"I thought that might get your interest. Sit down," Millie called. "Make yourselves comfortable. I'll only be a minute."

She disappeared into the kitchen.

Quent called out greetings to the four ranchers standing to one side of the room, discussing the latest problems with crops and weather. "'Afternoon Gus, Willie, Sam, Gordon. You all know Miss Ruby Jewel."

Though the ranchers answered him with nods and murmurs, their gazes were riveted on the woman beside him. Quent felt a moment of annoyance. Ruby Jewel seemed to have the same effect on men everywhere. But, he had to admit, it wasn't a deliberate effort on her part. She was simply a magnet for men's attention. Not that he didn't understand. Besides her obvious beauty, there was that charming manner. She just couldn't help herself. It was as natural for her to bestow a radiant smile on each man as it was for a cat to purr.

"We were just about to take a seat," one of the men called. "Glad you're joining us."

All four men fell over themselves to hold Ruby's chair and sit beside her. But since Quent was the closest he managed to beat them to it. As he took his seat, his thigh brushed hers and he could feel the heat clear through his clothes. Though his first reaction was annoyance, he had to admit that it was not an altogether unpleasant sensation. Especially since she was so busy trying to ignore him.

Millie emerged from the kitchen, carrying a platter of chicken. Damp little tendrils of red hair had slipped from the knot atop her head to cling to her cheeks. She was trailed by Birdie Bidwell, the neighbor girl who helped with the chores. Though Birdie was tall for thirteen, and clumsy, she made up for it by taking great care not to knock over anything as she served the guests. She seemed especially in awe of the glamorous Ruby Jewel.

"Help yourself," Millie called as she set the platter in the center of the table.

At once hands reached out and plates and bowls of steaming food were passed. But when the men saw Ruby sitting primly, her hands in her lap, they remembered their manners and deferred to her. When it came to impressing her, each of the ranchers seemed determined to outdo his neighbor.

"Rolls, Miss Ruby?" asked the bewhiskered Gus.

"Thank you." Ruby helped herself to one and passed the basket to Quent.

"Chicken, Miss Ruby?" Tall, mannerly Gordon actually ladled a piece of chicken onto her plate.

"My, these dumplings sure do look good, Miss Ruby. Will you have some?" Willie, toothless and skinny as a fence rail, held the platter for her.

"*Merci,*" she purred.

Birdie stood at one end of the table, removing serving dishes as they were emptied and returning to the kitchen for refills.

"I made enough for everyone," Millie cautioned as Birdie returned with another platter of chicken.

Millie, a pretty young widow, was neat as a pin, and kept her boardinghouse in perfect order. Her reputation as a fine cook earned her enough money to raise her three little daughters.

The large wood table had been set with Millie's collection of mismatched dishes and crockery. Despite an occasional crack in a cup, or chip in a plate, everything was clean and colorful, like their owner.

On a sideboard holding an assortment of desserts was a vase of wildflowers, adding their perfume to air already sweet with the fragrance of apples and cinnamon.

"Where are April, May and June?" Quent asked as he reached for a steaming biscuit.

"The girls are at school." Millie filled his cup with coffee, then moved around the table topping off the rest. "They'll be sorry they missed you, Quent. They love your silly jokes and teasing."

Ruby glanced at him in surprise. It would be easier to imagine the marshal engaged in a gunfight with a dozen outlaws than to picture him joking and teasing with three little girls.

"What brings you to town in the middle of the

week, Ruby?'' Millie, ever the proper hostess, set a
glass of lemonade in front of her.

Ruby sipped gratefully. ''I was here to meet with
my banker and Farley Duke about building my new
shop.''

''Shop?'' Millie paused on her way back to the
kitchen. ''What sort of shop?''

''A dressmaker shop.''

''Who's going to work it?'' Millie asked.

Ruby arched a brow. ''Why, I am.''

''You?'' Millie's eyes widened. ''You can sew?''

''Of course.'' Ruby set down her glass and met
the surprised looks of those around the table. ''Why
do so many people find this difficult to believe? I
was taught to sew all my own clothes when I was a
girl.'' She touched a napkin to her lips, then, noting
the hole in it, added, ''Why, I could even make you
a fine new lace tablecloth and matching napkins.''

Millie's chores were suddenly forgotten. She
walked back to the table and paused beside Ruby.
''Lace?'' She spoke the word with a trace of rever-
ence, as though it were magic. ''Really?''

Ruby nodded. ''And if you'd like, I could add
matching lace curtains for the window.''

Millie glanced toward the window, hung with a
pair of simple white cotton panels tied back with
faded strips of fabric. ''Lace curtains,'' she said with
a sigh. Then she suddenly shook her head, as though
forcing herself back to reality. ''I couldn't possibly
afford it.''

Before she could leave the room Ruby said, ''How
do you know if you can afford it, when you haven't

heard my price? If you'd like, you could pay me a little at a time, as you earn it.''

Millie kept her face averted. But it was plain, by her hesitation, that she was doing some heavy calculating. ''How soon...?''

Before she could finish her question, Ruby blurted, ''I could start as soon as the lace arrives from San Francisco. Since I'm sending an order by stage tomorrow, you could be enjoying your lovely things within a matter of weeks.''

''Oh, my.'' Millie's eyes were dancing with pleasure as she turned. ''A few weeks? Really?''

''*Oui*. Would you care to be my first customer?''

Millie paused for only a moment before saying softly, ''I've wanted lace for such a long time now.''

''After lunch I will measure the table and window and give you a price.''

Millie nodded. ''If I can possibly afford it, I'll do it.''

When she made her way to the kitchen to fetch plates for the desserts, there was a new spring to Millie's step. Behind her, Ruby was so excited she could hardly do more than pick at her food.

When she turned her head, she realized that Quent was studying her with a strange look on his face.

''Now what, Marshal?'' she said in a undertone. ''Are you going to accuse me of taking advantage of my neighbor?''

''No, ma'am.'' His voice was low, for her ears alone. ''I was just thinking I'd misjudged you. I believe you may have the makings of a fine businesswoman.''

She couldn't imagine why his words warmed her. After all, she didn't give a care what Marshal Quent Regan thought of her. Still, this simple lunch had taken on a festive note. The men's jokes were funnier, and the apple pie sweeter. And by the time she'd measured the table and window, and secured an agreement with Millie Potter, Ruby floated out the door on a cloud.

She lifted her skirts and strolled through town until she came to the stable where she'd left her horse and rig.

"Afternoon, Miss Ruby." Neville Oakley, blacksmith and owner of the livery stable, was a giant who stood over six and a half feet and weighed more than 350 pounds. Despite the heat of the day, he was standing in front of a roaring fire, shaping and forging a horseshoe. Rivers of sweat ran down his face and glistened on his bulging forearms.

The moment he caught sight of Ruby he dropped everything and hurried inside the stable to hitch her horse. Minutes later he emerged into the sunshine leading the horse and rig.

"Thank you, Mr. Oakley. What do I owe you?"

"It's hardly worth a thing, Miss Ruby. You weren't in town more than half a day."

Ruby glanced at this rough man, who seemed to have earned the scorn of most of the town's citizens. His hair, shaggy and coal black, seemed always plastered to his sweat-stained face. People whispered behind his back. It was said that in his youth he'd been a drunk and a bully, though no one had seen him take a drink in years, and no one could be found who'd ever had the misfortune to fight with him. But in a small town like Hanging Tree, a man's reputation could be his best friend or his worst enemy. No matter how long he lived, or how well, it seemed impossible to erase the mistakes of his youth. To make matters worse, Neville Oakley presented a truly loathsome image to behold. His clothes were always shabby, his leather apron stained and work worn. He was a man feared by the town's women and children and avoided by its men.

From her first introduction to the man, Ruby had felt a kinship with him. She knew what it was to bear the jeers and whispers of others. And she understood the pain of living with a reputation that would not be put to rest.

She held out a small, linen-clad bundle. "I am sorry, Mr. Oakley. I must insist that you take some payment. After all, my horse did eat your oats and drink your water. And my rig took up space in your barn."

"What's this?" He kept his hands at his sides, refusing to accept her offering.

"Lunch, Mr. Oakley. From Mrs. Potter's boardinghouse." Ruby pressed it to his chest and he was forced to accept it or have it fall to the ground.

He seemed overwhelmed by this unexpected act of kindness. But to make matters worse, Ruby forced a coin into his big palm.

He took a step back, nearly dropping everything in his haste to avoid touching her. "Careful, ma'am. You'll get yourself all sweaty and dirty."

She smiled. "Dirt washes off, Mr. Oakley. And I admire the sweat of honest labor."

When she climbed into her rig and lifted the reins she called, "Good day, Mr. Oakley. Thank you for taking such fine care of my horse and rig. Enjoy your lunch."

The big man watched until she drove away. Then he sat down in the shade of a tree and unwrapped the linen as though it were the most cherished gift he'd ever been given. In fact, it was the first gift he could ever recall having been given. He stared at the chicken and fresh biscuits, drizzled with honey. And at the oversize piece of apple pie. For the longest time he didn't move. Then, brushing something from his eyes, he began to eat, savoring every morsel.

Quent emerged from the stable where he'd been saddling his horse. He hadn't meant to eavesdrop. But now that he had, he was even more confused about Ruby Jewel.

Did she just have to charm every man she met? Was this why she'd gone out of her way to be kind to Neville Oakley? Or was there more to this young woman than he'd first suspected?

Damn her. Just when he wanted to dismiss her as a shameless flirt, she had to confound him again.

He urged his horse into a run. Since he was headed her way, maybe he'd just engage Miss Ruby Jewel in a little conversation. And see what he uncovered.

Chapter Seven

"Oh, Marshal." Ruby gave a startled glance as Quent pulled up beside her cart. Then her tone hardened. "Are you following me? Because, if you are, I can assure you, I've done nothing wrong."

"I'm not following you, Ruby." He slowed his mount to keep pace with her rig and wondered again at her reaction to him. Was it personal? Or was she reacting to the badge he wore? "I'm heading past your ranch to Widow's Peak."

She visibly relaxed. "I suppose I should be grateful for your company, since I find the long ride tedious."

At her admission he said, "Then why don't you let me handle the reins? That is, if you have no objection."

It was on the tip of her tongue to refuse. Instead, she stopped the horse and slid over to make room for him.

He tied his mount behind the rig, then climbed aboard and took up the reins.

"What will you do up at Widow's Peak?"

"Study the trails." He made light of his mission, attempting to put her at ease. "It's something lawmen like to do."

"Why do you study them?"

"To see how many horses have passed by, and how long ago."

"You can tell all this by looking at the ground?"

He nodded.

Impressed, she asked, "And what will that tell you?"

"If there are any strangers in the area."

"How long have you been a lawman?"

"Almost ten years." He grew thoughtful, staring off into the distance. Had it really been that long? There were days when it seemed like a lifetime ago. At other times, it seemed like only yesterday.

"What made you decide to wear that badge, Marshal Regan?"

He smiled then, and she thought how handsome he was when he wasn't frowning at her. "I guess it was probably decided at birth."

At her arched brow, he explained, "My father was a lawman. It just seemed the most natural thing in the world to follow in his footsteps. Of course," he added softly, "there was a time when it looked like I might end up on the other side of the law. But I finally saw the light, thanks to your father."

"You...broke the law?"

He nodded, his eyes narrowing. "I was young, wild and foolish. And, for a while, angry. A dangerous combination."

She tried to picture this lawman on the other side

of the law, but it was impossible. "What did my father have to do with your decision?"

"I guess he saw something in me that I wasn't able to see in myself. Your father was a remarkable man, Ruby."

"Tell me about him," she said softly.

He glanced at her in surprise. "I figured Onyx Jewel's daughter would know him better'n most."

She looked away, but not before he saw the pain in her eyes. "I hardly knew my father at all. His visits to Bayou Rouge were brief. And infrequent."

Quent didn't know why, but he wished he could find a way to soothe her. It gave him no pleasure to see pain. Especially in such lovely eyes.

As the sun dipped below a bank of clouds, Ruby shivered.

He shot her a glance. "You're cold."

She shook her head, but he ignored her protest and removed his cowhide jacket, wrapping it around her. The heat of his body still lingered in the folds, along with the scent of horse and tobacco. Scents that would always remind Ruby of her father.

With a sigh she snuggled into the comforting heat. "*Merci*, Marshal. I am accustomed to the heat of the bayou. I'm not yet used to such abrupt changes in the weather."

Quent didn't know why, but there was something about Ruby Jewel that touched a chord deep inside him. Despite her attempts to appear worldly, he sensed an innocence about her. An innocence and a vulnerability. And more than that, a deep well of sadness. It seemed suddenly important that he put a smile on her lips.

He lifted a hand to point. "If you want to know your father, look around you, Ruby. For as far as you can see in any direction, it's Jewel land. There aren't many men who could have carved all this out of an untamed wilderness. But your pa wasn't like other men." His tone warmed, revealing his deep regard. "Onyx Jewel was a legend even before his death at the hands of a coward. Your pa did something no other man did. He tamed this land and made it his home. And afterward, he traveled the world searching for the best cattle, the finest equipment. The folks here in Hanging Tree were grateful that, no matter how far Onyx Jewel went, he always returned home. To the soil. To his roots. To the people who loved and respected him."

Ruby was surprised by the depth of emotion revealed in those words. "I didn't know you cared so deeply for my father." She tried to be flip, but the words held a brittle edge. "I suppose it's easier to care for a rich man than a poor one."

"I didn't give a damn about his wealth." Quent's tone roughened as he eased the horse and rig into a swollen stream and guided them through the water. "Your pa was a good, decent man. He took the time to care about everybody in Hanging Tree. That says more about a man than the size of his fortune."

Ruby arched a brow. "How did he show his concern for the townspeople? What did he do for them?"

Quent shrugged. "He never talked about it. But I've heard stories."

"Stories?" She found herself staring at his hands, so strong and sure. So like another's hands, which had always been surprisingly gentle.

"Rumors. Repeated over the years. How he forgave debts. How he would order his wranglers to slaughter a heifer and deliver it to a poor widow or struggling rancher. How, after his wife died in childbirth, he sent his ranch foreman East with orders to fetch a doctor for the town, so no other rancher would have to suffer the same loss."

Ruby fell silent. Hadn't Mama told her how tender her father had become when he'd learned that she was having his child? It must have broken his heart when he learned that Madeline would neither marry him nor bring his infant daughter Ruby to live with him in Texas.

She felt tears sting her eyes, thinking about the pain her father had been forced to bear in stoic silence. Far away in Louisiana, she had thought of him merely as a rich stranger, who could have anything he desired. But now, seeing the primitive land he'd tamed, and the loneliness he must have endured, she felt his pain keenly. For all his wealth and power, he couldn't have the thing he most wanted. A wife and family around him, to give him love and comfort.

"Thank you, Marshal. For giving me a glimpse of my father."

"You're like him, you know, Ruby."

At the marshal's words, she turned to him in surprise. "In what way?"

"You have his enthusiasm for life. And his kindness toward people. All people."

"Now, how would you know that?" she asked.

He shrugged, thinking of what he'd witnessed at the livery. "I've seen how you deal with the folks in town. You make time for those the others don't even notice. That's a real gift. One that not all people are blessed with."

She was deeply moved by his words. "I can't think of anything that would give me more pride than to be compared favorably with my father," she murmured. "There haven't been too many things in my life to be proud of."

"And why is that?"

She felt the heat rise to her cheeks and turned away. "No reason. I...don't know why I said that."

But Quent wouldn't let it go. "What is it, Ruby? Why wouldn't you feel proud to be a Jewel?"

She swallowed, ashamed at having been trapped by her own words. "In my small town it was common knowledge that my father and mother were unmarried. There were those who never let me forget it."

Quent's jaw clamped tight, and he concentrated on handling the reins. But his heart went out to this young woman beside him. He knew only too well that self-esteem was a precious thing.

When they made it across the stream, the horse scrambled up the embankment, and the rig tilted precariously for a moment. Quent's arm closed around Ruby's shoulders, holding her steady until the rig righted itself. It was a simple gesture, but she found herself trembling at the strength in his touch.

He suddenly released her and drew hard on the reins, bringing the horse and cart to an abrupt halt. His hand went reflexively to the gun at his hip. Ruby followed the direction of his gaze and saw the darkened outline of a cluster of horsemen galloping toward them at breakneck speed.

"Who…?" Ruby felt a flash of fear.

He touched a rough palm to her lips to silence her. "Not a word," he cautioned.

In one smooth motion he leapt from the rig and lifted her in his arms. For the space of a heartbeat she felt strangely disoriented, her face inches from his, her breath mingling with his, her heart beating overtime. And then he set her on her feet behind a tree, where she was shielded from danger. And he boldly stepped out, to face alone whatever was to come.

She studied the broad back, the muscled shoulders. His hand holding the gun was calm, steady. He turned slightly, to assure himself that she was still hidden from view. She caught a glimpse of hard, steely eyes. And the glint of the badge over his heart.

Again she found herself wondering what would make a man willing to risk his life for others.

As the horses and riders drew near, Ruby saw Quent suddenly holster his gun. She chanced a quick look around the tree and let out the breath she'd been unconsciously holding.

"It's Diamond and Adam," she said on a rush of relief. "Riding with the wranglers."

As the party drew abreast of them, Diamond glanced from her sister to the marshal with a frown of concern. "We didn't expect to see you out here, Quent. Has there been some more trouble?"

"It's not what you're thinking." Quent gave her a reassuring smile. He didn't want to be the cause of any trouble between these two sisters. And he could see that everyone was willing to jump to conclusions about Ruby after her "incident." "I was just accompanying Ruby, since I'm on my way to Widow's Peak."

Diamond was instantly alert. "You looking for anything in particular?"

His tone was guarded. "I don't know yet. Just thought I'd look around. See if there's any kind of familiar pattern to the tracks. If you'd like, I can stop by your ranch on the way back and let you know what I find."

"I'd appreciate it," Diamond said. "If there's any sign of trouble, we'll post extra wranglers around the herd. But instead of our ranch, stop by Pa's." Though each of her sisters, as well as foreman Cal McCabe, owned a share of the huge spread, she still referred to the Jewel ranch as her father's. "Carmelita is fixing supper. If you don't mind stopping there, we'll see that Carmelita saves you some food."

"You just said the magic word." Quent walked to the rear of the rig and began untying his horse. "Wild mustangs couldn't make me miss a chance to enjoy Carmelita's cooking."

Before he could swing into the saddle, Ruby

stopped him with a hand on his arm. "You almost forgot your jacket."

"Keep it." He closed a hand over hers. "You still have a way to go. And it doesn't look like the sun is coming back."

She couldn't resist teasing. "Are you sure you can trust me, Marshal?"

"I wouldn't worry about it. I know where you live if I have to come after you."

Ruby's smile grew. Though his words could have stung, she had detected an underlying warmth in them.

He helped her into the rig and watched as she flicked the reins and followed behind the party of horsemen. He continued to watch until they disappeared over a ridge.

The silence of the day closed around him as he pulled himself into the saddle and started off at a fast clip.

Though the air had grown cooler, he was unaware of anything except the warmth he felt at the simple touch of Ruby. A warmth that lingered as his horse ate up the miles.

"You'd better set another place, Carmelita." As soon as Diamond warmly embraced the housekeeper, she added, "I invited Quent Regan to stop by."

"Ah, the marshal. That is good." Carmelita removed a tray of corn bread from the oven and turned away before Diamond could help herself to a sample. "The more men the better. I grow weary of trying to cook for this one." She pointed a wooden spoon at Ruby. "These last few days she has hardly eaten a thing. I think I am losing my touch."

"It isn't you, Carmelita," Ruby assured her. "I've just had more important things on my mind than eating."

"You see?" The housekeeper frowned. "What can be more important than food? What I miss the most is having men around. Men with hearty appetites." She sighed as she stirred a pot of venison stew. "At least when Cal lived here, he could eat almost as much as your father."

"But then he had to go and fall in love with Pearl and set up housekeeping miles from here," Diamond said.

"*Sí.* But at least while he was here, and Adam began courting you, I had two hungry men to feed." She glanced around. "By the way, where is Adam?"

"He's with the wranglers at the bunkhouse." Diamond managed to break off a piece of steaming corn bread before Carmelita's spoon came down on her knuckles. "He noticed Cal was still here. He wanted to talk to him before Cookie called the wranglers to supper and Cal headed home to Pearl." She turned away, stuffing the morsel into her mouth before she could be stopped.

"You will sit over there," Carmelita said sternly, pointing to the far side of the room. "Or there will be nothing left for supper."

Diamond's antics had Ruby bursting into gales of laughter. The two sisters were still giggling when the back door opened and Adam came in, followed by Quent Regan.

"What's so funny?" Adam asked as he brushed a kiss over the housekeeper's cheek.

"Some things do not change." Though Carmelita's words were terse, there was a twinkle in her eye. "I can see that marriage has not changed your wife. She is still that naughty child I was always scolding."

"And if she ever changes," Adam said with a wink in his wife's direction, "I'll find myself hunting the world over for the naughty woman I fell in love with."

Carmelita wiped her hands on her apron as she greeted Quent. "Welcome, Marshal. I am pleased that you could come for supper."

"Not half as pleased as I am, Carmelita. There's nothing I like better than good home cooking."

"And, according to Carmelita, nothing she likes better than working her fingers to the bone for some ungrateful man," Diamond said with mock sarcasm.

"My kind of woman." Quent followed Adam's lead by hanging his hat on a peg and washing his hands in a basin by the door.

"You will sit," the housekeeper said as she removed the first platter from the stove.

Within minutes the table was laden with steaming bowls of venison stew, a platter of beef lavished with red and green chilis, and corn bread still warm from the oven.

As they dug in to their meal, Diamond asked, "So we've been talking about Boyd Barlow. Did you see any sign of him up on Widow's Peak, Quent?"

He shook his head. "No trail. Nothing to make me

think he's still in the area. But on the way back I stopped by to see Frank and Nellie Cooper. Frank thought he spotted a horseman up in the foothills a couple of days ago.''

"It could have been one of our wranglers," Diamond said logically.

"That's what I thought. But Frank said this man was a stranger. And the horse he described sounded a lot like one stolen from a nearby ranch." Quent shook his head. "Still, Nellie thinks it's just Frank's age catching up with him. Says his eyes aren't what they once were.''

"Pa used to say ranching's for the young and the hungry,'' Diamond muttered.

Adam grinned at his wife across the table. "I guess that'd describe us. Young and hungry.''

"Or at least hungry," Quent said, filling his plate a second time. "Carmelita, this is the best venison stew I've ever tasted.''

She set a cup of hot black coffee beside him. "What you need is a wife to cook for you.''

"No, thanks. After spending days on end listening to Arlo's complaints about his wife, that's the last thing I want. Still, I'd be willing to settle for a house-keeper. But only if she can cook like you.''

"Wives can be good for other things," Adam said, causing Diamond's cheeks to turn scarlet.

To hide her embarrassment, she sputtered, "Arlo's wife is a fool. And ever since being befriended by Lavinia Thurlong and Gladys Witherspoon, she's become impossible. Sharing secrets, spreading gossip.

They're only happy if they're making someone else miserable.''

Adam chuckled. "Now, don't get started on your favorite subject.''

Ruby began moving the food around her plate. Recalling the scene at Durfee's Mercantile, she discovered she wasn't very hungry. Though she had reacted with indifference, the truth was, she'd been stung by Lavinia's words. She'd felt as she had when she'd been a child, listening to the cruel gibes and mocking laughter of the prim-and-proper girls at Notre Dame du Bayou.

Across the table Quent studied Ruby, lost in thought, and realized she'd been more deeply affected by those silly women in town than she'd let on. Though it was none of his business, he searched for a way to bring her out of her painful reverie.

"You'd have been proud of your sister today, Diamond," he said suddenly. "Did she tell you she managed to snag her first customer?"

"Who?" Diamond asked.

"Millie Potter." Quent watched as Ruby's little frown was gradually replaced with a smile. "Ruby had her talked into a new lace table cover before she'd even finished with lunch."

"Oh, Ruby, that's wonderful." Diamond closed her hand over her sister's. "Millie's boardinghouse is the perfect place to display your work."

Ruby nodded. "That's what I've been thinking. If I can get just one or two women to admire some of my handiwork, the others will come around."

"So you won't be making just gowns now," Diamond said.

Ruby shrugged. "I guess only time will tell. Sewing is sewing. I can make a gown, a hat, a rug, or a man's shirt. It matters not to me."

At the mention of a shirt, Quent glanced down at his own. "I've been meaning to mend these holes, but I never seem to find time. Think you could whip me up another shirt like this one?"

Ruby smiled. "Yours is a simple enough request, Marshal. But I would have to take your measurements."

"All right." He lifted his cup to his lips and studied her over the rim. "How about after supper?"

"After supper will be fine."

Carmelita approached the table with bowls of peach cobbler, topped off with heavy sweetened cream. While the others dug in to their dessert, Ruby nibbled hers and wondered why she suddenly felt too warm.

It was not the thought of measuring Quent Regan's chest and shoulders, she told herself sternly. It was merely the heat of the kitchen. And the result of all this food. But when the meal was over, Ruby insisted on helping Carmelita clear the table.

"Go," the housekeeper said, shooing her aside. "I do not want your help, Señorita Ruby."

"But the dishes..."

"Are my job, and I'm almost through with them. Go." Carmelita turned her around and gave her a shove.

"Come on." Diamond linked her arm with Ruby's. "You know Carmelita is going to have her way."

They walked to the parlor, where a fire already blazed on the grate. Adam and Quent were standing in front of the fireplace, smoking cigars, talking in low tones.

"You going to check out Frank Cooper's story?"

Quent nodded. "I've been thinking it's time I took a long, leisurely tour of the territory."

"That'd take weeks."

"Maybe, but..." Seeing the two women crossing the room, he let the words he'd been about to say die on his lips. Instead, he made a move to toss his cigar into the fire. "Sorry," he muttered. "I should have saved this for the ride home."

"Not at all." Ruby stopped him with a hand on his arm. "I like the smell of tobacco. Probably because the only time I smelled it in my house was when my papa came to visit. And that was always such a happy time for Mama and me."

Quent tried not to stare at her hand. But he could feel the heat of her touch clear through his sleeve. "It's nice that your ma didn't object. My father had to do his smoking in the barn. I guess I've always associated it with something that shouldn't be done in front of ladies."

"And when did you ever think of me as a lady?" Diamond asked as she glanced down at her buckskins and boots.

Quent grinned. "You'd be surprised how many men in Hanging Tree noticed you, Diamond, buckskins or not. The only trouble was, your father was a formidable obstacle. There weren't too many men who would have risked Onyx Jewel's temper. Or his gun.''

As the others laughed, Ruby said softly, "It must have made you feel very safe to have your father always here to watch out for you.''

Diamond dropped an arm around her sister. "I did feel safe. And loved. I only wish I'd known about you. And Pearl. And Jade. It makes me sad to know that while I was enjoying Pa's love, you and the others were denied so much.''

Ruby's hand went to the gold rope at her throat, and her fingers closed over the two stones, one onyx, one ruby. Beside her, Diamond touched a hand to the matching one at her own throat, containing an onyx and a diamond.

"Don't be sad for me," Ruby whispered. "Papa loved all of us. And he is, as he promised, with us still.''

The two sisters touched cheeks in an intimate gesture, before stepping apart.

"I have brought some refreshments." Carmelita entered with a tray containing several glasses and decanters. "And I will say good-night now. Rosario is here to take me home.''

"Thanks for the dinner," Diamond said as she pressed a kiss to the older woman's cheek. "It's the best food Adam and I have had in ages.''

"Oh. You don't like my cooking?" Adam teased. He kissed the housekeeper and added, "I appreciate this meal even more than Diamond. It gave me a break from my own cooking.''

"And I would have eaten cold beans and dried beef along the trail," Quent said as he brushed yet another kiss to Carmelita's cheek.

"Then you must come back often." Carmelita was blushing at all the compliments. Especially from such handsome men. "I like to cook. But I like even more to see someone enjoy my cooking."

With a swirl of skirts, she was gone.

Diamond filled two tumblers with whiskey and handed them to the men. Then, pouring tea into small fragile cups, she handed one to Ruby and sipped the other.

"Here's to your first customer," Diamond said, lifting her cup and clinking it against Ruby's. "To Millie Potter. May she be the first of many."

Everyone touched glasses and cups, then settled themselves comfortably around the fire, Adam and Diamond on a love seat, Quent and Ruby in nearby chairs.

"Tell me about the shop," Diamond urged.

"It will be small," Ruby said, "but adequate for my needs. Shelves along one wall to hold an assortment of fabrics. Windows, to display goods." As she spoke, she became more animated. Her eyes took on a liveliness, a light that hadn't been there moments before. "And a little room in back where the ladies can try on their gowns in private, if they wish, and where I can keep my accounts."

Diamond studied her while she spoke, then shook her head. "It's still hard for me to think of you as a businesswoman, Ruby. But it sounds as though you know exactly what you want."

"All I want is to feel useful here in Hanging Tree. To belong," Ruby said softly. "It's all I've ever wanted."

Quent's eyes narrowed slightly. Did she realize how much she'd just revealed? He tipped his glass and drained it. Standing, he said, "I'd better get going. It's a long ride back to town. And I'm sure Arlo's been asleep at my desk for hours."

"You can't leave until Ruby measures you for a new shirt," Diamond reminded him.

Quent looked distinctly uncomfortable. "Maybe we'd better leave that for another time."

"Don't be silly." Diamond took the empty glass from him and refilled it before handing it back. Turning to Ruby, she said, "Go get whatever you need, while we visit with Quent."

Ruby left the room and returned minutes later with a small pouch. Dumping the contents on a table, she rummaged through them until she located a measuring tape and slate and chalk.

Turning to Quent, she said, "I'm afraid you're too tall, Marshal. Would you mind kneeling here on the hearth?"

Kneel? Hell, Quent thought, he'd lie down and die as long as she asked him in that cool, breathless voice.

He did as he was told, and had to swallow back a smile when Ruby stood in front of him. If she knew what he was looking at, and just where his thoughts were right now, she'd lay him flat with a few well-chosen curses in that exotic mix of French, Cajun and English that she used so expressively.

He thought about closing his eyes and trying to concentrate on horse thieves. But there was no way in hell he was going to try anything noble right now. He was enjoying himself far too much. He kept his gaze fixed on the darkened cleft between those lush breasts. Damned if he wasn't near drowning in the smell of her, the touch of her.

Ruby wound a length of tape around Quent's shoulders. As her hand brushed his upper arm, she felt the strength in him. And felt, too, the way he reacted to her touch. Like a horse, quivering. It should have given her a sense of power. But instead, it only added to her feelings of inadequacy. *Mon Dieu,* could he hear the beating of her heart? Or the way her breath caught in her throat?

When she was assured that she had the right size, she stepped away to mark it down, grateful for the chance to move a little away and calm her labored breathing.

Quent, too, seemed deeply affected by this encounter. He stood, lifted the tumbler and took several long drinks of whiskey.

"Now your chest," she said.

He set the tumbler on the mantel and moved his arms out stiffly at his sides.

Ruby had never felt so unnerved in her life. With Adam and Diamond standing to one side watching, and Quent staring down at her in that quiet, watchful way he had, she became aware of the fact that she was the center of attention. Like an actress overcome with stage fright, she found herself momentarily paralyzed. Then, forcing herself to move, she reached around his back and drew the tape firmly about his chest.

"My. You are..." She could feel her mouth going dry. Could feel her heart beating like a bird caught in a trap. She swallowed. Loudly. Her voice sounded unusually loud in her ears. "A very big man, Marshal."

Her fingertips brushed his nipple, and he thought he'd die from the pleasure. If Adam and Diamond weren't here... Oh, the thought of what he'd like to do was driving him around the bend.

Nerves had Ruby letting go of the tape. For a moment she couldn't believe what she'd done. Then, biting back a curse, she dropped to the floor and fumbled around until she located it. She stood. And was forced to start over.

As her fingers guided the tape around his back, under his arms, across his chest, Quent stood very still, enduring the sweetest torture he'd ever known. If he were to move his face just a fraction, his lips would brush her temple. The thought brought a rush of heat that left him weak. For what seemed an eternity he forgot to breathe. His heart forgot to beat.

"There. I have it." She noted the size and jotted it down beside the others. "There is just one more measurement needed."

He groaned inwardly. He wasn't going to make it. If she touched him one more time, he'd lose whatever control he had left. And he'd embarrass her and himself by crushing her in his arms and kissing her until they were both breathless.

"Turn around, Marshal," she commanded.

She'd never know how grateful he was to obey. At least, for the moment, the proof of what he was thinking would be hidden from view.

She measured from his neck to his waist. The hair at his nape tickled the back of her hand, and she drew away as though burned.

Quent, too, felt the tremor when her hand brushed his collar. Little pinpricks of pleasure shot along his spine. The thought of those long, slender fingers running through his hair had him closing his eyes.

He heard the rustle of her skirt as she moved away.

"All right, Marshal."

He turned.

She kept her face averted as she busied herself at the table, returning everything to the little pouch.

For the space of several seconds he watched her, but she kept her lashes lowered, veiling her thoughts.

"Come on, Quent," Diamond called. "Adam and I will ride with you as far as our place."

Quent picked up the tumbler and drained it in one long swallow, then trailed the others to the door.

On the front porch Diamond and Adam kissed Ruby before mounting their horses.

Quent offered his hand. Ruby had no choice but to accept. The current that shot between them had the force of a bolt of lightning.

Though he frowned, he didn't let go of her hand. "Good night, Ruby. Thanks for supper."

"Good night, Marshal." She prayed her legs would support her a little longer. Just until he rode away. "I'll have your new shirt ready in a few days."

"There's no rush."

She glanced down at the big hand holding hers. "I don't mind. I'm grateful for the work."

He released her hand and forced himself to take a step back. Feeling more in control now, he strode toward his horse and pulled himself into the saddle.

"Good night," she called again.

As he urged his horse into the darkness, Quent turned for a last glimpse of Ruby, standing on the porch in a pool of lantern light.

Even now he could feel the touch of those hands, moving gently over him. And smell, in the clear night air, the fragrance of crushed roses.

Chapter Eight

Ruby flicked the reins, guiding the horse and rig along the dusty stretch of road heading into town. On the seat beside her, nestled between layers of brown paper to keep it safe from trail dust, lay the new shirt she'd made for Quent.

As she halted outside the livery, Neville Oakley lumbered forward.

"Morning, Miss Ruby."

"Good morning, Mr. Oakley."

He offered a hand and she stepped down, clutching the package.

"You look...pretty, ma'am."

"Thank you, Mr. Oakley." She gave him her brightest smile. "I won't be long. I have to see the marshal, and make a quick stop at Durfee's. There's no need to unhitch my horse."

"Yes, ma'am." He waited until Ruby disappeared up the street. Then he unhitched her horse and began rubbing it down before leading it to a stall, where it was given oats and water. That done, he thoroughly cleaned her rig.

Nothing was too good for Miss Ruby Jewel.

Ruby paused at the site of her new building. Farley Duke was directing a group of workmen who were unloading a pile of lumber from a wagon. When he caught sight of her he waved before continuing with his chore.

Ruby waved back and continued to watch in fascination as the men struggled beneath the load of wood until it was formed into several neat piles.

"Oh, Papa," she whispered. "Look at the wood for my shop." Her heart swelled with a rare sense of pride. "The shop I am building in your town. No," she suddenly corrected. "Not your town. It is my town now, as well."

As she continued along the dusty street, her heart felt lighter than it had in a very long time.

Outside the jail she paused to greet Arlo Spitz.

"Good morning, Deputy."

At the sight of her he set the broom against the wall and whipped his hat from his head. "Morning, Miss Ruby." He eyed the package in her hand. "What brings you to town this morning?"

"Business," she replied. The very sound of that word pleased her.

"With the marshal?"

She nodded. "Is he in?"

"Yep. But not for long." He leaned forward and lowered his voice, to convey the importance of what he was confiding. "The marshal got word about a rancher and his wife found dead."

"Here in Hanging Tree?"

"No, ma'am. About a week's ride from here. A local sheriff found them. Sent word for the marshal to come take a look."

"Are you going along, Deputy?"

Arlo puffed up his chest. "The marshal said someone has to stay here and take care of the folks in town."

"Yes, of course. How foolish of me not to think of such a thing." With a smile she swept past him and walked inside.

For a moment her smile disappeared as her gaze swept the empty cells and she recalled the night she'd been forced to spend here. Then she nudged aside the troubling thought. Today was a happy day. She wouldn't allow a dark cloud to spoil it.

Finding the office empty, she glanced toward Quent's private room. The door was open, and the shadow moving back and forth alerted her to his presence.

"Hello," she called.

Quent's tall frame filled the doorway. A bedroll was under his arm, and two fat saddlebags were slung over his shoulder. He carried a rifle in one hand.

"Good morning, Marshal. Arlo said you're leaving to hunt outlaws."

"That's right." He stayed where he was, drinking in the sight of her. "What brings you into town so early in the morning?"

"I wanted you to have your new shirt as soon as it was finished. But I didn't realize...I mean...I don't want to interfere with your work." She set the package on his desk. "You can open this when you get back."

"I'll open it now."

In quick strides he was across the room. He tossed his burdens aside and tore open the paper.

At first glance the shirt seemed ordinary enough. It was black, with black buttons. But when he touched it, he realized that she'd turned the fabric inside out, so that the tough outer sheen would wear like cowhide, and the soft inner nap would be against his skin.

"You...don't like it." She'd been watching his face. And she'd seen the way his eyes had narrowed slightly as he'd studied her work.

He didn't say a word. Just removed his cowhide jacket and began to unbutton his shirt. And while she watched in astonishment, he stripped off his old shirt and shrugged into the new one.

In those few moments she'd had a chance to see again the hard, chiseled body, the ripple of muscle. Her throat went dry at the sight of him.

"I...made it larger than the measurements, to allow for sudden movements." She was feeling suddenly shy. "I know that a lawman needs to draw his weapon, and occasionally engage in brawls."

He bit back the smile that hovered at the corners of his mouth. He was beginning to see what she thought of his job. "Occasionally."

"And I made the seams as strong as I could, so they wouldn't give way."

Now he was smiling. But he couldn't help himself.

"So, even if I'm knocked around and find myself bruised and bloody, my shirt will remain intact."

She lowered her head. "I believe you're mocking me, Marshal."

He touched a hand to her cheek. "I would never mock you, Ruby. I was just having fun with you. I couldn't resist." He couldn't resist moving his thumb across her lips, either, before he lowered his hand to his side. "It's a fine shirt. And I thank you. Now, what do I owe you?"

"Fifty cents."

"Fifty cents? What kind of price is that?" he demanded.

"That's the price Rufus Durfee is charging for his shirts."

"Durfee's shirts are made out of old feed sacks," he said irritably. "And this..." He looked up. "Where did you get this fabric?"

"I bought it in New Orleans. I was going to make a special shirt for my papa."

"You probably paid more for the material than I'd pay for a good rifle." He dug in to his pocket and unrolled several bills.

Seeing it, she shook her head. "I will take no more than fifty cents. It is only fair. Otherwise you could have bought your new shirt at Durfee's Mercantile, and you would have had it days ago."

"Ruby." He pressed a bill into her hand and closed his hand over hers. "I really want to keep this shirt. But I won't, unless you allow me to pay what's fair."

She continued to look troubled, though she finally nodded her head in reluctant agreement.

He surprised her by lifting her hand to his lips. She felt a rush of heat clear up her arm.

"Thank you," he murmured. "Now I really have to leave. But I'll think of you whenever I wear this shirt."

He tossed the saddlebags over his shoulder and tucked the bedroll under his arm. He picked up the rifle and headed for the door. But after only two steps he stopped, turned and walked back to her side. Without a word he circled her waist with the rifle and dragged her against him. His mouth covered hers in a kiss so hot, so hungry, it startled both of them.

She had no time to think, to formulate a defense. All she could do was stand there, being assaulted by so many emotions, she couldn't even sort them out. Her lips warmed, softened and opened for him. And she felt herself drowning in wave after wave of pleasure as she returned his kiss.

He certainly hadn't planned this. But now that it was happening, he wasn't about to stop. In fact, he couldn't stop if he wanted to. The heat was too intense. The need too overpowering.

He could feel her breath hitching, her pulse quickening, and knew he ought to pull back. Instead, he dragged her even closer, until he could feel the pounding of her heartbeat inside his own chest.

He cursed all these barriers between them. Saddlebags. Bedroll. A rifle instead of his open palm pressed to her back. But nothing could stop him from feeling. And with every movement of his lips on hers, the feelings intensified, until he thought about taking her here and now.

It was the warrior in him, he knew. He'd already been preparing himself for the thrill of the hunt. His blood was already hot for battle. But now, with Ruby in his arms, her taste warm on his lips, her exotic fragrance filling his lungs, he was sliding toward the very edge of some kind of madness.

It took all his willpower to stop. Lifting his head, he studied her through narrowed eyes. Her cheeks were flushed, her moist lips thoroughly kissed.

"I don't know how long I'll be gone." He nuzzled her temple and buried his lips in her hair. "But when I get back, we'll try this again. And see if we can't—" He shot her a quick, dangerous smile "—choose a better time and place to start a fire."

He took a step back, then turned and stalked to the door.

This time he made it out.

Ruby leaned weakly against his desk. From outside she could hear him giving last-minute orders to his deputy. She closed her eyes at the deep timbre of his voice, still causing little explosions all along her spine.

She waited until she heard the sound of hoofbeats signaling his departure. Then she sank into his chair, willing her heartbeat to return to normal.

Ruby shaded her eyes as she watched the workmen swarm over the roof of her shop.

"That's it, Miss Ruby." Farley Duke couldn't help swaggering just a bit. After all, he'd amazed even himself by finishing this job in half the time he'd predicted. "We can start on the interior tomorrow. You ought to be open for business in another week."

"Thank you, Mr. Duke. That's wonderful news." She stood watching a few minutes longer. Then she turned away. She had a need to celebrate. But how? She smiled. She would ask Carmelita to prepare a special supper for her sisters and their husbands.

At the stable she waited while Neville brought her horse and cart.

"Thank you, Mr. Oakley." Ruby gave him her usual bright smile as she accepted his outstretched hand and climbed aboard her rig.

"You're welcome, Miss Ruby. Will I see you tomorrow?"

She nodded. "And soon, Mr. Oakley, you will see me here in town every day."

Ruby flicked the reins and headed toward the ranch in a state of high excitement. There was so much to do. And much less time than she'd anticipated. For weeks she'd been working late into the night sewing as many ladies' gowns as she could. She hoped, by the time she moved in to her shop, to have enough variety to tempt every woman in Hanging Tree to stop by.

A large shipment had arrived by stage from San Francisco, containing bolts of fabric, spools of thread and buttons of every size and color. And the lace for Millie's tablecloth, napkins and curtains had arrived, as well. She had just now taken it to Millie's for her approval, and was delighted with her response. Ruby suspected that she would probably find it much more difficult to make her fine, even stitches on the delicate lace. But the result would be well worth the effort.

She smiled, thinking how lovely it would all look in Millie's boardinghouse. Perhaps, until the work was completed, she would hang it in the window of her shop, so that the other women of the town could admire the quality of the lace and drool just a bit. Yes, she would like it if they coveted her work.

She was so deep in thought, she didn't notice the horseman coming toward her. Even when she did, she wouldn't have recognized him had he not called out her name.

"Ruby."

Her heart turned over in her chest at the sound of that familiar, deep voice. "Quent."

As he drew near, she was shocked by his appearance. He looked like some sort of wild mountain man, with a growth of dark beard masking most of his features. But his eyes, when they focused on her, were clear and bright. And dancing with a wicked light.

"Now, how did I know you'd be the first thing I'd see when I returned to civilization?"

At his words a little thrill shot through her. "Maybe I planned it that way."

His lips curved into a smile. "Are you flirting with me, Miss Jewel?"

She couldn't help laughing. "And if I am?"

"A dangerous thing to do with a man who's forgotten how to behave in civilized society." He urged his horse closer, until he was near enough to touch her. "I want to see you. Tonight."

At the intimacy of his words, she felt her heart leap to her throat. "You're seeing me now, Marshal. Isn't that enough?"

"Not nearly enough." He reached out a hand and caught a tangle of her hair, wrapping the strands around his fingers. "I've had three weeks to think about you. About that kiss. About...things. And the things I've been thinking nearly drove me mad. So if you don't mind, I'd like to spend a little time just looking at you."

Her heart was hammering; the blood was throbbing in her temples. Even her laughter was strained and husky as she said, "Go ahead."

"Not here. Not now. Right now I look like a bear after a winter's hibernation."

She nodded, enjoying this light, teasing moment. "You probably smell like one, too."

"Probably." He chuckled, low and deep in his throat. "Would you care to find out?"

He saw the slight flush on her cheeks. For some reason he felt enormously pleased. "Well, we'll let it go for now. But after I've cleaned up, I have to see you."

"When?"

"Tonight. Is that a problem?"

She pretended to think a moment, until her laughter gave her away. "I was planning to invite my sisters and their husbands to supper to celebrate."

"Celebrate what?"

"The completion of the outer walls of my new

shop. Farley said he can begin on the interior to-morrow."

"That's wonderful news, Ruby. Congratulations."

His words warmed her as nothing else could. She felt the curl of pleasure deep inside.

"Thank you. I was planning to celebrate with a special supper. That is, if I get home in time to ask Carmelita to cook. Would you like to join us?"

Now it was his turn to pretend to mull over her offer. But she could hear the warmth in his tone when he finally said, "I'd rather have you alone. But I guess I could put up with the rest of your family."

"Then come for supper." She picked up the reins. "And Marshal," she said primly, "be sure to shave. So you won't be mistaken for a bear."

He stared after her until the little horse and cart disappeared over a ridge. Then he nudged his horse up the dusty street and dismounted at the jail.

"Marshal." Arlo bolted out of the chair as if someone had just lit a fire under him. "I didn't expect you back for a couple more days."

"I can see that." Quent couldn't even work up any feelings of anger for his lazy deputy. Right now it felt so good to be back. And, he realized, the weariness that had dogged him for the past few days had completely disappeared, thanks to the vision in red satin who had just invited him to supper.

"Can I get you anything?" Arlo began to stack the papers that had scattered all over the floor.

"Yeah." Quent trudged to his room and dropped his saddlebags and rifle on the bed, before running a hand over his bearded chin. "Run over to Barney

Healey's barbershop and tell him I'm heading over for a shave and a haircut. And I want him to start heating a tub of water. I'm ready for a nice long soak."

"Yes, sir."

"And Arlo," he called as the deputy headed for the door, "when I come back, I expect to find this place clean."

Arlo nodded before beating a hasty retreat. As he made his way toward the barber's, he scratched his head. Something had softened the marshal's usual taciturn attitude. Maybe he'd engaged in a satisfying gunfight with some outlaws. But then, he'd have brought their bodies back to town for burial.

The deputy decided not to try figuring it out. He'd just be grateful that, for now, he wouldn't have to face the marshal's wrath. And by the time Quent Regan returned to his office, it would be clean as the widow Purdy's parlor.

Chapter Nine

"They are coming," Carmelita called. "I hear a carriage."

Ruby threw open the door and stepped out onto the back porch. Reverend Dan Simpson was just helping his wife, Jade, from the fancy white-and-gilt carriage she had brought from San Francisco.

"Dan. Jade." Ruby hugged them both. "I'm so glad you could come to supper."

"We wouldn't miss it," Dan said with a grin.

Though Jade still dressed in the silk of her mother's homeland and carried herself with the cool elegance of one born to a life of opulence, she appeared to be more comfortable with the role of a simple, small-town minister's wife. The loving glances exchanged by the happy couple spoke volumes about their happiness.

They looked up as Pearl and Cal rode up in their wagon. In the back were their adopted sons, Gil and Danny. Riding alongside on their spirited mounts were Diamond and Adam.

"Looks like we're all here," Adam called as he

tethered the horses and strode hand in hand with his wife up the stairs.

Carmelita dried her hands on her apron before embracing their guests. She saved her biggest hugs for the two little boys. "Umm. It is so good to have children in the house."

Gil, nearly fourteen and tall as most men, looked offended by her comments. But six-year-old Danny was clearly enchanted by the housekeeper's cuddling.

"Soon," Carmelita added, "there will be another." She embraced Diamond, then stood back to cast a disparaging look at the way the young woman was dressed. "What is this?" Carmelita asked with a sniff of disapproval.

"One of Adam's old jackets." Diamond patted her swollen middle. "It's more comfortable than my own right now. Everything of mine is too snug."

"I thought by now you would switch to a pretty dress," the housekeeper remarked.

"You know me better'n that." Diamond and the others turned at the sound of approaching hoofbeats. "I didn't know anyone else was coming. It looks like…"

"Quent Regan." Ruby kept her tone deliberately casual, but she felt her heartbeat already starting to accelerate.

"I'm glad to see he's back in town," Cal muttered as he dropped an arm around his wife's shoulders.

Pearl shot him a love-filled look that had a lump forming in Ruby's throat. Love, it would seem, had transformed each of her sisters in some subtle way.

Quent slid from the saddle and tied his horse, then strode up the steps. For a moment, through the blur of faces, the only one he could see was Ruby.

"Good evening." He caught her hand and absorbed the expected jolt of pleasure. She made a dazzling picture, with that rich swirl of auburn waves framing the prettiest face he'd ever seen. And, as always, her red satin gown revealed a body so lush, it rivaled the lady in the portrait that hung in Buck's saloon.

"Good evening, Marshal." She couldn't help staring. His hair was freshly cut, his face clean shaven, revealing a proud, firm jaw and strong, even features. Best of all, he was wearing the shirt she'd made him. "You look..." She almost said handsome. Instead, she covered by saying, "Much less like a woolly bear tonight."

He grinned, sending her heart into a series of somersaults. "Amazing what a shave and haircut can do."

Ruby's family stood watching and exchanging puzzled looks.

Diamond whispered in Jade's ear, "When did this happen? When did these two enemies become... whatever they've become?"

The young woman shrugged and turned to Pearl, who seemed as surprised as the others. It was obvious to everyone watching that there was something happening here. These two had eyes only for each other.

"Adam. Cal." Quent was easy and comfortable with Ruby's family, shaking hands with the men and boys, greeting the women with a smile and, in the case of Diamond, a hug. When he spied Carmelita, his smile widened.

"Looks like I get to sample your good cooking again, Carmelita."

"And I get to cook for a man who likes to eat," she remarked with a laugh. "Come inside. All of you." She dropped an arm around Gil and Daniel. "I have a special treat for both of you."

As Carmelita hurried off to the kitchen, Ruby led the way to the parlor, where a decanter of whiskey and several tumblers rested on a small table. Ruby poured and handed them to the men. The moment she offered one to Quent, and their fingers brushed, she felt the sizzle along her arm.

It was a relief when Carmelita entered with tea for the women and glasses of lemonade for the boys. It gave Ruby a chance to turn away and hide the heat that stained her cheeks.

"You were gone a long time, Quent." Adam paused in front of the fireplace, and the other men gathered around, eager to hear about the marshal's journey. "Arlo said a rancher and his wife were killed."

"Arlo talks too much." Quent took a drink of whiskey and held his silence.

"I heard it was a young couple," Cal said. "New to Texas. Had only been here a year. You going to tell us the rest? Or do we have to wait and hear it from your deputy?"

Quent shrugged. "Arlo or his wife will probably have it all over the territory by tomorrow." He drank

again. "Young husband and wife from Kansas City.
it. They had a small, poor ranch. Not much to steal.
Looks like the gunman just walked in and helped
himself. Both were shot in the head. Wife was—"
he glanced toward the women, and kept his voice
low "—brutalized before she was killed."

"Got any idea who shot them?"

Quent merely shrugged.

"See anything or anyone suspicious on your journey?" Adam asked.

"No. But I've asked all the lawmen in the territory
to send me any reports of similar murders."

"Sounds like you're being pretty thorough."
Adam exchanged a glance with Cal before asking,
"You looking for anyone in particular?"

Quent chose his words carefully. No point in
alarming people without proof. "I only know I have
a particular hatred for killers."

"You don't think Boyd Barlow'd come back, do
you?" Cal shot a quick glance at Pearl and the boys
across the room.

Seeing it, Quent was quick to soothe. "Now, don't
go thinking the worst. That's my job. If he's smart,
he's already in Mexico. But I can't take any chances.
That's why I wanted to check out the area."

"No sign of him?" Cal pressed.

"I found a couple of campsites. Someone had
gone to a lot of trouble to clean them up, and make
it look like nobody had been there."

Adam and Cal looked at each other before Adam
said, "That doesn't sound like a drifter passing
through. It sounds like someone who's hiding out."

"My thoughts exactly." Quent sipped his whiskey while the others pondered his words.

Carmelita paused in the doorway. "Supper is ready."

The men drained their glasses, then trailed the women to the dining room. The table had been set with festive linens. The crystal and silver gleamed in the light of the candles that winked from the overhead chandelier.

"I don't remember this tablecloth," Diamond said as she sat in the chair Adam held for her.

The four women sat on one side of the table, with the four men across from them. Pearl and her husband chose the seats closest to their boys, who sat together at one end.

"That's because you haven't seen it before," Ruby said with a trace of pride. "I just finished sewing it."

"You made it?" Pearl sighed. "Oh, Ruby, it's lovely."

The three sisters examined the fine stitches and remarked on the exquisite handwork.

"I just know your shop is going to be a success," Jade said emphatically. "Once the townspeople learn of your fine talent, you won't be able to keep up with the demand."

"'You're right about that," Quent remarked. "I can attest to the fact that your sister's a fine seamstress. She made this shirt, and it's the finest I've ever owned."

At that her sisters turned to study her, then the man across from her.

"I've been admiring that shirt," Adam said with a laugh. "Now I know why." He turned to Ruby. "I hope you won't forget your family. I might be handy with a needle and thread, but there are a whole lot more things I'd rather do than mend my own clothes."

"Not to mention mine," Diamond added. "Adam didn't realize when he married me he was taking on twice the work."

"Diamond, for what I've gained, I'd take on a hundred times the work," he said.

"Talking about extra work..." Cal surprised them by pushing back his chair and rounding the table until he was beside his wife. He bent and pressed a kiss to Pearl's temple, then said, "I think, since we have the whole family here, we ought to share our good news. What do you say, boys?"

Gil and Daniel were grinning from ear to ear.

Cal urged Pearl to her feet, then dropped an arm around her shoulders, drawing her close. The others watched in puzzled silence.

"It's awfully soon. I was hoping to wait until after Diamond had her baby." Pearl smiled up into his eyes, then nodded. "But I can't wait to see their reaction. You tell them, Cal."

Her husband cleared his throat. "As foreman of the Jewel ranch, it is my pleasure to announce that Pearl and I are about to add another wrangler to our crew."

"He means," Pearl said with a laugh, "that we're going to have a baby."

"A baby?"

There was a collective gasp around the table. Then, as the fact sank in, Ruby shoved back her chair to embrace the happy couple. "I am so thrilled for all of you. Mama used to say that a child is a special gift from heaven, to remind us of the beauty of angels."

Hearing her, Quent was struck by the tenderness in her tone. It wasn't something he'd expected from this fiery beauty.

Suddenly there was a rush of hugs and kisses as Diamond and Jade and their husbands joined in the congratulations, hugging Pearl, then Gil and Daniel, before pumping Cal's hand. Hearing the commotion, Carmelita rushed in carrying a heavy platter.

When she heard the news she set the platter aside and fell, laughing and weeping, into Pearl's arms.

"For so long this house has been without the sound of children. And now. First Diamond. And now you. Oh, Señora Pearl," she said on a sob, "this makes me so happy. So..." She was too overcome to speak. She burst into tears and, dabbing at her eyes with the corner of her apron, fled to the kitchen.

Cal and Pearl stood, their arms around their two young sons, wearing identical grins of pure happiness.

"What do you think of all this, Daniel?" Ruby asked the little boy.

"Gil says it'll be neat to have a little brother to teach."

"A brother would be fun. But, of course, it could be a little sister," Ruby remarked.

The smile was wiped from Daniel's lips. His eyes

widened in surprise. It was clear he'd never even given that a thought. "What would we do with a little sister, Gil?"

The older boy shrugged, then ruffled his brother's hair. "I guess you'd have to put up with her tagging after you all day, while I was off with Dad running the ranch."

Everyone burst into roars of laughter at the pained expression on Daniel's face. But Ruby took pity on him and knelt down to draw him into her arms. "Do not despair, Daniel. Whether it is a boy or a girl, you will always be the big brother who can do no wrong."

"I will?" As the thought sank in, Daniel's smile returned.

"Oui," Ruby said, pressing a kiss to the top of his head. "When I was growing up in Bayou Rouge, I would have given anything for a gallant big brother."

Again Quent found himself witnessing a side of Ruby he hadn't expected. There was a gentleness, a tenderness she kept hidden, except from those most in need.

When at last their interest returned to food, they began to pass around the platters of chicken and beef, laden with spicy chilis, and the basket of corn bread.

Before they began to eat, they joined hands and bowed their heads as Jade's husband spoke from the heart. "Bless this food, and those gathered here. And bless, especially, Diamond and Adam, Pearl and Cal, Daniel and Gil, and the precious new lives they're so eagerly awaiting."

"Amen," the others intoned.

"Diamond, when are you going to stop riding and roping?" Pearl asked as she lifted her fork to her mouth.

"Why should I stop?" Diamond seemed genuinely surprised by Pearl's comment.

"Why, because you need to slow down now," Pearl said. "You'll want to spend more time at home, resting and knitting little clothes."

"Knitting? Me?" Diamond couldn't help laughing at the thought.

"Pearl is right," Jade put in. "You should give up riding your horse, and get yourself a proper carriage."

"Give up Sunrise?" Diamond tossed her head. "I've been riding her since she was a frisky filly. I wouldn't dream of giving her up."

"You'll soon have no choice," Jade said in that calm, logical tone that always set Diamond's teeth on edge. "If you get any bigger, you won't be able to fit in the saddle. And you really ought to give up your buckskins and gun belt, too. It just doesn't look right for a new mother."

Ruby, seeing that her sisters' thoughtless comments were spoiling Diamond's mood, interrupted. "Do not fret, *chérie*. Babies have a way of being born, no matter how their mothers dress, or what their choice of travel. But know this. You and Adam will be loving parents. As will you, Pearl and Cal. And your children will consider themselves very lucky."

The smile returned to Diamond's eyes. Across the table Adam shot Ruby a look of gratitude.

Carmelita, having composed herself, entered with a tray laden with slices of hot apple pie. While everyone murmured their approval and began devouring the dessert, she circled the table, filling their cups with coffee. When she paused beside Diamond's chair, and then Pearl's, she couldn't resist touching a hand to their hair.

"You will make beautiful mothers," she whispered.

Diamond hugged her, then, to no one's surprise, announced that she'd like a second slice of pie. Pearl's smile was so bright she seemed to glow.

"By the way," Jade said to her sisters, "I hope I can count on all of you to help with the town's first social."

"When?" Ruby asked.

"How can you ask such a thing?" Jade demanded. "Ruby, where has your mind been?"

"On her new shop," Diamond said. "And all those fancy gowns she's been sewing all night, every night. How many do you have now?"

"Nearly a dozen," Ruby replied. "I want enough to fill the shop when it opens. Which will be sooner than expected. That's why I invited you here tonight. To celebrate the fact that the outer walls of my shop have been completed. I should be open for business within a week or two."

"And here we are, spoiling your celebration by barging in with our own news," Pearl said.

"Not at all." Ruby was quick to soothe. "There's

nothing I would like more than to celebrate all good news with my family.'' She turned to Jade. "Now, tell me about the town social.''

"It's going to be held on the last Sunday of the summer. Dan and I thought it would be nice to get the ranchers together with the folks from town.''

"They've been doing that for years,'' Diamond remarked. "Every time there's a hanging. That's how the town got its name.''

"That's why we're planning this town social,'' Danny said with a laugh. "We thought that might be more fun than a hanging.''

Though Diamond merely shrugged, the others looked interested.

"Why now?'' Ruby asked.

"Because by summer's end the crops will be harvested, and the wranglers will be preparing for the long cattle drive. Since they'll be on the trail for a couple of months, we thought this was the perfect time to bring everyone together, before the winter cold sets in.''

"What are you planning?'' Ruby asked excitedly.

"A potluck supper. A few games of chance for the men, and maybe a quilting bee for the ladies. Some races for the children. And dancing.''

"Oh, my.'' Pearl sighed. "I haven't danced since I left Boston.''

Cal gave a laugh. "Well, don't look at me. I've never danced. Wouldn't know how.''

"I'll teach you,'' she said.

"Fair enough. Then I'll think of a couple of things to teach you.'' Across the table he winked at his wife, and her cheeks turned a becoming shade of pink.

By the time they retired to the parlor for brandy and coffee, they felt happily content. The women were busy discussing food for the social. The men's talk, as always, centered around work.

Finally, when the glasses were empty, and their cigars had been smoked, Adam took a look at his wife and tossed the remains of his cigar into the fireplace. "Come on, Diamond. I'd better get you home before you fall asleep in the saddle."

"I have been feeling a little tired lately." Diamond stifled a yawn. "Think it's because of the baby?"

Pearl nodded. "I feel the same way. But I really don't know."

Her sisters looked at each other, then shook their heads as they were forced to admit that their knowledge of childbirth was sadly limited.

Diamond turned to Carmelita as she began to gather the tray and glasses. "Will this feeling pass?"

"*Sí.* But for now, you should do what your body demands, and sleep."

"Come on, Diamond," Adam called. "We have a ranch to run in the morning. Although it looks like I might be running it alone pretty soon," he said, kissing the top of her head. "You have something even more important to consider."

She shot her sisters a look of surprise. "I never thought I'd consider anything more important than the ranch chores. It seems like I'm learning something new every day."

"We'll ride out with you," Cal said. "Morning chores start awfully early."

Pearl nodded, and looped her arms through Gil's and Daniel's. The others followed them out the door. On the porch they kissed good-night, prepared to take their leave.

"You coming, Quent?" Diamond called sleepily.

"You go ahead. I'll be along," the marshal said.

"But we're going your way and—" Her voice was abruptly cut off as her husband gave her a gentle nudge in the ribs.

"You take your time, Quent. We'll see you later." Adam's voice was warm with unspoken laughter.

"Yeah. Thanks." Quent stood on the porch beside Ruby, watching until the others rode away amid the clatter of carriage wheels and horses' hooves.

Ruby continued peering into the darkness, feeling suddenly shy and awkward. "Would you like to come in for another piece of Carmelita's pie?"

"No, thanks. I've had enough."

"Coffee, perhaps? I could make you some café au lait, the way we made it in the bayou."

Quent shook his head.

"There must be something..." Her voice trailed off as he placed a hand over hers, resting on the porch railing. The feeling that shot along her arm had her trembling.

Quent spent a very long time watching the path of a shooting star. When he spoke, his voice seemed lower, deeper. "You know why I stayed. It wasn't more food or drink I wanted."

His words sent a shiver along Ruby's spine. She turned to study his profile. "I think—"

"Don't think." When a breeze caught a strand of

her hair, he lifted a hand to it. "Just let me look at you."

She stood very still, absorbing the shock of his touch.

He studied her in the glow of moonlight and felt his throat go dry. "I guess I knew that day in my office that one kiss would never be enough. I'm going to have to kiss you again."

He framed her face with his big hands and stared down into her eyes. He lowered his head slowly, so slowly she felt her heart stop and her breath back up in her throat. And then, when she thought she couldn't bear to wait a moment longer, his lips found hers.

The kiss was unlike any they'd shared before. He kept his eyes open, watching her. His hands remained lightly touching her face, the thumbs moving ever so gently across her jaw. His lips brushed hers with the softness of a feather, the merest whisper of mouth to mouth.

She was so deeply affected, she couldn't move. She held herself stiffly, afraid that if she so much as breathed too deeply, her bones would snap like fragile glass.

The feel of his work-roughened hands against her skin was so incredibly erotic. The thought of them touching her, all of her, had the blood pounding in her temples. She lifted her hands to his wrists, and felt the throbbing of his pulse. Its erratic rhythm matched her own.

Though he kept the kiss soft and light, she could feel the tension vibrating in him. Could feel the surge of blood pumping through his veins.

When at last he lifted his head and stared down at her, his eyes narrowed in concentration. He traced a finger around the outline of her lips, and felt her trembling response.

His voice was rough. "You know there's something between us, Ruby. It's been there from the first time we saw each other."

He combed his fingers through her hair, drawing her head back. She waited for another kiss, but he held back, as though testing himself, gauging just how much inner strength he could summon. And then, with a sigh, he covered her mouth with his. Against her lips he muttered, "God knows, I've tried to deny it. But no more. No more."

As he took the kiss deeper, her arms glided up his arms, feeling the tightly bunched muscles. Her arms slid higher, to his shoulders, and then encircled his neck as she gave herself up to the pleasure. A pleasure unlike any she'd ever known.

How could one man's mouth do such clever things? With only his lips, his teeth, his tongue he took her on a wild ride, climbing, climbing, until her lungs were starved for air.

She couldn't hold a single coherent thought. All she could do was feel. The wild beating of a runaway heart. The heating of her blood, until she thought her flesh would surely melt. The mingling of his breath and hers. And his taste. Dark. Mysterious. Dangerous. And distinctly male.

She breathed him in, filling herself with the scents of horses and leather and whiskey. When his lips left hers, to explore the sensitive hollow of her throat, she clung to him, and moved in his arms. A sigh of pleasure escaped her lips. A sigh that soon turned to a soft moan as his lips moved lower, to the swell of her breast. Despite the barrier of chemise and gown, she felt her nipple harden. And was shamed by her body's betrayal.

"Señorita Ruby, I will leave now. Rosario is here...." The door slammed. Carmelita's voice trailed off when she realized what she'd interrupted.

Two heads came up. The two darkened figures straightened.

Ruby was grateful that Quent kept his arms around her, for she feared that without his support, she would surely fall.

"Thank you, Carmelita." Her voice wavered, the words stilted, formal. "Good night."

"*Sí.* Good night. Would you like to ride along with us, Marshal? Rosario and I would enjoy your company."

"Thanks, Carmelita." Quent's tone was rough with frustration. "But I think I'll stay awhile."

"*Sí.*" There was a hint of suppressed laughter in the housekeeper's voice. "There is a chill in the air tonight. Perhaps the two of you should go indoors, where you would be more comfortable."

When the door closed behind her, Quent turned to the woman in his arms and pressed his lips to a tangle of hair at her temple. "Maybe I ought to go now, while there's still time."

She panicked at the thought of him leaving. "Time?"

"To come to our senses. If I stay, Ruby, I know where this will lead. And so do you."

Ruby struggled to calm her wildly beating heart.

He was giving her a choice. It would be her decision, to send him on his way or to give in to the desperate longing of her heart.

Oh, why did it have to be Quent Regan's touch that unlocked all this longing? Of all the people in the world, why did it have to be a lawman? He was wrong for her. They both knew it. Still, knowing didn't change anything. As he'd said, there was something between them. Something she could no longer deny. She wanted him, as she'd never wanted anyone.

Oh, Papa, she thought. *Is this how it was between you and Mama?*

Until this moment Ruby hadn't understood how Madeline St. Jacque and Onyx Jewel could have been swept away by passion. Or how they could have flouted convention to be with each other again and again. But now she was experiencing the same desperate need. And she was about to make the same terrible mistake.

"Don't go," she whispered as the clatter of carriage wheels faded, and Carmelita and Rosario were swallowed up by the darkness. "I want you to stay."

"Dear God, Ruby." His hands tightened at her shoulders, and he pressed his forehead to hers. "Do you know what you're saying?"

She nodded.

He hauled her roughly against him and covered her mouth with his in a kiss so hot, so hungry, it left no doubt of his intentions.

Chapter Ten

Quent swept Ruby into his arms and carried her across the porch. He braced a foot against the door, kicking it inward. Then he headed toward the stairs.

He'd thought he'd have to ask which room was hers. But there was no need. As he paused outside an open door, he caught the faint whiff of sweet crushed roses. Without a word he strode inside, then paused beside the bed and set her on her feet.

Moonlight streamed through the window, painting her with soft golden light.

He framed her face with his hands and kissed her forehead, her temple, her cheek.

She stood, her face lifted to his, trembling beneath his touch.

He'd thought of this. Planned it in his mind. All those nights on the trail, alone under the stars, he'd thought of her. And what he'd do when he returned. The vision of her had played in his mind, teasing him, tempting him, driving him half-mad with desire.

But now they were here, together, and his fantasies had been nothing compared with reality.

"Ruby, you're so lovely you take my breath away." He kissed the tip of her nose, the corner of her mouth, the curve of her jaw.

And still she waited, trembling, for the moment when his mouth would claim hers.

Instead he explored her ear, his tongue plunging, his breath tickling, until she sighed and tried to draw away. But he pulled her closer. And his hands began an exploration of their own.

His strong, work-roughened fingers trailed the slope of her shoulders, touching, kneading, before sliding down her arms.

"Quent..."

"Shh." He touched his lips to hers, silencing her.

It was the softest of kisses. And all the while his clever hands continued to touch, to excite, to arouse. When she twined her arms around his neck, his hands moved up her sides until his thumbs encountered the swell of her breasts.

She started to pull back, but he distracted her by taking the kiss deeper. At that she leaned into him, wanting to give more. Wanting to give all. His thumbs stroked her already erect nipples until she moaned and clutched at him.

"How many clothes are you wearing?" he muttered.

"A dress, a chemise, petticoat..."

Her words stilled as, with great patience, he unfastened the row of tiny buttons and slid the gown from her shoulders. It pooled at her feet, dark and shimmering in the glow of moonlight.

He cupped a hand to the back of her head and pressed light kisses over her upturned face.

"I want to see you. All of you," he murmured as he untied the ribbons of her chemise.

It parted, revealing pale, creamy flesh.

It occurred to Ruby that she had no feelings of shame. She had always known that one day a man would see her, as Quent was now. And it would be right. So right. As it was now.

"Ruby, you're so beautiful." Because he wanted to crush her to him, he deliberately kept his hands light, easy, as he drew her close for another slow, drugging kiss. "I want to touch you. All of you."

"And I want to touch you." She reached a hand to the buttons of his shirt, but her fingers fumbled.

"I'll do that." He helped her, shrugging out of his clothes. They joined hers in a heap at their feet.

He drew her close, and she was surprised at how beautifully their bodies fit together. Hers all soft and curving; his hard and muscled.

"You're trembling," he murmured against her temple. "Are you afraid?"

"No." She whispered the word against his throat and was surprised by his low moan of pleasure. "Well, maybe a little."

Pleased at her newly discovered power, she ran openmouthed kisses along his throat, as he'd done, and heard his moan turn into a growl.

"You needn't be afraid," he muttered. "I should be the one trembling. You make me weak, Ruby."

Growing bolder, she pressed more wet kisses to

his shoulder, then gently nipped his flesh. "I'm trembling because you're here with me. Touching me."

With a shudder he put his arms around her, pinning her to the length of him.

He drew her down until they were both kneeling. He surprised her by catching her hand and lifting it to his mouth, where he pressed a kiss to the palm. He watched her eyes darken with desire as he kissed her wrist, the inside of her elbow, the top of her arm. And then his lips covered hers in a kiss that spoke of all the hunger, all the longing he'd kept hidden inside him for so long.

She gasped and started to pull back, but his hands were at her back, holding her. And then those same clever hands were moving, seducing, arousing, and she moaned and pulled him close.

He could feel himself starting to lose control. But it was too soon. He'd waited so long, and he wanted to savor every precious moment, every delicious taste of this sultry woman in his arms.

"Do you want me to tell you all the things I've been wanting to do to you?" he growled against her throat.

She dug her fingers into his hair and lifted his head until she could see his eyes. "No."

He blinked.

A slow smile crept across her lips. "I'd rather you showed me."

It was as though her words were a key that unlocked a secret door. A door that revealed a caged beast.

He dragged her into his arms. The hands stroking

her were no longer gentle. And his mouth savaged hers until her lungs screamed for air.

"Do you know, Ruby? Have you any idea what I want?" He laid her down on the floor, cushioned only by their discarded clothes, and feasted on her lips, while his hands worked their magic. Suddenly greedy, he reveled in her gasps of pleasure, her moans of desperation.

Now he took her on a wild ride, climbing, then falling, and all the while pleasuring her. Pleasure beyond belief. And always keeping the final release just out of reach.

She was hot. So hot she couldn't seem to get enough air into her lungs. The heat rose, clogging their throats, bathing them in a fine sheen.

Outside, the night was alive with sound. Insects chirped. A night bird sang. On a distant rise a coyote cried for its mate, but neither of them heard.

Their world had been reduced to this room, and the pleasure each brought the other. Here the sounds were muted. A sigh. A moan. A whisper.

Quent watched her face as she lost herself in the pleasure. At first she lay floating on a cloud of sensations. But as the lovemaking increased, the feelings intensified, and her body became alive with need.

He felt a thrill of power. This was how he'd wanted her. How he'd known she would be. Wild. Raging. Lost in him. Her face flushed with pleasure. Her body a mass of nerve endings. And desperate for what only he could give her.

"Tell me," he whispered against her throat. "Tell me you want me."

"I do. I want you."

He could feel his control slipping. Slipping. The caged beast had been unleashed, and was stalking, seeking relief.

He levered himself above her. "Say my name, Ruby. I want to hear my name on your lips."

"Quent," she whispered.

"Yes," he said in a voice husky with desire. "Say it again."

Her eyes opened. "Quent. Quent." Oh, what a lovely name. Why had she never spoken it aloud before?

She smiled dreamily. "I want you, Quent."

He plunged into her, mad with need.

And froze.

"God in heaven." The oath was torn from his lips as he realized what he should have known all along. Hadn't his heart always known?

"Quent, what is it?" She gripped his upper arms, feeling the ripple of fear as he started to pull away.

He couldn't stop. Not now. Not when she was so high. But there was something she had done wrong. Or something, perhaps, she should have done.

"You're..." He could feel the need tearing at him, desperate now for release. But still he halted, one step away from paradise.

"You should have told me, Ruby. You've never..." He swore again, hating himself. Seething with frustration. "You're a virgin."

"Oui." Her smile bloomed. "You are my first." She lifted a hand to his cheek in the sweetest of gestures. "Are you sorry?"

"Sorry?" He ran a hand through his hair in a gesture of helplessness. "It's every man's dream. I guess I should be flattered. But I didn't realize..." He knew his willpower was about to be tested to the limit. He pressed his forehead to hers, praying he could find the strength to do the honorable thing. "A man has certain obligations."

She wrapped her arms around his neck and drew his mouth down to hers. "Please, Quent," she whispered against his lips, "you cannot leave me like this. Please."

His heart was pumping so hard, he thought it might explode. And his breath was coming in shallow gasps.

And then she wriggled. And moved. And wrapped herself around him, drawing him fully into her.

And he was lost.

One moment he was trying desperately not to hurt her. The next he was driving hard and deep, feeling pleasure beyond anything he'd ever known.

She moved with him, strong and sure, her young body keeping time with his, wanting more. Wanting all.

And then she forgot everything as she began spiraling out of control.

He felt the shudders as they swept through her, and heard her little cry as she reached the crest.

And then he followed her, his body exploding, shattering.

Limp, exhausted, they lay, still joined. He pressed his lips to her hair, breathing in the sweet, earthy fragrance that he knew would stay in his memory for a lifetime. From now on, the perfume of roses would always remind him of this night, and this rare, surprising woman.

"Ruby. Ruby." He whispered her name like a prayer.

She had gone so quiet, it worried him. He was already beginning to fill with remorse.

"I'm sorry, Ruby." He wanted to move, to get up. But it seemed too much effort. And so he lay, lifting one hand to brush the hair from her eyes. "I should have stopped this before it got so out of hand. I just didn't know..."

She caught his hand and brought it to her lips. "Shh. I've never known you to talk so much. Usually the words have to be dragged from you."

Surprised, he levered himself up so he could see her eyes. "You don't sound sorry."

"About what?"

"About...what we just shared."

"Are you sorry?" she asked.

"No. Of course not. But I thought..." He looked at her more closely. She looked...satisfied. Like a kitten that had just lapped the cream off the milk bucket. "You're not angry that I...took your virtue?"

"You didn't take it. I gave it. There's a difference." She arched herself up to brush her lips over his.

At her incredible gesture of tenderness he felt himself harden once more inside her. "You'll be a little sore in the morning."

She ran her hands along his arms and smiled. "A small price to pay for so much pleasure."

His lips curved. She was flirting. They had just shared the most incredible experience of a lifetime, and she was flirting. He was thoroughly aroused again.

"Think you could stand a little more pleasure?"

"Is it possible?" she asked.

"Um-hmm." He gathered her close and pressed a kiss to her eyes, her nose, the corner of her mouth.

She turned her face so that their lips mated.

"Do you know how long I've been wanting you, Ruby?" he muttered inside her mouth.

She came up for air. "How long?"

He ran a rough fingertip down her spine and watched as she shivered. "Since the first time I laid eyes on you. You rode into town in that red satin gown, stirring up every man from eighteen to eighty."

"Including you?"

"Including me." He began to move, and was rewarded by her sudden gasp of pleasure. "And I haven't been able to stop looking at you since."

And then he could see nothing but her eyes as they locked on his. And the look of surprise, and then pleasure, as the two of them were lost in a passionate dance as old as time itself.

"I'm sorry Onyx had to die before his time." Quent's voice was soft against Ruby's temple. They lay tangled in the sheets. Sometime during the night he had scooped her up and carried her to her bed.

"He was a good friend, and I miss him like hell. But I'm glad something good could come of his death. And I know I'd never have met you if you hadn't come to Hanging Tree to visit his grave."

She nodded. "I'm sorry, too. I wanted so desperately to know my father. But I was eager to come here, to see for myself what it was that kept him here. I knew, even before I arrived, that I would never go back."

"Why?"

"There were...unhappy memories in Bayou Rouge. People said cruel things about my mama because she never married my papa."

"But no matter how painful some memories are, it was your home."

"No. This is my home. Only this."

He drew her closer, wishing he could shield her from all the old scars. But all he could do was hold her. And give her whatever pleasure he could.

"I vowed I would live my life as I pleased, and not care what others said." She traced the dark hair that curled on his chest. "But that isn't always possible." She glanced up to see him watching her closely. "I know what they say. That I must be like my mama because I wear gowns that are too revealing, or too tight. And though it sometimes hurts, I just keep on doing it, to show them that they cannot control me."

It was so easy talking to Quent. He had a way of listening, really listening, to what she was saying. And he didn't pass judgment.

"Sister Dominique said it was my way of defying authority."

"She sounds like a wise woman."

Ruby nodded. "She was my friend. My only friend at Notre Dame du Bayou. I wonder what she would think if she knew that I had found three sisters here in Texas?"

"She'd think you were lucky. They're fine women, Ruby. You're all good for each other."

"Oui." Ruby smiled then, and wrapped her arms around his neck, pressing herself close. "And you and I are good for each other."

"Careful." His hand made a slow pass along her spine, loving the way she fit against him, all soft and curvy. "You keep moving against me like that, I may have to see just how good we really are."

"Oh, we are good." She pressed slow, languid kisses down his throat, across his chest, then lower, until he gave a hiss of pleasure.

"Too damned good," he muttered thickly as he lost himself once more in her.

"What are you doing?"

The sky was still dark, with only the faintest dawn light beginning to unfurl. Beneath the blanket, Ruby rolled herself into the warmth that still lingered from Quent's body.

"I've got to get dressed and get back to town." He was standing across the room, sorting through the pile of discarded clothes. "By now, Arlo has had plenty of sleep. It's time I sent him home to Effie."

Ruby stretched and folded her hands behind her

head while she watched him bend, then straighten. He was magnificent. It was the only word that came to mind when she looked at him.

All night their lovemaking had been by turns frantic, then gentle. At times a wild frenzy, sending them to the edge of madness and beyond; at other times as slow and easy as comfortable old lovers.

"You are so beautiful," she said.

He turned and gave her a wicked grin. "I don't believe I've ever heard that said about me before."

"Well, you are. You have a beautiful body. It's so lean and muscled, and sun kissed."

"Go on." He picked up his shirt and untangled his gun belt.

"The first time I saw you I was frightened of you."

"Of me? Why?"

"It was..." She swallowed. "The badge, I suppose."

He turned, then crossed the room and sat down on the edge of the bed, still holding his clothes. "Why does my badge bother you, Ruby?"

"It doesn't bother me exactly. Well, it does, but..." She shrugged and looked away. "I don't know why."

He caught her chin and lifted her face until she was forced to meet his eyes. "I think you know. Could it be that you see this badge as a symbol of authority? Like the ones you vowed to defy?"

She pushed his hand away. "Maybe. I don't know."

"Maybe it would help if you knew why I decided to become a lawman," he said gently.

"I thought it was because your father was a lawman."

He caught her hand and studied the pale, creamy flesh. So unlike his own callused, sun-darkened skin. "When I was younger, and sowing my wild oats, I resented having a father who was a lawman. I'm afraid I broke his heart a number of times. As many times as I broke the law. I ran with a pretty wild bunch. Oh, we didn't do anything too bad. But we drank, and shot up a couple of saloons, broke up some furniture. Looking back, I can see that I was headed in the wrong direction."

"What happened to change things?" she asked.

His tone hardened. "An outlaw, fresh from a jail-break, came back to settle an old grudge against my father. The coward shot my father in the back, then ran. When Onyx Jewel found out I was going after the killer, he pinned my father's badge on my shirt and deputized me. Said he expected me to see to...not vengeance, but justice." Quent shook his head. "I couldn't believe that a man like Onyx would trust me with something as precious as my father's badge. That trust changed everything."

"Did you catch the killer?"

He nodded. "It took me nearly two weeks, but I found him."

"Did you...kill him?"

Ruby saw his eyes narrow.

"I wanted to. More than anything. But that damned badge pinned to my shirt stopped me. I

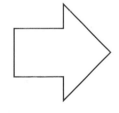

NO COST! NO OBLIGATION TO BUY! NO PURCHASE NECESSARY!

PLAY "LUCKY 7" AND GET FIVE FREE GIFTS

HOW TO PLAY:

1. With a coin, carefully scratch off the silver box at the right. Then check the claim chart to see what we have for you—FREE BOOKS and a gift—ALL YOURS! ALL FREE!

2. Send back this card and you'll receive brand-new Harlequin Historical™ novels. These books have a cover price of $4.99 each, but they are yours to keep absolutely free.

3. There's no catch. You're under no obligation to buy anything. We charge nothing—ZERO—for your first shipment. And you don't have to make any minimum number of purchases—not even one!

4. The fact is thousands of readers enjoy receiving books by mail from the Harlequin Reader Service®. They like the convenience of home delivery...they like getting the best new novels BEFORE they're available in stores...and they love our discount prices!

5. We hope that after receiving your free books you'll want to remain a subscriber. But the choice is yours—to continue or cancel, anytime at all! So why not take us up on our invitation, with no risk of any kind. You'll be glad you did!

***THIS SURPRISE MYSTERY GIFT
CAN BE YOURS FREE AS
ADDED THANKS FOR GIVING
OUR READER SERVICE A TRY!***

PLAY "LUCKY 7"

**Just scratch off the silver box with a coin.
Then check below to see the gifts you get.**

YES! I have scratched off the silver box. Please send me all the
gifts for which I qualify. I understand I am under no obligation to
purchase any books, as explained on the back and on the opposite
page.

247 CIH CCNN
(U-H-H-10/97)

NAME

ADDRESS   APT.

CITY   STATE   ZIP

7	7	7	**WORTH FOUR FREE BOOKS AND A SURPRISE MYSTERY GIFT!**
🍒	🍒	🍒	**WORTH THREE FREE BOOKS**
⬤	⬤	⬤	**WORTH TWO FREE BOOKS**
🔔	🔔	🍒	**WORTH ONE FREE BOOK**

Offer limited to one per household and not valid to current Harlequin Historical™
subscribers. All orders subject to approval.

© 1990 HARLEQUIN ENTERPRISES LIMITED   **PRINTED IN U.S.A.**

THE HARLEQUIN READER SERVICE®: HERE'S HOW IT WORKS

Accepting free books places you under no obligation to buy anything. You may keep the books and gift and return the shipping statement marked "cancel". If you do not cancel, about a month later we'll send you 4 additional novels, and bill you just $3.69 each plus 25¢ delivery per book and applicable sales tax, if any.* That's the complete price—and compared to cover prices of $4.99 each—quite a bargain! You may cancel at any time, but if you choose to continue, every month we'll send you 4 more books, which you may either purchase at the discount price…or return to us and cancel your subscription.

*Terms and prices subject to change without notice. Sales tax applicable in N.Y.

BUSINESS REPLY MAIL
FIRST-CLASS MAIL   PERMIT NO. 717   BUFFALO, NY

POSTAGE WILL BE PAID BY ADDRESSEE

HARLEQUIN READER SERVICE
3010 WALDEN AVE
PO BOX 1867
BUFFALO NY 14240-9952

NO POSTAGE
NECESSARY
IF MAILED
IN THE
UNITED STATES

found myself thinking about Onyx Jewel trusting me to do the right thing, to honor my father's memory. And then I thought about my father, and the fact that he'd spent his whole life living by the rules. And I just had no choice. No matter how badly I wanted revenge, I had to swallow my feelings. I brought the outlaw back alive.''

Ruby felt tears sting her eyes. How like her father to trust a half-wild young man who'd defied his own father and broken the law. Onyx Jewel would understand. As he would have understood her, had he known her better.

He lifted her hand to his lips. "So you see, Ruby. I owe it to my father, and to yours, to wear that badge and see that the people of Hanging Tree are kept safe from madmen who think their guns give them the right to defy the law.''

"Where is your father buried?" she asked suddenly.

He arched a brow. "At the edge of town. Right beside my mother's grave. She died when I was ten.''

"I'd like to visit their graves," she said softly.

"Why?"

She sat up, unconcerned about her nakedness, and wrapped her arms around his neck. "To tell them what a wonderful, honorable son they have.''

He framed her face with his hands and studied her before bending close for a kiss. Against her lips he muttered, "Now you've done it.''

"What?"

He took the kiss deeper. "Made me late. Arlo's going to have to stick around until morning.''

Chapter Eleven

A cool, crisp breeze blew down from Widow's Peak, ruffling the grass, putting a chill on the morning. Quent Regan opened the back door of the jail, breathing deeply. This was the kind of day he savored. Not too hot. Not too cold. Just right.

And in an hour or so, he'd see Ruby. That would make the day perfect.

He smiled as he walked back to his desk and picked up the latest assortment of paperwork which was piling up. Mainly because he'd spent so much time lately thinking about Ruby.

Damned if that woman didn't affect him like no other. He couldn't recall the last time he'd felt so good. So alive. So...complete. That was it. With Ruby, he felt complete.

He shook his head. Next he'd be thinking about marriage. And young ones. Hell, it didn't seem like such a bad idea. The thought of sharing the rest of his life with Ruby had him grinning like a fool.

He looked up as Birdie Bidwell entered, carrying a covered breakfast tray. He inhaled the fragrance of hot coffee and freshly baked biscuits, and gave her a wink. "Looks like Millie outdid herself this morning."

"Yes, sir." Birdie removed the linen square and began arranging the food on his desk. "Which is pretty amazing, considering how upset she is."

"What's she upset about?" Quent lifted a steaming cup to his lips.

"It seems she was robbed last night."

Quent burned his tongue and set the cup down with a clatter, sending coffee sloshing over the rim. That, in turn, caused him to burn his hand, and he was forced to bite back a stinging oath.

His eyes narrowed. "What was stolen?"

The girl shrugged. "A pretty little brooch, near as I can figure. Don't know why she's so weepy over a trinket, but she's been crying ever since she discovered it missing."

The breakfast was suddenly forgotten. Quent crossed the room and grabbed up his hat, before heading for the door.

"What about your tray, Marshal?" Birdie called in dismay.

But he was already stalking toward the boardinghouse at the end of town.

He didn't bother with the front door, but made his way to the back and rapped sharply. Millie opened the door, then stepped back to allow him entry.

He could see for himself that she'd been crying. Her eyes were swollen, her nose red from blowing it. "Birdie said you were robbed."

"Ohhh." She couldn't speak. Her lower lip was quivering, and she bit down hard.

"Birdie said it was some sort of trinket."

"It was…a brooch." Tears started again, but Millie didn't try to hold them back. Just talking about it had her heart breaking. "A pretty little swirl of gold set with some sparkly stones. It was the last thing Mick gave me before he…" The tears became a flood, and she broke into sobs. "It was all I had left of Mick."

"I don't believe I ever saw you wear it," Quent muttered helplessly. In all the years he'd known Millie, he'd never seen her cry. She was the strongest, bravest woman he'd ever known. After her husband died, she'd turned her place into a boardinghouse to support her three little girls. And she'd been working, without complaint, ever since.

"It was too fine and pretty to wear." Millie swiped at her eyes with the back of her hand. Her voice wavered, but she forced herself to go on. "I…just kept it on my dresser, where I could look at it and…remember the night Mick gave it to me. Oh, Quent." She was hiccuping now, her voice breaking with each word. "Who would do such a cruel thing?"

Quent drew an arm around her shoulders and led her to a chair. Kneeling in front of her, he took both her hands in his. "When did you notice it missing?"

"This morning. After I'd tidied up my bedroom. Before coming down to start breakfast."

"Are you sure it was there yesterday?"

She nodded. "Yesterday morning. It's the last

thing I look at every morning before I go downstairs and start my work.''

"Were April, May or June in there? You know how children are, Millie. Maybe one of your girls picked it up to admire it, then just forgot where they set it.''

She shook her head. "The girls weren't in my room. Besides, they know how important that brooch is, Quent. It's the only thing they have of their father, too.''

"All right.'' He squeezed her hands. "Now think, Millie. Was anyone else in your room? Birdie, maybe?''

She choked back her tears, struggling to make her mind work despite her loss. "I didn't have any overnight guests, so Birdie wasn't needed upstairs yesterday. There wasn't anyone at all. Wait.'' She frowned. "I forgot. There was one. Ruby. Ruby Jewel.''

Quent felt his blood freeze. "What was Ruby doing upstairs?''

"She brought over a sample of the lace to show me.'' Millie blew her nose loudly. "You remember, Quent. The lace tablecloth she's making for me.''

"Yeah.'' He struggled to keep his tone even. "Do you recall how long she was upstairs?''

"A couple of minutes, I guess. I was just putting away some fresh linens, and Birdie told her where to find me. She laid the lace on my bed, and we both stood back admiring it.''

"And then what?'' His stomach was tied up in

knots. He'd have given anything not to have to hear any more.

"Let's see." She wiped her eyes, sniffed, then said, "I remember. Ruby suggested we go downstairs, where I could get a better idea how the lace would look on my table and at my windows."

"Who went down the stairs first?" He wasn't looking at her now. He couldn't. Instead, he stared at her hands while he rubbed them gently between his. But he was no longer certain who was in greater need of comfort.

"I think I did. Yes." She bobbed her head, remembering. "Ruby stayed behind to roll the bolt of fabric, then followed behind me."

He cleared his throat. Still, it hurt to ask the question. "And there was no one else who went upstairs yesterday?"

Millie Potter thought a moment. Then her eyes went wide. "Quent, you don't think..." Her hand went to her mouth. "I'd heard the rumors, of course. I guess by now everyone in town has heard the gossip about Ruby's night in jail. But I never believed she did what they said." Fresh tears rose to the surface, and she blinked them away. "Her father was the richest man in Texas. What would she need with...?" The tears spilled over, running down her cheeks. Scalding tears of pain and anger. "Not Mick's brooch. Oh, no, Quent. No. She wouldn't. She couldn't. Not Mick's..."

"I'm not saying she did, Millie." He handed her his clean handkerchief, then patted her shoulder before getting to his feet.

"Where are you...? You're going to...confront Ruby?"

"Knowing what I do, I have no choice." He pulled the door open. "Don't worry, Millie. I'll get to the bottom of this."

Once outside, his features changed dramatically. The frown between his brows deepened. His jaw was clenched so hard, his teeth ached. His hands were balled into tight fists. He jammed his hat on his head and headed down the dusty street.

Before he'd taken ten steps, he saw her, standing between Farley Duke and Byron Conner. Her hands were motioning here, there, everywhere. And her mouth was going a mile a minute. Whatever she was saying, she had the two men smiling and nodding, and staring at her with big calf eyes.

Oh, she was slick. But she wasn't going to get away with it.

"Ruby." He stalked to within a few inches of her, then halted. He saw the way her smile grew, as if she were actually happy to see him. She was a crafty one.

"Good morning, Quent." Ruby's heart tripped over itself. She couldn't take her eyes off her tall, dark, masterful hero. If anything, he looked better in the light of day than he had last night in her bed. "Isn't it a lovely day?"

"I'd like a word with you, Ruby."

"But of course." He seemed flustered. But maybe he'd caught Arlo sleeping in the office again. That would explain his almost brusque behavior. "As soon as I finish with Mr. Duke and Mr. Conner."

She turned to the foreman of her crew. "I have decided I want a pedestal built in one corner, for my customers to stand when I am measuring hems."

Farley nodded. "I'll see to it, ma'am."

"And," she said to her banker, "I have sent for several large looking glasses."

"That shouldn't be a problem, Miss Jewel," Byron Conner said. "As long as you stay within the budget we agreed on."

"But they are very expensive looking glasses," Ruby admitted. "And they are being shipped all the way from New York."

"New York." The banker looked suitably impressed. "Do you really need something that fancy?"

"The salesman assured me they can be positioned in such a way that my customers will be able to see either side of their reflections. They will add a great deal to my business."

He gave a grudging nod. "If you say so, Miss Jewel. But we'll have to cut corners someplace."

"I'll find a way," she told him. "Leave it to me."

As the two men walked away, Ruby turned expectantly toward Quent. "Now, Quent, you have my complete attention."

His voice was as cold as his eyes. "And you have, once again, found a way to have mine."

Her smile faded slightly. "I don't under—"

"My undivided attention, Ruby." He closed his fingers around her wrist. "What did you just tell Byron Conner? That you'd find a way to pay for those expensive looking glasses?"

She nodded.

"Even if it meant having to hurt Millie like that?"

"Hurt Millie?" Her brows creased together. "Quent, you are making no sense. I am confused."

"Well, that makes two of us." Seeing a carriage heading through town, he caught her roughly by the arm and steered her to the side of the road. "What you did makes no sense, either. But then, I'm sure you have a reason that will suit your twisted logic."

"Reason? Reason for what?"

She tried to pull free of his grasp, but he tightened his fingers, dragging her close.

"For stealing. Again."

"Stealing?"

"Oh, that's right. I forgot. You don't call it stealing, do you? I believe you call it your petit vengeance. But what did Millie ever do to you?"

"Something has been stolen? From Millie?"

"No more lies. I'm not going to believe this innocent act a second time." His words were a low rasp of fury. He'd been fighting his temper ever since he'd seen Millie's first tears. Now, seeing Ruby all fresh and dewy, with that throaty voice washing over him, his temper reached the boiling point. Especially since, despite everything he knew, his body reacted to the nearness of her. "Not this time, Ruby. This time you're going to admit the truth. And you're going to make restitution to Millie."

She yanked her arm free and drew herself up until her chin jutted defiantly. "You seem to think I have something of Millie Potter's. You are mistaken. And

I consider your accusation unforgivable. I demand an apology, Quent.''

"Damn you!" His temper exploded. He caught her by both shoulders and lifted her off her feet, dragging her so close that his hot breath burned her cheeks. "Don't you think I can see through this? You figured, since you've got the marshal eating out of your hands, you can do whatever you please. Well, this time you went too far. This wasn't a harmless little bauble. That brooch was a gift from Millie's dead husband. She's over there crying her eyes out. Now, I'm warning you, Ruby, if I don't get the truth out of you, I'll lock you in a cell and throw away the key. Do you understand me?''

If Ruby's eyes had been guns, Quent would have been lying dead in the street. Her voice frosted over. Her accent thickened. "What you accuse me of is despicable.''

"My thoughts exactly. Hand it over, Ruby.''

She swore in a mixture of French, Cajun and English. "I do not have Millie Potter's brooch. Furthermore, I have never even seen it. But this much I have seen. The devil himself. Who would lead on an innocent woman, and then use her...moment of weakness to bully her into a confession for a crime she did not commit.''

Quent snapped. "That does it, Ruby. I've had enough of your lies. You're not going to sweet-talk your way out of this. If you don't tell me right now, I'll...''

"You'll what?'' she demanded.

"I'll throw your hide in jail. And you'll stay there until you tell me where I can find Millie's brooch."

"You wouldn't dare."

"Just watch me."

With that he picked her up, tossed her over his shoulder and stalked off to jail.

With everyone in the town watching and whispering.

The news spread like a prairie fire. Effie Spitz told Lavinia Thurlong, who told Gladys Witherspoon, who couldn't wait to tell everyone she met that Marshal Regan had hauled Ruby Jewel off to jail. Again. Deputy Arlo Spitz told his wife it was for stealing Millie Potter's brooch. Arlo's wife, Effie, embellished the tale so much that by the time it made the rounds, it sounded as though Ruby Jewel ranked right up there with Jesse James.

"Rufus Durfee's been looking for a pouch of tobacco that's been missing from the shelf for close to a week now." Effie lowered her voice. "He thought his boys, Amos and Damon, might have taken it so they could smoke out behind Neville Oakley's livery. But I wouldn't be surprised if the marshal found it in Ruby Jewel's pocket. I'll bet, with all the other things she does, she smokes tobacco, too."

Her husband shot her a look. "Next you'll have her drinking whiskey and dancing with the customers at Buck's saloon."

Effie flushed before saying defensively, "Well, you know what they say about women like Ruby Jewel. If she'll steal, she'll probably break other rules, as well. And you can't deny she's a thief. She'll probably help herself to anything that isn't nailed down.''

"Effie," he muttered, "if you know what's good for you, you won't let Marshal Regan hear you talking like this.''

"And why not? I'll bet he's going to keep his own belongings under lock and key from now on. Why, I wouldn't be surprised at anything I hear about that bold hussy. I told you the first time I laid eyes on her, in that fancy red satin gown and feathered bonnet, that she was wild and wicked. Didn't I, Arlo?''

Her husband walked away, muttering under his breath. Besides, he was in a hurry to get to work. He didn't want to miss a moment of the fireworks that were bound to take place between Ruby Jewel and Quent Regan.

Effie hurried away, eager to spread the word. After all, it wasn't every day the little town of Hanging Tree had such delicious gossip. Imagine one of the richest women in Texas turning out to be a common thief.

When Diamond rode into town a little while later, she was surprised to see a crowd of people milling about. Not one to stand around and join in gossip, she dismounted in front of Durfee's Mercantile, and ambled inside.

Several women stood to one side whispering and giggling behind their hands. When they caught sight of Diamond, they lapsed into silence.

"Howdy, Rufus," she called, heading toward the

counter in an uneven gait. The bigger she got, the harder it was to walk. Especially in boots and chaps.

"Morning, Diamond." Rufus Durfee made a great show of removing his spectacles and wiping them on his apron, to avoid her eyes.

"Quite a crowd today, Rufus. What's going on?"

"Oh, this 'n' that." He replaced his glasses. "Something I can help you with?"

"Your wife used to make those little sweet-sour pickles. Bread-and-butter pickles, I believe she called them. Every year when she'd do them up in those fancy jars, Pa used to buy them as a special treat."

Rufus nodded.

"Do you still sell them?"

"Yes, indeed."

Diamond smiled. "Oh, Rufus. I've been thinking about those pickles all night. Thought I'd treat myself."

He shot her a strange look. "You rode all the way into town for Ida Mae's pickles, huh?" He walked to a shelf and lifted down a small glass jar. "How many would you like?"

"How many do you have left?"

"Pickles?"

"Jars," she said.

He blinked, paused, counted. "Eleven jars left."

"Good. I'll take 'em all."

"All?" He seemed momentarily puzzled, then lifted down the jars and set them on the counter. "I'll have to charge you a whole dollar, Diamond."

"Fair's fair." She whipped out her money and picked up a jar. Twisting off the lid, she popped a pickle into her mouth and said, "Would you mind putting them in my saddlebags, Rufus? I thought, while I was in town, I'd amble over and see how Ruby's shop is coming along."

She was almost out of the store when Rufus found the courage to say, "Maybe you'd better stop by the marshal's office first."

She heard a ripple of muted laughter from the cluster of women. She glanced their way, then turned toward Rufus. His face was beet red.

"Why?" Her eyes narrowed in sudden suspicion. "What's happened?"

"It's your sister. She's in jail for stealing Millie Potter's jewelry."

In the time it took to reach Quent's office, Diamond had muttered every rich, ripe swearword she'd ever learned from her father and his wranglers. And by the time she threw open the door and stormed inside, her temper was in full bloom.

"Where've you got Ruby?" she demanded.

Quent looked up from the papers littering his desk. "Back there." He nodded toward the cells.

She crossed the room and came to a halt at the door to the cell. Ruby stood just inside, spine stiff, head high. The bunk behind her wasn't even wrinkled. It was obvious she was not about to give in and sit.

Separated by bars, the two sisters faced each other.

"All right, Ruby." Diamond's voice cut, sharp and deep. "The way I hear it, you stole from Millie Potter. At least, that's what the townspeople are saying. Now I want to know what you have to say."

"I stole nothing. I have never even seen Millie Potter's jewelry."

"Then why are you here?"

Ruby's eyes narrowed to tiny slits. "Because that *cochon* of a marshal has decided to be both judge and jury. He hears only what he wishes to hear."

At his desk, Quent pretended to be busy concentrating on his papers. But he was listening intently. And every word spoken by Ruby was like a knife to his heart. How he wished he could believe her. He wanted to. Desperately. But the truth was, he could no longer trust himself or his judgment where Ruby Jewel was concerned.

"I'll listen," Diamond said softly. "Just tell me the truth, Ruby. Did you go to Millie's boardinghouse yesterday?"

"*Oui.* I wanted her approval on my choice of lace before I started sewing her new tablecloth."

"Did you stay on the porch, or did you go inside?"

"I went in."

"But you confined yourself to the kitchen," Diamond said, hoping fervently that Ruby would answer in the affirmative.

"I would have. How I wish I had. But Birdie sent me upstairs to find Millie. I laid out the lace on her bed. Then I suggested we take it downstairs so that she could see it in the dining room."

"Damn," Diamond muttered. "And then?"

Ruby shrugged. "She approved. I left. I was returning home when—" she glowered at Quent's back "—I ran into the marshal and invited him over for supper and...other things.'' She felt her cheeks redden at the thought of the things they'd shared. ''A mistake I will not be foolish enough to make again.''

Quent flinched.

''And you didn't see any jewelry while you were in Millie's home?'' Diamond asked.

Ruby shook her head. ''I was eager to show her the lace. I recall that the bed was covered by a threadbare quilt. I remember thinking that Millie saves all her good things for the paying customers. I had planned to surprise her with a new quilt, as payment for being my first customer.''

''That was sweet, Ruby.''

Quent found himself thinking the same thing. Now, who would have believed that she'd do such a nice thing, just to repay her first customer?

''Can you tell me anything else about Millie's room?'' Diamond prodded.

Ruby thought. ''There is a dresser beneath the window. A table beside the bed, with a basin and pitcher of water. The curtains at the windows are as threadbare as the bedcover. The ends are ragged. I only noticed because they kept blowing in the breeze.''

Hearing this, Quent's head came up sharply. ''You're certain the curtains were blowing?''

Ruby shot him a frigid look. To Diamond she said, ''You may tell the marshal that I do not wish to speak to him. Ever again.''

Swearing, he crossed the room and gripped the bars of her cell. ''This is important, Ruby. Are you sure about the curtains blowing?''

Instead of answering, she turned her back on him. "Diamond, I do not wish to dignify any of the marshal's questions with a reply."

He spun away, snatched his hat from a hook on the wall and stormed out.

"What could be so important about curtains blowing?" Diamond mused aloud.

Ruby shrugged. "If he tries to blame me for the ragged state of Millie Potter's curtains, I swear I will scratch out his eyes."

Diamond studied her half sister. Despite the dingy surroundings, Ruby held herself like a queen. But it was obvious that she was struggling to hide a case of nerves. Her hands were locked together, the knuckles white.

Seeing the direction of Diamond's gaze, Ruby unclenched her hands. But moments later her fingers began worrying a section of her skirt.

"Seems to me you're attaching a lot of importance to the marshal, Ruby. He's just doing his job."

"His job is to find criminals, not to persecute the innocent. And I attach no importance to him. He means nothing to me. Nothing. He is as insignificant as—" She snapped her fingers "—that."

"Uh-huh." Diamond remained unconvinced. She'd seen the look in Ruby's eyes before she'd turned her back on the marshal. What was worse, she'd seen the same look in Quent's eyes.

The two of them were about as miserable as she and Adam had been, when they'd found themselves head over heels...

Both young women looked up when Quent strode into the jail, followed by Millie Potter.

Millie rushed to the cell and lifted her hand, opening it so that both Ruby and Diamond could see what she held.

"Oh, Ruby," she cried. "Please forgive me. But when I couldn't find this..." Tears filled Millie's eyes. But this time they were tears of joy.

In her open palm a pretty bejeweled brooch caught and reflected the glittering sunlight streaming through the narrow window of the cell.

"It was Quent who suggested I check the bottom edge of my curtains. And sure enough, there it was. Yesterday the wind must have whipped the curtains so hard that a jagged edge caught and snagged the brooch. By this morning the wind had died down, and the curtains were hanging limply. I might not have found my precious brooch ensnared in the hem for days if it hadn't been for Quent."

Ruby was speechless.

As for Diamond, she was so delighted, she hugged Millie Potter. "I'm so glad you found it, Millie. I know what a treasure this must be." She turned to Quent. "I guess you'll be releasing Ruby now."

He nodded. He'd been watching Ruby's reaction. And he thought he'd detected tears. "If you two don't mind, I'd like a minute alone with my..." He caught himself in time. He'd almost said prisoner. "With Ruby."

"I'll be outside," Diamond said.

Before she took two steps, she popped a pickle

into her mouth, then caught Millie's arm. The two women exited together.

When they were alone, Quent turned the key in the lock and opened the door of the cell. Before Ruby could leave, he barred the way.

Knowing the others were just beyond the door, he kept his tone low. "I hope you'll forgive me, Ruby. I know how much pain I've caused you by jumping to conclusions."

She was still too raw. The humiliation had been even greater this time, since it had been witnessed by half the town. She gritted her teeth. She would not give him the satisfaction of a single word.

She tried to walk past him, but he stopped her with a hand on her arm. "Don't do this, Ruby. I need to know that I'm forgiven."

"You need?" Her voice was thick with anger. "And what about what I needed? I needed your trust. But you withheld it, choosing instead to believe the worst about me. And all the while I believed that you...cared for me."

"I do care for you, Ruby. Deeply. But you'd stolen trinkets once before. I caught you red-handed. Whether I care for you or not, I just figured..."

"A *cochon* who does not trust me cannot claim to have feelings for me. Now step aside."

Reluctantly he did just that. But as she walked past him, he caught her gently by the arm. "I want to see you tonight. I need to."

She kept her face averted. "That is impossible."

He closed his other hand on her shoulder. "I hope,

Ruby, in time, you'll forgive me. I think you must have feelings for me, as well."

She shot him a look of cold fury. "Whatever feelings I had for you are gone. You shattered them with this clumsy display of authority."

He caught her chin, hoping to force her to look at him. "Don't say that, Ruby. I know you still have feelings for me."

She refused to look at him. Instead, closing her eyes, she asked, "And why would you think such a ridiculous thing?"

"Because of that French word you used. *Cochon.* Sounds like something a woman might say to a man she...cares about. What does it mean, anyway?"

Now she did look at him. And there was a gleam in her eyes that would have warned him of her growing temper had he not been so distracted by guilt. "It means pig."

With her head high, her chin jutted at a dangerous angle, she swept past him and took her leave.

Chapter Twelve

"You all right?" Diamond asked when Ruby emerged from the jail.

Ruby took several deep breaths, then lifted her head, determined not to cry. "I'm fine. You go ahead. I'll be along later."

"Aren't you heading back to the ranch?"

Ruby nodded.

"So'm I. We'll ride together," Diamond said. "Where's your rig parked?"

"At Neville Oakley's livery."

"Come on, then. Looks like we'll have to walk through the whole damned town."

"You don't have to walk with me," Ruby said softly. "I can manage alone."

"Yeah, alone. That's what we both used to do." Diamond took her time choosing another pickle from the jar. She popped it into her mouth, crunched, swallowed. "Now we don't have to do anything alone anymore. We're family, remember?"

For a moment Ruby's throat was too tight to

speak. But she squeezed Diamond's hand and began walking.

"Millie Potter wanted to stay and apologize. But she had to get back to the boardinghouse to see to her pot roast. She said she hoped you'd stop by later so she could tell you how sorry she is."

"*Oui.* It is not Millie's fault."

In front of the mercantile Diamond untied her mount and led it, choosing to remain by Ruby's side. Seeing the little clusters of men, women and children pointing and whispering as they passed, her head came up and her chin jutted in just the same way as Ruby's. Despite the differences in their garb, and their very diverse coloring, their profiles were identical. Proud. Defiant. Filled with disdain.

The two sisters sailed through town like royalty, refusing to acknowledge the people who were rude enough to stare.

At the livery Neville Oakley put aside his bellows the minute he caught sight of the two Jewel sisters heading his way. He hurried into the stall and retrieved Ruby's horse, then hitched it to her rig.

As the women walked up, he finished checking the harness, then brushed a speck of dust from the seat.

"Good day, Miss Ruby," he said. "Miss Diamond."

Before Neville could offer a hand to Diamond she pulled herself into the saddle.

Neville turned to Ruby and assisted her into the rig. As he handed her the reins, he was shocked to feel her hands. They were as cold as ice.

Without thinking, he closed his big, sweat-stained

hands over hers and whispered, "You mustn't give a thought to what others say, Miss Ruby. The only thing that matters is what is in your heart."

"*Oui*. Thank you, Mr. Oakley." Suddenly she was holding herself together by the merest thread. The jeers of the townspeople were hard enough to take. Harder still was the kindness of this rough giant, who had tasted such similar cruelty all his life.

Ruby knew if she didn't escape quickly, she would embarrass herself by bursting into tears.

She flicked the reins, and the horse and rig took off at a fast clip. Riding beside her, Diamond happily chewed another pickle. And pretended not to notice her sister's churning emotions.

Ruby sat on the wide front porch of the ranch house, working her fine stitches through the lace. Late-afternoon sunshine filtered through the branches of the oak, making shifting patterns at her feet. The day had grown warm enough to work without her shawl, but there was a bite to the air, with a hint of the cooler weather that would soon soothe the scorched Texas landscape.

Her mind wasn't on the approaching season. Or the fact that it was so different from her childhood home in Louisiana. Right now, the town of Hanging Tree was too painfully similar to Bayou Rouge. At least, the people were.

The door opened and Carmelita walked out carrying a tray. "I made coffee just the way you like it, hot and strong. And your favorite sugar cookies."

"No, thank you." Ruby straightened for a moment and lifted a hand to massage the back of her neck.

"But you have eaten nothing today."

"I'm not hungry, Carmelita."

The housekeeper frowned. She'd heard about Ruby's humiliating morning. Even before Diamond had returned, one of the wranglers had come from town and told Cookie, who in turn had repeated it to her. But she could think of no way to broach the subject without embarrassing Ruby further. What was worse, she was pretty sure, by the disarray she'd found in Ruby's room this morning, that Quent had stayed the night. That would make this misunderstanding between them all the harder for Ruby to bear.

"You will go blind sitting in the hot sun sewing those little stitches all day. You should take a rest."

"I'm not tired." Ruby looked up and forced a wan smile. "Really, Carmelita. I'm fine."

"You are not fine. But I do not…"

At the sound of an approaching horse, both women looked up. Seeing the marshal, Ruby sucked in an angry breath. But before she could scoop up her precious lace and make her escape, Quent managed to swing from the saddle and stride across the porch.

He removed his hat and greeted Carmelita with an uncomfortable smile.

"I made these for Ruby," the housekeeper said, "but she seems to have lost her appetite. Would you care for some?"

She held out the tray, but he shook his head.

"No, thanks. I've lost my appetite, too. I came to talk to Ruby. Would you mind leaving us alone?"

Ruby's scowl grew. "Whatever you have to say, you can say in front of Carmelita. There are no secrets here. Especially now that you've managed to bare mine to the entire town."

The housekeeper hesitated, glancing from one to the other. From the sound of things, this could turn into war.

Seeing her dilemma, Quent touched her arm. "I promise I'll be brief, Carmelita."

He held the door while she maneuvered the tray inside. With a swish of skirts she was gone.

Ducking her head, Ruby picked up her needle. "Say whatever you came to say. And then leave me alone."

"I came here to tell you how sorry I am about this morning."

She stabbed viciously at the cloth. "All right. You've had your say. Now go."

"Not until you tell me you've forgiven me."

She refused to look at him. Working the needle with quick, efficient thrusts, she remembered what her mother had told her so many years ago. *Remember,* chérie, *a wise woman does not bend. If someone should bend, it must be the man.*

"I will not forgive. Ever. Nor will I forget," she muttered.

She was startled when he dropped to his knees in front of her. "Ruby, I haven't been able to stop thinking about you. About what we shared last night. And about what I did to you this morning. I know it was unforgivable. But I've come to ask your forgiveness anyway."

"Why should I forgive?" She was working the needle furiously now, her fingers flying across the snowy lace, her gaze fixed on the fine, even stitches.

"Because I can't work. I can't concentrate. All I see is you, being made the object of ridicule for the whole town. And all because of me."

"*Oui.* It is your fault." She turned the lace and started to hem another edge. "You carried me off to jail, and locked me in a horrible little cell. Like…" She clamped her mouth shut, fighting tears of fury.

"Like what?" he prodded.

She shook her head. "Like Sister Clothilde. She was a cruel woman who enjoyed meting out punishment. When I was her pupil at Notre Dame du Bayou, for the slightest infraction of her rules she would lock me in a hot dark closet, and demand that I beg for release. But I would not beg. I would endure anything before I would show her how much she hurt me."

At her admission he felt his heart turn over. God in heaven. What had he done to this wounded, vulnerable woman? He had locked her up, not once, but twice. And she had fainted rather than admit her fears.

Quent caught her chin, forcing her to meet his eyes. When she tried to pull away he tightened his grip.

"Look at me, Ruby. Damn you," he said through gritted teeth, "look at me."

She did. And what she saw caused her heart to stop. There was anger in those dark, narrowed eyes. And frustration. But there was something else. Something so deep, so penetrating, it reached all the way to her soul.

"I have a job to do," he muttered thickly. "A job that nice people don't want to think about. There's no time to worry about feelings, mine or anyone else's. There's just the law."

Without realizing it, his touch gentled. His thumb began to stroke her jaw. His voice, too, softened, as did his gaze. "But with you, Ruby, all the rules have changed. I can't trust my judgment anymore. I find myself wanting to protect you. Even from the law I've sworn to uphold."

His gaze burned over her. "Do you understand what I'm saying? This morning, when I heard about Millie's loss, and the fact that you'd been the last person in her room, I didn't give a damn about her brooch. All I thought about was you."

He pressed his forehead to hers, sending along her spine a flare of heat that had nothing to do with the weather. "And I was afraid. Afraid I'd stopped being a good lawman. Because the truth is, I found myself worrying more about how to protect you than I did about finding what was lost. That's why my temper got the best of me. I was trying to hide my fear."

Ruby couldn't swallow the lump that had formed in her throat.

When she remained silent he lifted his head and studied her. Then he pressed his lips to her temple, sending a series of shock waves through her veins. "I guess I shouldn't have come. You have a right to withhold your forgiveness." His lips grazed her temple, and she felt a slow, liquid heat begin to build deep inside her. "I behaved like a fool."

His warm breath tickled her ear, sending a series of delicious tingles up and down her spine. She knew that if she but turned her face a fraction, she would find his lips, warm and firm and tempting. But though she yearned to kiss him, she remained very still. Only the pounding of her heart revealed just how deeply moved she was.

"And you're the one who had to pay for my foolishness, Ruby."

She swallowed, hard, and tried to form a word. But none would come.

His voice revealed his pain. "I can see now that I've asked too much of you. You can't forgive me. I guess I should have known. It was an impossible situation, after what we'd shared last night. But I had to try. I had to tell you how much I care, and how truly sorry I am about…everything."

He got to his feet and started across the porch.

Ruby thought about calling him back, but her throat was too clogged to speak. Tears filled her eyes as he pulled himself into the saddle.

"I won't bother you again," he said, touching a hand to his hat. "Goodbye, Ruby."

As he wheeled his horse and started away, Ruby finally managed to get to her feet. The mounds of snowy lace spilled from her lap, slowing her progress.

She stepped carefully over it, then watched in horror as horse and rider started out at a fast clip.

"Quent."

The breeze carried her voice away.

"Quent. Wait."

She knew she couldn't be heard over the sound of his horse's hooves.

Lifting her skirts, she started after him. "Quent. Please. Wait," she shouted as she raced across the flat stretch of grass.

But still he kept riding, oblivious to the sounds of her cries.

Determined, she lifted her skirts higher and ran as fast as she could. Her lungs ached from the effort, but she kept going, shouting until her parched throat couldn't form another sound. And still she ran, silently, watching as the chasm between them continued to widen.

She cried out as horse and rider dipped below a crest. Dejected, defeated, she dropped to the ground, gasping for air. And wept as though her heart had shattered.

It took all of Ruby's courage to return to town the next morning. But as she dressed in her best gown and studied her reflection in the mirror, she harbored the faint glimmer of hope that maybe, if she confronted Quent Regan in his office, they could still find a way to resolve this horrible misunderstanding.

Perhaps he would look at her and smile. She would then explain that her feelings had been deeply wounded. He would say that he understood completely.

Of course. A half smile touched her lips as she indulged the fantasy. He would gather her close, and she would feel her heart beat once more. Because, in truth, her heart felt like a stone in her chest. Hard and cold and lifeless. And only Quent's touch would bring it back to life.

She rode the entire distance lost in her fantasy. As she reached the edge of town she straightened her spine. She would approach him boldly, as a woman would approach a man who cared for her. But not too boldly. Perhaps she could look…subdued. *Oui.* That was the look she would strive for. But as she drew nearer, she realized that she would even crawl to him, if that was what it would take to remove this latest barrier between them.

When she stopped at the livery, Neville emerged from the stable, wiping his hands on his pants.

"Good morning, Miss Ruby." He took the reins and offered a hand as she climbed from the rig. "Will you be in town long?"

"I don't know." She gave him a too-bright smile, to hide her nerves.

"It doesn't matter how long you're here. I'll take good care of your horse and rig," he assured her.

"Thank you, Mr. Oakley. You always do."

She made her way along the dusty road until she came to the jail. She paused a moment to pat her hair, then smoothed down her skirt with damp palms. Taking a deep breath, she pushed open the door and stepped inside.

Arlo was already asleep in the chair, his hat over his face, his feet on the desk.

She peered around. Seeing no one, she made her way to the small room in back. The bunk was neatly made up, the blankets taut and smooth. But there was no sign of Quent.

As she turned, Arlo's feet hit the floor and his hand went to the gun at his hip.

"Oh, it's you, Miss Ruby." He grinned crookedly, embarrassed at having been caught asleep. "You shouldn't sneak around like that. A body could get herself killed."

"I was looking for Marshal Regan."

"The marshal isn't here."

Her heart fell. She'd spent so much time preparing for this. What to say. How to act. How not to act. And all for naught. "Where did he go?"

"Off on another tour of the territory."

She was fighting a wave of tears, and struggled to hold them back. "Did he say how long he'd be gone?"

The deputy shrugged. "You never know with Marshal Regan. Could be a couple of days. Could be a couple of weeks."

"Weeks?"

He nodded. "Texas is mighty big, Miss Ruby. The marshal's got a lot of territory to cover. Just depends on what he's looking for and what he finds."

She leaned weakly against the desk, feeling as though at any moment her legs would fail her. "Did he...did he say anything?"

"Said plenty. All of it nasty. I've never seen him in such a foul mood."

She forced herself to walk to the door. As she started out he added, "You ought to be glad he's gone. I don't know what burr got up his...saddle, but

I don't think I've ever seen him that mad before. Thought he'd skin me alive just for losing a couple of Wanted posters.''

Before she could close the door he called, "What'd you want to see him about, Miss Ruby? Maybe I could take care of it.''

"No. That's all right." Her lips were trembling, and she struggled to hide her churning emotions. "It was…nothing important.''

She needed to get to her rig and put this town behind her. This town and its horrible, damnable marshal.

As she passed her shop she heard her name called.

"Morning, Miss Ruby. What do you think?''

She paused, swallowing back tears. Through the open door of her shop she could see several workmen inside, putting up shelves on one wall.

Farley Duke beckoned. "Your looking glasses arrived from New York. We set them up on either side of the pedestal. Is that how you wanted them?''

She looked around, noting the pedestal in one corner, and the tall looking glasses positioned on either side. "They're…perfect, Mr. Duke.''

She needed to get away from these workmen until she could compose herself. She crossed the room and opened a door, peering inside at the comfortable back room that would be used as a changing room and office. Her personal room, she thought. All hers. Right now she wished she could just close the door and wallow in the misery she was feeling.

She took several deep breaths, then walked around slowly, examining everything, from the floors to the ceilings. When she had her emotions under control, she walked up to Farley Duke and extended her hand.

"Mr. Duke, it is all that I'd hoped it would be. Please thank the workmen for me."

He returned her handshake. "I will, Miss Ruby. And you can be sure they'll be happy to hear that you're pleased with their work."

"I'm very pleased. I hope your wife will drop by my shop soon to see some samples of my work."

His smile faded. His face reddened. "Well, ma'am, I can't speak for my wife. She's been awfully busy lately. With the house and the children and the sawmill and all..."

"Yes, of course." Ruby turned away to hide a fresh wave of pain. How could she have been so foolish as to believe his wife, or any of the others in town, would put aside yesterday's gossip? Even though Millie's brooch had been found, the taint of suspicion lingered.

"Well, Miss Ruby, I'll say good-day now." Seeing that the shelves had been properly hung, Farley Duke followed the workmen from the shop.

When the door closed behind him, she sank onto the pedestal. And buried her face in her hands.

What if all this fine work had been in vain? What if no one ever came to her shop? What if the women in Hanging Tree decided, as they had with Neville Oakley, to treat her as a social outcast?

It didn't matter, she told herself, squaring her shoulders. Even with Quent Regan out of her life, and the entire town having taken sides against her, she would endure. Hadn't she always endured the disapproval of others?

No amount of gossip was going to quench her dream. No matter what people said about her, they couldn't deny her talent with needle and thread. And wasn't that, after all, the important thing? Let them ridicule her, as long as they paid her for her services.

As for Quent Regan, she would simply put him out of her mind. And get on with her life.

Chapter Thirteen

"Señorita Ruby. What are you doing?"

Carmelita stepped from her rig and waved her husband off before hurrying toward the wagon parked beside the back door of the ranch house. It was already packed with a desk and chair. Several wranglers were wrestling a chaise across the porch, under Ruby's direction.

"Don't worry, Carmelita. I asked Diamond's permission. These are just a few things I'm taking to my shop in town."

"But why? What need have you of all this?"

"It's just so far to ride from the ranch into town and back. If I ever find the day too long, I'll just stay in town and sleep in my shop. That's why I had the workmen add a back room."

"But this is your home." The housekeeper looked as if she might actually cry. "You are all I have left. Who will I cook for? Clean for?"

Ruby put her arm around the woman. "You make it sound as though I'm leaving for good. I'll still spend more nights here than in town. But I'm going to have to spend my days there. And I want to make it as comfortable as I can.''

"*Sí.*" The housekeeper brightened. "I will go with you. I will help you arrange your furniture, and make you something good to eat while you work.''

Ruby gave her a gentle smile. "No, Carmelita. This is something I have to do by myself.''

Carmelita dabbed at her eyes with the corner of her apron. "What about supper? I could make you food so hot your mouth would think it was back in Louisiana.''

Ruby kissed her cheek. "You're so good to me. But save it for tomorrow. Today I must settle in. And don't bother making supper. I've taken along some of your corn bread and cold chicken.''

"Then I will fix you something more. Some tortillas and chili peppers. Some—''

"I have more than enough, Carmelita.'' Seeing that the wranglers had already loaded the chaise aboard the wagon, Ruby climbed into her small rig, which was abloom with nearly a dozen gowns, petticoats, bonnets and shawls, all new, and all waiting to be displayed. "Don't wait for me tonight. I'll be home late.''

With a wave of her hand, she was gone, leading the way to town.

As their tiny procession made its way up the main street, Ruby noticed a number of carts and wagons parked in the dusty street. At this time of year ranchers and their families often came to trade the fruits of their harvest for seed and farm implements at Durfee's Mercantile. There was even a cluster of men and boys outside Barney Healey's barbershop. Children played hide-and-seek among the wagons and horses, while the women browsed the shelves of the mercantile.

Ruby halted her rig in front of her shop, then began directing the wranglers as they lifted down the furniture from the wagon and carried it inside.

"I'd like you to put the chaise over here in my private room," she called. "And that little stand beside it. I think the desk should be along this wall. Yes. That's fine. And the chair here, beside the fireplace."

It took several hours before she was satisfied. Long after the wranglers had returned to the ranch, she continued working alone, changing, rearranging, until finally she sank down and studied her shop and, through the open door, her new office and sitting room.

In the shop there were giant woven baskets filled with bolts of bright fabric standing guard in one corner of the room. On the shelves were trays of buttons, both plain and fancy, and all manner of trims to be used for making bonnets. Feathers, plumes, ribbons, pins were arranged in dishes and jars.

Framed in the window for all the town to see was Millie Potter's nearly completed lace tablecloth. For dramatic effect, Ruby had draped the remainder of the lace over two bolts of red satin. It made a stunning picture.

Along one wall, hanging from wooden pegs, were the ready-made gowns of pink organdy, yellow gingham, bleached muslin.

My shop, Papa, Ruby thought as she drank it all in. *My very own. Do you see it, Papa? Do you have any idea how much it means to me?*

She was so caught up in the excitement of the moment, she didn't even hear the door open.

"I see you've settled in."

At the sound of Millie Potter's voice, she jumped.

"Sorry," Millie said quickly. "I didn't mean to startle you."

"It's all right. Please." Ruby got to her feet. "Come in."

"I didn't know if I'd be welcome, after what's happened."

"It wasn't your fault." Ruby rubbed her damp palms along her skirt. She hadn't realized how nervous she'd been about seeing Millie again. Or any of the other women from town. "It was a natural conclusion."

"It's kind of you to say, Ruby." Millie stepped closer and placed a hand on Ruby's arm. "But it never should have happened. I had no right to think such a vile thing of you...."

"We'll speak of it no more." Ruby caught Millie's hand and led her to the window display. "What do you think of your tablecloth?"

Millie touched a hand to her throat. "Oh, my, Ruby. It's so beautiful, it takes my breath away." She stepped closer. "May I touch it?"

"But of course. It's yours. And I hope very soon it will be on your table."

"Do you think it can be done in time for the town social?"

"I have no doubt of it."

"Do you mean it?" Millie's eyes danced with excitement as she fingered the soft, creamy lace. "It just doesn't seem possible." She sighed and looked around the shop. "Oh, Ruby, this is a lovely place. When I get more time, I'll come back and look at everything. But now I'd better get back. Several wagonloads of families just got into town. That means I'll be cooking and cleaning for a houseful. And I'd like you to join us for supper," Millie said, catching Ruby's hand.

It was on the tip of Ruby's tongue to accept. She knew that she would be shunned by most of the townspeople, and she desperately needed a friend. And the smile on Millie's face was sincere. Furthermore, there would be potential customers seated around Millie's table tonight. And she needed customers. But she also needed to spend some time alone in her shop, finishing her work.

"*Non*. I cannot come for supper. Perhaps another time?"

"All right. But very soon. Promise?"

"*Oui*. I promise."

As soon as Millie left, Ruby picked up the lace and got to work. The sunlight streaming through the big window of her shop made the task easier. She sat, head bowed, fingers flying.

She looked up as she caught a glimpse of several strangers peering at the delicate lace in the window, then pointing at the row of pretty gowns and bonnets. Her heart nearly stopped when they opened the door and entered.

"Hello," she called. "Welcome to my shop." Oh, such lovely words those were. *My shop.* "Are you interested in buying dresses? Or perhaps bonnets?"

"I'd like to see the lace," a plump, gray-haired woman said.

While Ruby led her to the bolt of fabric, two other women examined the gowns that hung along the wall.

"Look at these, Hannah," one woman remarked to her friend. "I've never seen anything like this at Durfee's Mercantile."

Ruby flushed with pride.

"Did you make all these?" the one named Hannah asked.

"*Oui.* And I can tailor them to fit," Ruby assured her. "Would you care to try some on?"

The two women looked at each other, then nodded.

Ruby opened the door and showed them the private room. "You may undress in there, and then, for a better view, you might want to use these looking glasses."

"Oh, how fine," one of the ladies said.

Ruby felt herself absolutely glowing with pride.

"Now about this lace..." began the plump woman.

At once Ruby hurried to her side and began to explain how much fabric she used for a table cover, and how much more was needed for curtains and napkins.

"Can you sew it yourself?" Ruby asked. "Or would you like me to do the hems?"

"I think I can do it," the woman said. "If you'll just measure out the fabric I need."

Ruby began measuring and cutting. While she did, the door opened and a thin, ragged young woman entered.

Ruby looked up, noting the threadbare gown covering a painfully frail body. The woman kept her head down, avoiding Ruby's eyes.

"I'll be with you in a minute," Ruby called.

The young woman said nothing as she began examining the dresses along the wall.

While Ruby collected the money for the lace, Hannah emerged from the back room wearing a pink gown. She stood, preening and posing in front of the looking glasses.

"Why, that gown would need very little work to fit you," Ruby remarked. "Just a tuck here and there, and a simple hem."

"I'll only be in town today," Hannah said. "We have to leave at dawn to get back in time to see to the ranch chores. Do you think you can have it ready by tonight?"

"Of course." Ruby calculated the time needed and decided she could do without lunch.

"Oh, do you mean it?" Hannah asked. "I'd hardly dared to ask."

"If you'd like, you may pick it up before supper." While she assisted the woman onto the pedestal and knelt to pin the hem, Ruby saw the shabby woman fingering the jars displaying the fancy buttons.

"If you'll give me a few minutes, I'll help you," she called.

Just then the second woman came out of the back room, wearing a pale blue gown. "I'm going to have mine ready by tonight," Hannah announced smugly.

The second woman scowled. "That isn't fair." She turned to Ruby. "Do you think you could have mine ready, as well? You see, our families are traveling together."

"*Oui*. If you wish to buy it, I'll see that it's ready before you leave," Ruby assured her, and found herself wondering how she would manage without a single break. No matter. The success of her shop was much more important right now than mere food or rest.

Ruby's heart was beating overtime as she pinned and measured, and, after much discussion between the women, made arrangements to deliver the gowns to Millie Potter's boardinghouse as soon as they were finished.

"I think I'll want a bonnet to go with this," Hannah said. She tried on every bonnet in the shop, and finally settled on a simple one, with a pale pink feather that dipped provocatively over one eye.

While Ruby made the sale, the other woman said, "Well, I can't afford another bonnet, Hannah. But I do think I'd like some fancy buttons to set this gown off."

"Of course." Ruby crossed the room to the jars of buttons. "I have some here that would be the perfect shade of blue...."

She picked up the jar and shook it. Then she set it down and picked up a second jar. The blue buttons were gone. And so was the shabbily dressed woman who had been eyeing them.

Ruby's first reaction was surprise. How had the woman managed to disappear so quickly?

Then the surprise turned to anger. How dare she! That no-good, miserable thief.

And then suddenly she felt a wave of shame. Was this how others had felt when she or her mother had practiced their petit vengeance?

The irony of the situation wasn't lost on her. How strange that the fates should send a thief to her shop, on her very first day of business. As a reminder of her past sins? she wondered. It was a humbling experience.

"What about those buttons?" came a voice, jolting Ruby out of her reverie.

"They...are gone. But I have these." She shook several pretty mother-of-pearl buttons from a jar and offered them to the woman.

"I suppose so." The woman studied them for a moment, then nodded. "Yes. I'll take them."

Ruby concluded the sale, assuring the women that their gowns would be ready before they left town.

When they were gone, she walked outside and peered in all directions. The stranger was nowhere to be seen.

She thought about reporting the theft to Deputy Arlo Spitz. Thought about it and instantly rejected it. In her mind's eye she could see him dragging the poor shabby girl off to jail, to the jeers of the townspeople.

She shook her head. Though she wanted the buttons back, the thought of what might happen to the thief was too offensive.

With a sigh, Ruby returned to her shop and bent to her work. Her customers were her first obligation. She would deal with the thief later.

Quent reined in his mount at the top of a hill that offered a sweeping view of the countryside. Within a few short weeks, if the weather followed its usual pattern, Widow's Peak would be snowcapped from the first storm. Next spring Poison Creek, now just a narrow strip of water meandering between parched hills and gullies, would become a raging torrent.

He was reminded of the words from his mother's Bible. "To everything there is a season." A time for planting, and a time for harvest.

It had been a fine summer. The harvest would be rich. And the ranchers would have enough profit, from the crops and their herds, to survive another year.

Survival was everything in this tough land. Only the strongest made it.

He rolled a cigarette and scratched a thumbnail over a match, then held the flame to the tip, inhaling deeply. He'd always thought of himself as a survivor. Tough as rawhide. He'd faced fists, knives, guns. He'd been involved in bare-knuckled saloon brawls, ambushes, gunfights. He'd faced down his fears more than once in this lifetime.

But Ruby Jewel was a first.

The first woman he'd ever met who made him tongue-tied. Who left him weak in the knees and honest-to-God scared. When he was near her he couldn't think. Couldn't take charge of his emotions. The damned woman got under his skin, churned his gut, addled his mind.

He couldn't stop thinking about her. About the way she looked after a night of lovemaking. All soft and sleepy and content. Or the way she'd felt in his arms. That voluptuous body fitting so perfectly to his. As if she'd been made just for him.

For a while there, he'd started to think this was his season. His season to love, to plan for the future. Hell, he'd even been letting himself think about settling down and having a family.

The thought of Ruby was driving him mad. He couldn't eat or sleep. Couldn't concentrate on his work.

He took one last deep drag on the cigarette, then tossed it aside and nudged his horse into a trot.

He'd already gone farther than he'd intended on his first day. But damned if he didn't feel like riding right through the night. It would be better than lying awake under the stars in a bedroll, cursing the wind and the cold and the coyotes. Cursing Ruby Jewel, for being so beautiful and unforgettable.

And cursing himself, for being such a brainless fool.

On a distant hillside, tucked inside a cave for concealment, a figure huddled close to a small fire. A stolen calf from a nearby ranch roasted over a spit. He tore off a hunk of meat and ate until his hunger was abated. Then he leaned back and plotted his next move.

The young rancher and his wife had been easy. The minute they'd spotted the badge, they'd let down their guard. The only trouble was, their ranch had yielded little of value. He would need money when he was ready to flee.

When he was ready.

He smiled and tipped his head back, draining the last of his whiskey. There were still things he had to do here. The first was to find another victim. One who could yield cash, and a couple of good horses. Only this time, he'd find someone who was so isolated, his death would go unnoticed for weeks, even months. No point bringing the law down on him until he was ready.

The law. His smile widened. That was the most important thing he had to do here. Deal with the law. Or at least one lawman.

His smile faded, to be replaced with an almost feral snarl. Marshal Quent Regan would taste his vengeance. The vengeance he'd sworn on his brother's grave.

Chapter Fourteen

With a gesture of weariness Ruby rubbed the back of her neck and blew out the lantern. It was a good thing she'd told Carmelita not to expect her. Who would have believed she would work this late into the evening? But she had wanted the gowns to be perfect. After all, these two customers were important. If the townspeople should notice and admire what they were wearing, they might be willing to put away their own prejudices and come to her shop.

Moonlight drifted in the window, illuminating the chaise longue in the corner of the room. Ruby was grateful now that she'd insisted upon bringing it here. She was too tired to face the ride back to the ranch. Instead, she would curl up under a quilt and spend the night.

Just as she turned she saw a shadow drift past her window. It appeared to be the figure of a child. Now, why on earth would a child be prowling the town at such an hour?

She dismissed the question from her mind as she bent to the chaise. Just then she heard a slight muffled sound. She turned. The figure had stopped outside her shop and was now peering in the window. A moment later the door began to open ever so slowly.

Heart pounding, Ruby pressed herself back against the wall. With every second that she wasted, the intruder was advancing deeper into the room.

Her hand closed around the heavy base of the lantern. Taking pains to move silently, she crept forward until she was directly behind the shadowy figure.

"Don't move," she commanded in her sternest tone.

When the figure turned, Ruby raised her arm, prepared to defend herself.

Seeing the weapon in her hand, a frightened voice cried, "Please. Don't hurt me."

In the moonlight Ruby saw wide, terrified eyes in a woman's pale face.

Taking a step back, Ruby set the lantern down with a clatter and held a match to the wick until it caught. Light flooded the room, making the woman cringe.

"You!" Ruby said in a strangled voice. "So, the buttons you stole weren't enough. You came back for more."

"No. Yes. Please, I'm sorry." Tears shimmered in pale gray eyes and the woman sank to her knees on the floor.

Holding the lantern aloft, Ruby studied this stranger. She was much younger than she'd appeared at first glance. Perhaps no older than fifteen or sixteen. With a hungry, haunted look about her.

"You're not much of a thief." Ruby's stern, heavily accented voice cut like a knife. "A few puny buttons will bring you little profit."

"I was desperate. I only took them because they were small enough to fit in my hand. I thought...that is, I'd hoped...I could trade them."

"For what?" Ruby demanded.

"For some food."

Ruby felt as if she'd taken a blow. It took her a moment to catch her breath. "And did you? Trade the buttons for food?"

The girl shook her head. "I was afraid. Afraid you had reported them stolen and someone would recognize them if I tried to barter them."

"So you're hungry." Ruby thought about the linen-wrapped parcel of food that she'd brought from the ranch. There'd been no time to eat it. And, in truth, no inclination, since she'd had little appetite lately.

"Have you no family?"

"No." There was a catch in the frightened voice, but the stranger offered nothing more.

"How long have you been without food?"

The girl shrugged. "A couple of days."

The thought of going days without food was so shocking, Ruby had to busy herself for a moment setting the lantern on a table, adjusting the height of the flame, so that she could buy time to think. "So you came here looking for something to steal?"

"No." It was a choked cry. "I came to Hanging Tree to look for work. But I couldn't find anything," the girl said, "except at a place called Buck's."

Ruby experienced a sickening jolt. She knew how the girls at Buck's saloon earned their living. Cowboys, often fresh off the trail, were crude and rough. And often cruel.

"So you have no work. And no money. And you came back here tonight to find something even more valuable to steal?"

"I...didn't come back to steal," the girl said.

"Then why did you come back?"

The girl's gaze darted to the chaise in the corner. "I saw this room when I was here before. I thought I could sleep here, and no one would be the wiser."

Ruby took a good, hard look at this girl, who knelt before her. Could it be she was too weak to stand? Or was she just very good at playacting?

On impulse she caught the girl's hand and helped her to her feet.

The trembling in the girl's limbs was no act. Nor was the pallor on her cheeks.

Ruby led her to the lounge, and the girl sank down gratefully. Ruby removed the linen-clad packets of food from a shelf. When she unwrapped them, the girl's eyes widened.

"What is your name?"

"Patience. Patience Carter."

"My name is Ruby Jewel. Here, Patience," Ruby said, placing the food in her lap. "You must eat something."

"You mean you're giving this to me?"

Ruby nodded.

"But why? I...stole from you."

Ruby gave a nod to the food. "Eat. And then we'll talk."

She watched with satisfaction as the girl began to eat. It was obvious, from the way she choked down the food, that she was starving.

"Oh, Patience." Ruby sighed as she turned away and began to pace. "What am I to do with you?"

"I suppose you'll want to summon a sheriff," Patience said before biting into another piece of corn bread.

"The thought has crossed my mind."

Ruby could see the way the girl was struggling to hold herself together. Any minute now she would probably lose control and start to cry. If she didn't faint first. She removed a jug of buttermilk from a bucket of water and poured a cup.

"Drink," she said.

The girl drained the cup in several long swallows.

"Do you sew?" Ruby asked suddenly.

The girl seemed confused. With a mouth full of chicken she nodded, then swallowed and said, "A little. I don't think I'm very good. But my ma taught me a few stitches before she died. I was able to patch my clothes. And my pa's."

"*Bon.* That is good." Ruby resumed her pacing, then turned. "Would you like to learn a trade? I could teach you to sew."

"You could?" Puzzled, Patience set down the corn bread she was about to eat. "But why would you do that for someone who stole from you?"

"Because you need work. And a place to stay. And I need an assistant."

"An...assistant?" The girl's eyes lit up. "Do you mean it?"

Ruby nodded. "I do. If you really want to work."

"Oh, yes, ma'am. Truly I do."

Ruby turned away and folded the quilt, draping it over the foot of the lounge. "Finish your meal. Then, if you wish, you may sleep here on the chaise."

"I...can see that you were about to sleep here."

"Millie Potter will have room at her boarding-house."

"But why should you give up your bed? You've given me enough already," the young woman protested.

Ruby smiled. "Yes, I have. But tomorrow you will begin to pay me back. I'll expect you to help me clean and sew and even deliver some of my goods. Do you think you can do that?"

Patience nodded.

"*Bon*. That is very good. Tomorrow I'll see just how well we work together. Now I'll say good-night."

As she stepped from the shop and pulled the door closed, she could see the young girl's face, mouth still gaping, eyes wide as saucers.

Under the cover of darkness she made her way to Millie Potter's. And as she walked, she thought about the strange fate that had brought this girl to her door.

"Oh, Papa," she whispered. "Quent told me you always went out of your way to help the people of your town. I want to be like you. But what if I've made a terrible mistake? What if I'm being a fool for trusting this stranger?"

At the door to the boardinghouse, Ruby knocked and waited. When the door finally opened, Millie, in night clothes, peered at her.

"Ruby."

"I know it's late," Ruby said apologetically. "But I wonder if you might have a room left."

"I'll always make room for you," Millie said with a smile. "I'm afraid I have only the smallest one left, though. All the other rooms are filled. But the bed is comfortable."

"That's all I need. Thank you, Millie."

"Come in. I have coffee. And I've baked some cinnamon biscuits for tomorrow's breakfast."

"Thank you. Please don't fuss."

"I don't mind. You go ahead into the parlor. I'll be right along," Millie said, hurrying down the hall.

The parlor was dark except for the glow of embers on the hearth. Ruby shivered and drew her shawl around her shoulders.

"Here we are." Millie Potter bustled into the room carrying a tray. She set it on a table with a clatter, then began filling cups with hot black coffee. "Wait'll you taste these cinnamon biscuits."

She handed a cup to Ruby. "You're up late."

"*Oui.*" Ruby sipped, then set the cup aside. "I hired an assistant today. A young woman named Patience Carter. Do you know of her?"

Millie nodded. "I met her briefly. She came looking for a job. I had to tell her I didn't need her. What do you know about her?"

"Very little," Ruby admitted. "Except that she has no family and is in need of money."

"How did you happen to hire her?"

"She…came into my shop in need of a job. And I got very busy today and realized I needed help."

"And you hired a perfect stranger?"

Ruby felt a need to explain her bold actions. "She is just a poor girl, Millie, struggling to survive."

"Maybe. Maybe not." Millie pursed her lips, thinking. "Maybe you ought to have Quent Regan check out her story when he gets back to town."

"No," Ruby said quickly. Too quickly.

Millie arched a brow, studying her in a strange way.

"I don't…wish to trouble the marshal."

"But that's his job. At least let him talk to her. He can find out where she's from, and then notify a lawman from her territory, to make sure she isn't in any trouble."

Ruby closed her eyes, wishing she could agree to her friend's suggestion. Suddenly overcome with weariness, she said, "Forgive me, Millie, for putting you to so much trouble. But if you don't mind, I really need to go to my room now."

"Of course."

As Millie led the way down the hall to the little bedroom off the kitchen, she pondered all she'd seen and heard.

Everyone in town said Quent Regan had left town in a vicious temper. He'd been pacing like a wildcat in a cage.

Unless she missed her guess, the reason for all that pent-up anger was the woman trailing behind her. The woman who was close to tears over nothing.

Maybe Quent Regan had finally met his match in Ruby Jewel.

If those two ever went head-to-head, Millie would have to put her money on Ruby.

Ruby washed and dressed, then examined her reflection in the chipped looking glass in the small, cramped bedroom. Morning sunlight streamed through the window, making last night's lack of sleep all the more noticeable. There was no denying the dark circles around her red-rimmed eyes.

It was all Quent Regan's fault. She couldn't escape him even in sleep. His image had been there, like an annoying gnat. And though she'd swatted and scratched, she hadn't been able to evade his sting.

To make matters worse, as she stepped from the room she could hear his deputy's voice, chatting with Millie Potter.

Both Arlo and Millie looked up as she entered the kitchen.

"Good morning, Ruby. Look who's joined us for breakfast."

"*Oui.* I see." Ruby forced her lips into a thin smile. "Good morning, Deputy Spitz. I thought you usually took your breakfast at the jail."

"Good morning, Miss Jewel." He eyed her over the rim of his cup, and she had the distinct impression that he and Millie had been discussing her. "The day is too fine to stay indoors. This gave me an excuse to walk through the town."

"Coffee?" Millie asked.

"*Oui.* Please." Ruby took a seat at the table.

"How did you sleep?" Millie was watching her closely. Almost as closely as Arlo. "Was the bed soft enough? Did you have enough blankets?"

"Everything was grand, Millie. I slept like a baby," Ruby lied. Without thinking, she poured a liberal amount of sweet cream into her coffee, then sprinkled cinnamon and sugar on top.

"What are you doing?" Millie asked.

"This is café au lait. Coffee and cream. The way I always drank it in Bayou Rouge," Ruby explained. "Would you like to try it?"

Millie made herself a cup, sipped, then sighed. "Oh, Ruby, that's tasty. How about you, Arlo? Care to try it?"

"No, thanks. I'll just drink plain old Texas coffee," he said.

"How about some of those cinnamon biscuits you missed last night?" Millie moved a plate of warm biscuits closer to Ruby, along with jam and honey. "I think Arlo's already eaten half a dozen."

Ruby shook her head. "No, thank you. But if you don't mind, I'll take a few with me. For my assistant."

"Assistant." Arlo perked up. "You've already hired an assistant at the shop?"

"Yes, I..." Ruby felt both of them staring at her and fought to ignore the flutter in the pit of her stomach. "I couldn't resist hiring her."

"Business must be very good," Arlo remarked.

"A little slow, of course, since I'm just beginning. But I sold two gowns yesterday, along with a bonnet and a length of lace."

"Isn't that wonderful?" Millie cracked eggs into a bowl and began to beat them. "Arlo likes his eggs scrambled. How would you like yours?"

"No eggs, thank you. I'll just finish this coffee and be on my way."

As Millie turned to the stove Arlo said conversationally, "I looked in on your shop on my way here."

"And what did you think?"

"Looked a bit prissy for my taste."

"Well, what did you expect? It is a ladies' shop."

"I found the door ajar. Closed it before I headed over here."

Ruby blanched. Coffee sloshed over the rim of her cup. She took no notice. All she could think of was all those lovely gowns and bonnets. The bolt of expensive lace. The buttons, and feathers, and... All gone? Oh, sweet heaven. And all because of her foolish belief that she could be like her papa.

She scraped back her chair and got to her feet.

Millie turned. "Where are you—?"

"I'm sorry, Millie. I must go."

As Ruby started down the hall, Arlo jumped up to follow.

"What about your eggs?" Millie called after him.

There was no reply. He was already halfway out the door. He wasn't about to miss this. It was the most exciting thing that had happened since the marshal left town.

Ruby stopped outside her little shop. With a quick twist of the knob, she strode inside, with Arlo right behind her.

"Patience," she called as she swept through the empty shop.

There was no response.

A quick glance at the wall assured her that the gowns were still where she'd left them. As were the bonnets, the feathers, the jars of buttons.

She let out an audible sigh as she strode toward the back room. She opened the door and looked around. The chaise was empty, the quilt tossed carelessly to one side. Nothing else in the room appeared to be out of place.

"Well," Arlo said from behind her. "At least your new assistant didn't strip your shop bare before she left."

"But where would she have gone?" Ruby started to pace. "She has no home, no family."

"Is that what she told you, Miss Jewel? How do you know it was the truth?"

"I don't understand. Why would she lie?"

"She could be a runaway," Arlo said. "Maybe she was tired of ranch chores. It happens sometimes. A woman marries young, hoping to escape a hard life, only to find that marriage and young ones and her new chores are even worse than the life she ran from."

Ruby shook her head, trying to deny what she was already starting to believe. "She did look like someone on the run. She was starving. And exhausted." And, she thought, her boots had been caked with mud, her gown threadbare. "But she seemed so sincere.''

''If you'd like, Miss Ruby, I'll check out the Wanted posters, see if anything shows up about her.''

''Yes, thank you, Arlo. I suppose I should...''

They both turned at the sound of footsteps. Patience raced through the open doorway, then skidded to a halt when she saw the deputy. She visibly paled.

''Patience,'' Ruby called. ''When I found the shop empty, I thought... Where were you?''

''There's a lovely little stream just over that meadow outside of town. I wanted to wash before you got here this morning, Miss Jewel.''

Little drops of water still glistened in her corn-silk hair. And her face, though still pale, was scrubbed clean. As was her gown.

''You walked all that way just to wash?''

Patience bobbed her head, as eager as a child. ''I didn't want you to be embarrassed by your new assistant.''

Seeing the way Ruby and Arlo were watching her, her smile faded. ''Maybe I'm not your assistant anymore. Have you changed your mind, Miss Jewel?''

Ruby ignored the look in the deputy's eyes and hurried across the room. ''Of course I haven't changed my mind. You're still my assistant.''

''Oh, thank you, Miss Jewel. I'll work hard. I'll do anything you want.''

''I know you will, Patience. And your first assignment is to go to Millie Potter's boardinghouse at the end of town.''

The smile was back on the young girl's face.

"Yes, ma'am. And what do you want me to do there?"

"I want you to tell her you've come to eat the eggs she scrambled for the deputy."

Though Patience looked confused, Ruby urged her to the door. "Go now. And tell Millie Potter to add your meal to my bill."

The shy smile bloomed. "Yes, ma'am. I will. And…" She started away, then called over her shoulder, "I won't be long."

When they were alone, Ruby avoided Arlo's eyes and began folding the quilt. "I'm glad I was wrong. I'm glad we were both wrong," she amended, still feeling the sting of guilt.

"I hope you'll take some advice, Miss Ruby."

She set the quilt at the foot of the chaise and began smoothing the wrinkles.

"Just remember. Sometimes a stray will bite the hand that feeds it."

She waited until he walked away. Then she sank onto the chaise and stared after him. Her hand reflexively went to the rope of gold at her throat, from which dangled an onyx and a ruby.

"Oh, Papa," she prayed. "I'm making such a mess of things. I wish you were here to help me sort them out."

Then, as she fingered the two precious stones, she felt a sense of peace. Hadn't Onyx Jewel told her, when he'd presented this gift to her on her sixteenth birthday, that he would always be with her?

She took a deep breath and added, "I'll keep trying, Papa. I know that's what you would have done."

* * *

Patience returned from breakfast eager to work. The first thing Ruby demanded was that she try on several of the gowns.

"But why?" Patience asked.

"Because you are working in my shop now. And I can't have my customers seeing you in that." Ruby pointed to the shabby gown and worn boots. "What would they think if we were not properly dressed?"

"But I couldn't afford even one of your gowns," Patience protested. "Let alone several."

"You will earn them," Ruby said, leading her toward the changing room.

They finally settled on two simple muslins, one pale pink, one buttercup yellow, along with a creamy white pinafore to keep them clean.

Studying her reflection in the looking glass, the young woman was stunned. A chance to earn her keep. And two new gowns. All within the space of a day and night.

When Ruby asked for a sample of her sewing, Patience took up needle and thread and made a variety of stitches on a piece of white fabric. Pleased, Ruby said, "A worthy assistant. I believe Sister Dominique would be impressed. But for now, come and I'll show you what services we offer our customers."

When that was done, she took up Millie's lace table cover and began to sew, all the while watching as Patience began to wait on first one customer, then another.

Not one woman, Ruby noted, was from the town. All were from outlying ranches. Which only proved to her that the women of Hanging Tree still thought of her as an outsider. One unworthy of their patronage.

Another reason to resent Quent Regan. But she couldn't resent him. She was too busy missing him. And hating herself for such foolish feelings.

Chapter Fifteen

As Jade's white-and-gilt carriage rolled through the dusty street of Hanging Tree, it caused the usual stir. After all, it was far more suited to the streets of San Francisco. As were the women who rode in it.

Jade brought the matched team of whites to a stop in front of Ruby's shop. Then she and Diamond and Pearl stepped down.

"My, oh, my. Will you look at that." Patience stared in openmouthed surprise at the three regal beauties heading toward the shop.

Ruby looked up, then set her sewing aside and hurried to hug her sisters.

"Patience," she said when she'd greeted them, "I'd like you to meet my sisters, Diamond, Pearl and Jade."

"How do you do?" Patience couldn't help staring at these exotic women, who all looked so different from each other.

"Patience works for me," Ruby explained. "As my assistant."

That caused the three to study this stranger more

closely. Pale yellow hair had been carefully washed and combed. And the neat muslin gown fit her perfectly. It was obviously one of Ruby's creations.

Satisfied, they turned to Ruby.

"We've come to fetch you home," Pearl announced.

"Carmelita's fit to be tied," Diamond said. "She hasn't been able to sleep, just worrying about you here in town."

"But I still have so much work to do," Ruby protested. "With the town social ready to begin, there are many ranchers coming into town, bringing me new customers. And I have only two hands."

"Then you'll just have to keep those hands busy sewing at the ranch," Jade said. "And no arguing. You can't put Carmelita through another night of worry."

Reluctantly Ruby nodded. "You're right, of course. It's been selfish of me not to think about her."

"Good. You'll come with us now?" Diamond asked.

Ruby nodded, then had a sudden thought. "*Oui*. And I'm bringing Patience along, as well."

When the girl looked as though she'd refuse, Ruby said, "Now that my sisters have places of their own, the ranch house is practically empty. And Carmelita is always complaining about nobody to cook for. I'd like you to come with me. I promise you'll enjoy it. Besides, I need you to help with the sewing."

Patience swallowed, then nodded her head.

"Good." To her sisters Ruby said, "I'll take my

own rig. It's been at Neville Oakley's livery since yesterday morning.''

"Come on, then.'' Diamond, whose buckskins looked as though they'd burst if they were stretched any tighter, led the way to the carriage. "You can ride with us as far as the livery.''

"I'll need a few minutes,'' Ruby said as she began to gather up the gowns that still needed tailoring. Patience worked alongside her, gathering up Ruby's sewing supplies.

When everything was in readiness, they climbed in beside Pearl, Jade and Diamond. Jade flicked the reins.

As soon as they rolled up to the livery, Neville Oakley set aside his bellows and hurried to hitch up Ruby's horse. A few minutes later he led the horse and cart from the stable.

"Thank you, Mr. Oakley,'' Ruby called.

As he helped her into the cart, she said, "This is my assistant, Patience Carter.''

"Hello, Mr. Oakley.'' Patience placed her hand in his.

For a moment he seemed robbed of speech at the sight of this frail, delicate creature in the simple gown and worn boots. Then, swallowing, he managed "Ma'am.''

Patience was lifted effortlessly to the seat beside Ruby.

At a flick of the reins, the two carriages rolled out of town. And as they ate up the miles to the Jewel ranch, the air was filled with the sound of women's voices, laughing, chatting, catching up on each other's busy lives, and making plans for the big event of the year, the town social.

Along a riverbed far from town, Quent knelt beside his horse and drank.

He'd checked at every ranch. Talked with every wrangler. There had been no reports of stolen horses, no sightings of strangers in the area.

He'd studied the trail for any sign of a makeshift camp and found it remarkably clean.

Why, then, did he have this prickly feeling along his scalp? As though he were being watched.

He got to his feet and stood beside his horse. While he pretended to check the saddle, he studied the surrounding hills. Birds wheeled overhead. A herd of deer moved lazily across a dry gulch. There wasn't a single thing out of place.

He was a man who'd always relied on his instincts. And right now every instinct was warning of danger.

But where? And who?

He'd come out here for one reason. To make himself a target. He figured if Boyd Barlow was still in the area, he wouldn't be able to resist the chance for revenge. He'd remained in the open, riding across hills and valleys in plain view. And each night he'd made a campfire that could be seen for miles. But though he'd baited the trap, there'd been not a single nibble.

He pulled himself into the saddle. It was obvious that he'd been wrong. He'd been away too long. It was time to head back to town. He'd never have stayed away so long in the first place, except for Ruby. After the way he'd treated her, he had a need to be alone with his thoughts. But his thoughts were proving to be too troubling. What he needed now was to be around people.

In a way, he dreaded the thought of returning. It meant having to look at her, and reading the censure in her eyes. It meant looking, but never touching. He didn't know whether he could handle the knowledge that she would never again smile at him, speak with him. Touch him and lie with him.

But he'd been running long enough. It was time to go home and try to get on with his life.

Boyd Barlow held the rifle to his shoulder and squinted through the site as the marshal crested a ridge. His finger actually trembled on the trigger as he imagined squeezing it slowly, and watching the lawman tumble from the saddle and fall to the dirt.

It would be so easy.

But it wasn't good enough. Not after what the marshal had done to his brother.

He'd had plenty of time to think about this. He didn't just want Quent Regan dead. What he wanted, he thought, lowering the rifle, was to be close enough to see Regan's face when he was mortally wounded. To watch the blood pool around him, as his life slowly slipped away, just as the marshal had watched his brother's blood ooze and his life end. He wanted Quent Regan to know who'd pulled the trigger. In fact, he wanted everyone to know who had cut down this stinking lawman.

That's why he'd decided to choose a public place to kill Quent Regan. And it didn't get any more public than the marshal's own town. During the town social. When everyone would be there to witness it.

Oh, he knew all about the social. And all about the town. He had his own methods of gleaning information. And when he put his plan into action, he'd be able to walk through the town without anyone recognizing him.

Soon, very soon, everyone would know the name Boyd Barlow. The man who killed Marshal Quent Regan, the fastest gun in Texas.

Carmelita stood on the porch and watched until the two wagons rolled to a stop. Then she hurried down the steps to hug Ruby. "At last, you are home. I was so worried."

"I'm sorry, Carmelita. I shouldn't have stayed away so long without sending you word."

"*Sí*. I had you dead, wounded, starving, going without sleep."

"And that was only the first hour," Diamond said dryly as she awkwardly climbed the stairs.

"And you, Señora Diamond," Carmelita scolded. "Look at you. You should not be riding around the countryside in your condition. You should be confined to bed until this baby is born."

"This baby might not come for weeks yet. I'd go crazy lying in bed for that long." Diamond pressed her hands to the small of her back. "Though I must admit, I don't think I could take another mile in that carriage." She glanced around. "Where's Adam? I told him to meet me here, so he'd have a good supper."

"He is inside, talking with Cal and Dan and Marshal Regan," the housekeeper said.

At that, Ruby's heart stuttered, then began racing. Quent Regan here?

Before she could smooth down her skirts, or touch a hand to her tousled hair, the door opened and Adam, Cal and Dan emerged from the house, followed by Quent.

While Diamond, Pearl and Jade smiled their pleasure at the sight of their husbands, and greeted them affectionately, Ruby and Quent merely stared at one another.

He looked as he had the last time he'd returned from the wilderness. His hair long enough to curl over the collar of his shirt, the shirt she'd made for him. His cheeks and chin covered by a dark, shaggy growth of beard. His eyes seemed even more penetrating than she'd remembered. As though they could see clear through to her soul. He was a handsome, commanding presence, as wild, as primitive as this place he called home. And she hadn't realized how much she'd missed him until now, when he was standing here before her.

She felt her heart lurch.

When she finally managed to find her voice she said, "What are you doing here, Marshal?"

"I had some business in the area. Thought I'd pay a neighborly visit."

"I invited him to stay for supper," Carmelita said. "But he refuses."

"I need to get back to town. I'm sure by now Arlo has my paperwork in a shambles."

Carmelita stared at the stranger still seated in Ruby's rig. "And who is this?"

"I'm sorry." With much effort, Ruby pulled her scrambled thoughts together. "This is Patience Carter. My new assistant. Patience, our housekeeper, Carmelita Alvarez, and the marshal of Hanging Tree, Quent Regan."

"Marshal?"

Quent noticed the way the young woman avoided his eyes before turning to the housekeeper. "I hope you don't mind an extra mouth to feed. But Ruby insisted."

"Of course she did. The house has become too empty. All my birds have flown away."

"Well, this chicken has come home to roost," Adam said after giving his wife a long, loving look. "At least for the night."

"What do you mean?" Diamond demanded.

"I mean that you can't hide your discomfort anymore. I think we should move back here, where Carmelita can keep an eye on you."

"Now you are being sensible." A wide smile split Carmelita's lips.

Pearl nodded. "I think you should listen, Di. I'm really afraid you'll end up having that baby all alone while Adam's miles from home."

Seeing that Diamond was about to argue, Carmelita caught her hand. "You will go inside and sit," she ordered. "And I will fix you tea."

"Coffee," Diamond called to her retreating back. "Hot and black."

"*Sí.* Tea." The housekeeper hurried away. "And

while I am gone, the rest of you will talk some sense into Señora Diamond.''

The others merely grinned. Carmelita Alvarez was the only person who could bully Diamond into taking care of herself. Whether she liked it or not.

''Well, what are we waiting for?'' Diamond demanded. ''Let's go inside.''

As the others followed her indoors, Quent started down the steps.

''Can't we persuade you to stay for supper?'' Adam called.

''Another time.'' As he passed Ruby, Quent inhaled the sweet, dark fragrance of roses.

The pain was so sharp and swift, it felt like a knife in his heart. He'd known it would be painful to see her again. But he hadn't been prepared for this.

Mustering all his willpower, he pulled himself into the saddle and took off without a backward glance.

As he rode away, Ruby stood alone, watching until he disappeared from view.

From inside she could hear the voices and laughter of her family. For some strange reason, they only added to her misery.

She had never felt so alone, or so wretched, in her life.

Ruby carefully folded the length of lace and wrapped it in brown paper, then placed the bundle in a basket, which she carried over her arm. As she drew near the boardinghouse, she saw the wagons and carts of several boarders, in town for the social. Only the most prosperous ranchers would pay to put their families up at Millie Potter's. The rest would sleep in their wagons, or under the stars.

All around town could be seen the glow of campfires. The air was sharp with the tang of roasting meat. But the sweetest smells of all came from Millie's kitchen. As Birdie Bidwell opened the front door to admit Ruby, the fragrance of Millie's pot roast and freshly baked bread wafted on the air.

Birdie's freckled face bore a dusting of flour. A smear of chocolate ran from the corner of her mouth to her chin.

"I see you've been busy, Birdie."

"Yes'm. Been baking and cooking for hours and it's only midday."

"Well, your customers will be glad of all your hard work."

"Yes'm. Table's going to be crowded." She glanced at the basket on Ruby's arm. "That the tablecloth we've been hearing about?"

"This is it." Ruby started toward the dining room. "Would you like to give me a hand with it?"

"Yes'm. But Mrs. Potter said I was to call her as soon as you arrived."

Birdie's shout brought Millie out of the kitchen. Wiping her hands on her apron, Millie watched as Ruby and Birdie cleared the big, scarred wooden table of the few things clustered in the center. A chipped sugar bowl and dainty cream pitcher. A vase of wildflowers. A sturdy water pitcher. All were set on a sideboard. Then Ruby unfolded the cloth.

"Oh, my" was all Birdie could manage.

Ruby gave the cloth a slight shake. It drifted across the table and began to settle.

"Oh, Ruby." Millie clapped her hands to her cheeks in a gesture of delight as Ruby and Birdie took either end and straightened it out. "Just look at it. It's like something the angels might have spun."

"It is that," Birdie said with a trace of awe. "Like the dew that covers the ground early in the morning. Or the snowflakes up on Widow's Peak."

"I couldn't have said it better myself," came a voice from the doorway.

Ruby glanced over to see Quent leaning casually against the wall.

Her heart did a series of flips and she knew her face was suffused with color. She wanted to turn away, to hide the blush. But she couldn't help drinking in the sight of him. His commanding presence seemed to fill the room.

"You're early, Quent," Millie said. "Most of my boarders are still upstairs, washing up from their travels. Supper won't be served until we get this table set and the last of the meat cut. Which reminds me…" She started back to the kitchen. "I'll see to the food, Birdie. You set this table."

"Yes'm."

"I can help," Ruby volunteered. Anything would be better than having to stand here, feeling Quent's dark gaze boring into her. He hadn't even spoken to her. And she had the feeling, from the way his eyes narrowed on her, that he would prefer not to.

"No, you won't help in here," Millie said firmly. "You've done enough. You and Quent go along to the parlor. Birdie will bring some lemonade and biscuits.''

''Is lemonade the best you can do?'' Quent's tone held a note of disapproval.

Millie glanced at him in surprise. ''Quent Regan, you've been grouchy as a bear since you got back to town. If you want something stronger, I suggest you see Buck over at the saloon.''

''Guess I'll make do with lemonade,'' he muttered as he held the door for Ruby.

She had no choice but to lead the way to the parlor. Once there, instead of taking a seat, she walked to the mantel, to avoid facing Quent. Spotting a tintype of a very young Millie Potter and a handsome young man, she picked it up to examine it more closely.

''It doesn't do them justice.'' At the sound of Quent's voice, Ruby steeled herself. He was standing directly behind her, peering at the picture over her shoulder.

''They were the most popular couple in Hanging Tree,'' Quent said. ''Mick was always laughing, teasing. And Millie just naturally liked people. Everybody loved them. Funny,'' he mused. ''Mick's hair was as red as Millie's. They looked more like brother and sister than husband and wife. And he was so proud of those three little girls. Always called them his angels.''

''It must be very hard for her.'' Ruby started to set the photo down, but nerves had her fumbling, and she dropped it. ''Oh. *Mon Dieu.*''

She and Quent reached for it at the same time, and

managed to catch it before it hit the floor. In their eagerness to save the picture from shattering, their fingers tangled. A bolt of lightning would have been less shocking. As they straightened, they found themselves face-to-face, their lips nearly touching.

For a moment they froze, neither one able to move. Ruby chanced a quick glance at Quent's eyes. There was a strange look in them. One of guarded invitation. She had the distinct impression that, were she to move her face just a fraction, she would find his mouth warm, and firm, and inviting. The mere thought of it had her nearly overcome by a blaze of heat. But before she could push aside the paralysis that gripped her, Birdie's voice had them both stepping apart with twin looks of guilt.

"Mrs. Potter said, since this is a special day, with the new lace cloth and folks in for tomorrow's town social and all, that she wanted you to enjoy some of her best elderberry wine."

The girl set down a tray containing a decanter and two glasses, before hurrying away.

Ruby shot another glance at Quent, and felt her heart sink. It must have been her imagination. Now there was no welcoming warmth in those narrowed eyes. They were once again cold, bleak, forbidding.

"It isn't whiskey," he said, filling two glasses, "but it's better than nothing."

He offered one to her, then turned away and downed his in one long swallow.

While she sipped, he filled his glass a second time and drank it more slowly. And all the while he stood,

staring morosely out the window, not making any
attempt at conversation.

"Supper's ready," Millie called.

Upstairs, doors opened and closed, and footsteps
sounded on the steps.

"Time to head to the dining room." He couldn't
hide the relief in his voice. "I hear the others coming."

He walked to the door, then stood back, waiting
for Ruby to precede him.

As she led the way down the hall, she had to swallow a burning in her throat. Not tears, she told herself
firmly. It was merely the elderberry wine. And if
truth be told, she was glad for this interruption. Marshal Quent Regan had made it plain that he had not
forgotten their last encounter. Perhaps it was just as
well that she hadn't caught up with him and accepted
his apology.

She was better off without this man. And his temper. And his arrogance. And his dark, brooding attitude.

And his kisses that set her on fire.

Chapter Sixteen

It was a day of frantic activity. Ruby had promised her three sisters new gowns for the social, as well as new shirts for their husbands. And as a surprise, she was making Pearl's boys new outfits. Daniel's was to be short pants and a white shirt. Gil's was to be a new suit, as befitted a young man of fourteen.

She glanced at the row of dresses and shirts hanging neatly on hooks in the shop. It gave her a sense of pride to know that her talent was going to make her family so happy.

On top of that she had made a new dress for Birdie Bidwell. Without the girl's measurements, she'd had to guess at her size. But she knew, no matter how it fit, Birdie would be delighted.

If she hadn't been so busy, she would have delivered the dress herself, just so she could see the girl's face. But she'd had to settle for sending it with Patience.

Her fingers flew across the fabric. One last dress, and she would be finished for the day.

She was so engrossed in her work, she didn't even pause when she heard the door open.

"How did Birdie like my surprise?" she asked.

When no one answered, she looked up. And froze.

Quent was standing just inside the door. Dressed all in black, with his guns at his hips, he looked completely out of place in this fussy, frilly room.

"I...thought you were Patience."

"Where is your assistant?" He remained where he was. His voice was gruff, to hide the emotions churning in his gut.

"I sent her to Millie's boardinghouse, to deliver a package."

"I came to give you a report on her."

Ruby shot him an angry look. "What do you mean, a report?"

"Arlo and Millie told me that you didn't know anything about her before you hired her. I thought I'd try to find out a little about her background."

"I don't care to..."

Seeing her angry reaction, he crossed to her and held out a hand. "It's all right, Ruby. I'm not here to report anything bad."

She hadn't even known she'd been holding her breath, until this moment.

She sighed, "I'm glad."

When he didn't volunteer anything more, she said, "As long is there's nothing unpleasant, I'll listen to the report."

His voice fell. "I didn't say it wasn't unpleasant."

"What do you mean?"

"It's a familiar enough story. She grew up on a

hardscrabble ranch on the banks of the Rio Grande. Her mother died a couple of years ago. Her father wasn't much good with the soil, but he knew a little about horses. So he worked other people's ranches. After her mother died, Patience went with him, helping out in the kitchens or the fields. Last year her father was thrown while he was breaking a mustang. Patience took him back home, but he never recovered. He just kept failing. And then, when he died, there was nobody who'd buy the ranch. And no way for one young girl to keep it going. As far as anyone could tell me, she just walked away one day. And kept on walking until she got to Hanging Tree.''

''That's pretty accurate, Marshal. But you missed a couple of things.''

At the sound of the young girl's voice, Quent and Ruby glanced up to see Patience standing in the doorway. Her lips were quivering, but to her credit, she held her head high. ''I thought burying Pa was the hardest thing I'd ever done. But it wasn't. Surviving was. Trying to stay alive while I made my way to Hanging Tree. And once here, when I couldn't find work, or a place to sleep, or food to eat, I wondered how I'd get through another day. Maybe Miss Ruby is too nice to tell you the truth about me. But I think you ought to know. I stole from her.''

Quent fixed his gaze on the girl who stood trembling in the doorway.

''When I came back later, hoping to sneak into the back room to sleep, Miss Ruby caught me. She could have turned me over to your deputy. She had every right. But instead she gave me food, and offered me a job. And even though she didn't know anything about me, she trusted me. She even made me feel like I was helping her instead of the other way around.''

She swallowed, then began removing the crisp white pinafore. ''I suppose you'll want to take me over to the jail now, Marshal.'' She hung it neatly on a hook.

''Now, why would I want to do that, Patience?'' he asked.

She turned. ''I just told you. I stole from Miss Ruby's shop.''

Quent glanced at Ruby. ''Did you make a report?''

''No. I...no.'' Ruby shook her head.

Quent showed no emotion. But his voice gentled. ''Then I guess I'll just have to forget what you said. Unless the owner reports the theft, it's out of my hands.''

He touched a hand to his hat, then crossed the room. ''I'd better get back to work.''

''Will you be coming to the social tomorrow?'' The words were out of Ruby's mouth before she could stop them.

He shrugged, still frowning. ''I probably won't have time. With so many strangers coming into town, I'll probably have my hands full keeping peace in the town.''

Ruby's heart fell.

Ruby and Patience watched as he strolled away.

Then, as Ruby bent to her sewing, she said softly, ''I guess we'd better get back to work, as well.''

Without a word Patience removed the pinafore from the hook and pulled it on. As she did, one tear rolled down her cheek. She lifted a hand to brush at it before turning to greet a new customer.

Behind her, Ruby also brushed away a tear. And blamed it on the fact that she'd been straining her eyes.

The sky was a clear, brittle blue, without a single cloud to mar the beauty. The merest hint of a breeze whispered through the leaves of the trees. It was a perfect day for a town social.

By the time Ruby's wagon rolled into town, the main street was littered with carts and rigs of every size and description. She and Patience could see throngs of people trudging up the hill toward the church. The men wore dark suits and wide-brimmed hats; the colorful gowns of the women gave them the look of beautiful butterflies. Children ran ahead or danced around their parents, propelled by boundless energy.

When they pulled up to the livery, Neville Oakley hurried forward to help them down. His smile was warm, his greeting cordial, until he held out his hand to Patience. At the sight of her his mouth opened, but he made not a sound.

"Good morning, Mr. Oakley," she said, as she had every morning.

And, like every morning, there was no answering greeting. Instead, Neville Oakley merely stared. And swallowed.

The young woman's smile faltered a bit as she and

Ruby followed the others, making their way through the throngs headed to the Golden Rule.

Reverend Dan Simpson kept the service mercifully short. After a brief sermon about seeing the goodness in every man, and the importance of being good neighbors, he led the congregation in a spirited hymn. Then, as he called for dismissal, he reminded everyone that this was a special day.

"Let us give thanks for this opportunity to break bread with our neighbors, and to share the fruits of our labors."

Ruby, making her way down the aisle beside her sisters, spotted Quent at the rear of the church. But by the time she got there, he was nowhere to be seen.

She touched a hand to her chest and wondered if she'd ever get used to the empty, hollow feeling around her heart.

Outside, the children gathered for the first of their contests—the three-legged races. The winners would be awarded blue ribbons and Carmelita's sugar cookies.

Pearl and Cal were hoarse from cheering when Daniel and Gil won. The two boys proudly displayed their ribbons as they ate their cookies in front of their friends, who jealously watched.

Some of the men held a horse race, which Adam handily won. Forced to watch from the sidelines, Diamond patted her swollen middle. "Next year," she reminded her sisters, "that'll be me winning that ribbon."

Pearl dropped an arm around her shoulders. "Adam will share it with you, Di."

"It's not the same as winning it myself." She forced a smile to her lips as Adam started toward her. "I don't think I'll ever get used to just standing around while my husband has all the fun."

"Speaking of fun." Jade pointed toward a cluster of men who had gathered inside the corral of Neville Oakley's stable for a shooting match. "I think this might be a good time for us to get as far away as possible and start our quilting bee."

Though many of the women drew away, Ruby moved closer, until she was leaning against the fence. It wasn't that she had an interest in the contest. But she'd spotted Quent among the contestants.

There were more than a dozen men holding rifles, while Doc Prentice explained the rules to them. Soon the air was filled with the volley of gunfire. Several of the men, including Cal and Adam, hit the target every time. But Quent Regan was the only man who hit not only the target but the bull's-eye with every shot.

Watching him, Ruby felt her heart constrict. He was so self-assured. So quietly competent. And so deadly accurate with a gun. The badge on his shirt was a constant reminder of that fact.

While the men patted him on the back, he laughed and accepted their congratulations. But when he looked up and saw Ruby watching, his laughter faded.

Feeling the heat staining her cheeks, she pushed her way through the crowd and went in search of the quilting bee.

* * *

By midday the men had set up long wooden planks across sturdy tree stumps, while the women hurried to their wagons to fetch the food they'd so lovingly prepared. Soon the tables groaned beneath the weight, and children twitched and fidgeted, as all those wonderful fragrances assaulted them, trying their patience to the limit.

As soon as the reverend led them in prayer, then called for the feasting to commence, long lines began to form. Everyone filled their plates, then sought shady spots to eat. Families from far-flung ranches gathered to share the news of crops and herds.

Ruby filled her plate and joined her family. As she took a seat on the grass, Diamond, sprawled out beside her in the shade of a tree, shouted, "Quent. Over here. Come and join us."

Ruby suddenly found her appetite gone as the marshal walked over.

"Sit here," Diamond said as she got slowly to her feet. "I'm going back for seconds."

Then she was gone, and Quent had no choice but to sit on the grass beside Ruby.

Across from him Pearl said, "You men are all alike. I see you chose the spiciest dish on the table."

"It's great," Quent said as he took a mouthful. "What's it called?"

"Gumbo," Pearl told him. "Ruby made it."

"You did? I didn't know you cooked."

Ruby felt oddly pleased that he'd chosen her dish. And even more pleased that he liked it. "With Carmelita in the kitchen, I rarely get the chance. But Daniel and Gil brought me a bucket of fish from

Poison Creek and I gave them my word I'd make them my gumbo. I don't know if it will be as tasty as the catfish we had in the bayou, but I do know it will be as spicy.''

He took another bite. It was as hot and spicy as the woman who'd made it.

"I don't know how you found time to cook, with all the sewing you've been doing,'' Pearl remarked.

Ruby saw Quent turn to her, and was forced to endure his quiet gaze. She flushed. "It wasn't easy. But I gave the boys my word, so I had to keep it.''

Just then Arlo arrived, breathless. "Marshal, there's an argument heating up over at Buck's saloon. Two ranchers been putting away a lot of whiskey and eyeing the same filly. Buck sent me to fetch you before it gets out of hand.''

Quent handed his empty plate to his deputy and said wearily, "Looks like I'll skip the cakes and pies.'' He tipped his hat to the women, then spared a quick glance at Ruby before saying, "Excuse me.''

While all around her the others cleaned their plates and helped themselves to more, Ruby sat very still, wondering how long it would take before her heart would stop betraying her like this. Each time Quent Regan came near her, the reaction was always the same. A wild, fluttering of pulse beat, then a numbness. As though even her heart had lost the will to continue.

The children ran off their meal, playing tag and hide-and-seek. Men dozed in the shade of trees, their hats over their faces. Women gathered over their quilts, fingers flying as they exchanged gossip or family recipes or tales of childbirth.

"You're going to have a boy," the widow Purdy told Diamond.

"I am?" Diamond looked mystified. "How do you know?"

"Carrying low. All in front. Yep. Definitely a boy." The old woman turned to Pearl. "And yours is a girl."

Pearl gasped. "How did you know...? I mean, I haven't even told anyone except my family that I was having a baby."

Watery blue eyes peered into Pearl's clear blue ones. "I can see it in your eyes. There's a light there that gives it away every time."

"She's never been wrong," her daughter said with a trace of pride. "Ma called every one of her grandchildren by name before they were born."

The widow Purdy leveled a gaze on Jade. "Do twins run on your side of the family, or the reverend's?"

Jade was momentarily speechless.

"No matter whose side. It's twins. Boys," the old lady said matter-of-factly.

Diamond, Pearl and Ruby could only stare at her in stunned surprise.

At their accusing looks, Jade swallowed, then said softly, "I'm not even sure myself yet. It was just too soon to mention it. Except to Dan."

"You can be sure," Martha Purdy said. "When Ma says it's so, it's so."

With laughs and shouts, the four sisters leapt to

their feet and embraced. Then Jade accepted the congratulations of the other women, before hurrying off to tell her husband what the old woman had said.

When at last the others took up needle and thread and continued to sew, Mrs. Purdy remarked, "Looks like you'd better find yourself a beau, Ruby. These sisters of yours are leaving you in their dust."

"That suits me just fine, Mrs. Purdy. I would much prefer the role of doting aunt to overworked mother."

Just then the marshal walked by and gave a tip of his hat to the group of women. When he saw Ruby, his smile disappeared, replaced with a frown.

Distracted, Ruby pricked her finger. With a hiss of pain, she lifted it to her lips and sucked at the drop of blood.

"Uh-huh." The old woman peered at her over the rims of her spectacles. Then she merely smiled.

Chapter Seventeen

Long before dusk settled, the sound of a fiddle summoned the townspeople to the meeting room of the Golden Rule. To make room for dancing, the chairs had been lined up against the walls. At one end of the room stood a raised platform, on which were Farley Duke with his fiddle, Barney Healey wheezing out tunes on the mouth organ, and Nellie Cooper, playing the tinny piano. At the other end of the room the last of the desserts were set out on a long table, along with bowls of punch.

Some of the men disappeared from time to time, to sip from a jug supplied by Beau Baskin. Of course, Beau had to take a sip for every one taken by the others. And very soon Beau's eyes started to cross, and he was walking like a sailor on a rolling ship.

When the music started, Pearl and Cal were the first to step onto the dance floor. Pearl, in the new pink gown supplied by Ruby, offered her hand to her handsome husband, and they began to move in a slow circle. Their two sons looked equally handsome in their new clothes, with their faces shining and their hair slicked back.

Daniel and some of his friends stood to one side of the hall, eyeing the platter of cookies. Whenever they thought no one was looking, they would snatch another cookie, or fill another cup with punch.

Fourteen-year-old Gil was too old for snitching cookies and punch. Besides, the minute he laid eyes on Birdie Bidwell, wearing her new frilly white dress, with her hair tied back in white ribbons, all he could think about was getting closer to her. And the only proper way for a boy to get close to a girl was to ask her to dance. So he did. And she floated around the room in his arms. It was the first time anyone in Hanging Tree had ever seen Birdie look anything but clumsy. In truth, she looked absolutely graceful, blushing and smiling up into Gil's eyes, being held in his arms.

Jade and Dan, on opposite sides of the hall, were still busy directing the social. Jade was folding the quilts that would be raffled off. Dan was trying to keep the men from slipping away to drink. But at the first strains of music, they looked across the room, then drifted toward each other and came together in a dance.

Adam searched the crowded room until he located Diamond sitting with a cluster of women. Judging by the look on her face, it was the last place she wanted to be. Taking pity on her, he approached and said, "Want to dance?"

She accepted his hand and got awkwardly to her

feet. As soon as they were out of earshot she hissed, "You know I don't dance."

"Want to go back and gossip with Lavinia and Gladys?" he muttered.

She put a hand on his shoulder and allowed him to lead her to the floor.

"Oh," she said between gritted teeth, "I'll be so glad when I can walk without waddling."

"You look beautiful," he whispered.

For a moment she merely stared at him. Then she said, "How can you say that? I'm fat and clumsy and ugly."

He drew her as close as her swollen middle would allow, and pressed his lips to hers. "Diamond, you're so beautiful, you take my breath away."

She had to blink back the tears that sprang to her eyes. But she was flushed and radiant as she allowed him to lead her slowly through the dance.

Ruby, watching from across the room, felt tears in her own eyes, as well.

Beside her Patience said, "All three of your sisters look so happy. They're positively glowing. And their husbands are so handsome, and so in love."

"*Oui.*" It was all she could manage over the lump in her throat.

At a little gasp from Patience, Ruby turned to where her young friend was looking. Making his way across the room was Neville Oakley. His hair had been neatly washed and combed. And he was wearing a clean shirt and trousers.

"Good evening, Miss Ruby, Miss Patience," he said.

"Good evening, Mr. Oakley. My, you look fine," Ruby said with a smile.

"Thank you." His big hands hung at his sides. He was staring at Patience with hungry eyes. "You look as pretty as a sunflower."

Ruby glanced at the young woman beside her, who was blushing clear to her toes.

"Will you dance with me, Miss Patience?"

She nodded, too overcome to speak. He took her hand and led her to the floor. And as they started to dance, Ruby felt the lump in her throat getting too big to swallow. To some in the crowd, Neville Oakley probably looked like a big, clumsy giant, and Patience like a small, helpless waif. But to Ruby they looked like a happy, perfectly suited couple.

"Beau Baskin had better watch himself now," came the voice of Arlo Spitz. "Here's the marshal. And he looks mad enough to spit bullets."

Ruby tore her gaze from Neville and Patience.

Quent Regan stood framed in the doorway, studying the crowd. The anger his deputy had mentioned was evident in the frown line between his brows, and the tight set of his jaw.

When he spotted Ruby he started across the room. She felt the pull of his dark gaze, and her heart started doing somersaults. Several times Quent was stopped by friends and neighbors. Though he paused to shake a hand, or offer a word, he continued making his way toward her.

Mon Dieu. He was going to ask her to dance. Her heartbeat accelerated. She reached for a fan and began waving it frantically, in the hope of cooling her heated flesh. And all the while she watched him, feeling her cheeks growing more flushed with every step he took in her direction.

"May I have this dance, Miss Ruby?"

For a moment Ruby was too distracted to hear. But when the voice came again, louder, she turned her head. And felt a stab of bitter disappointment. Byron Conner was standing directly beside her.

"Mr. Conner." The fan slipped from her hand.

The handsome young banker gallantly bent and retrieved it. She closed it and set it aside, just in time to see Quent, still watching her, pause beside Millie Potter.

"Well, Miss Ruby? May I have this dance?"

"*Oui.* Of course." Flustered, she allowed him to take her hand and lead her to the dance floor.

As they began to move together, she peered over his shoulder in time to see Quent take Millie's hand and lead her onto the floor.

Moments later they danced by, and Ruby heard the lilt of Millie's laughter. And the deeper sound of Quent's chuckle.

It cut, sharp as a razor.

"You're a very good dancer, Miss Ruby," Byron said. "And easily the prettiest lady in the room."

"*Merci.*" She forced a smile to her lips. But her voice lacked conviction. And she thought her heart was surely breaking. In fact, as she moved in Byron's arms, she was certain she could feel the sharp, brittle shards as her heart shattered into a million tiny pieces.

* * *

The dance floor grew more crowded as the music became livelier. There were bursts of laughter as the musicians broke into jigs and reels, bringing even the most reluctant dancers to their feet. Even the frail widow Purdy, who seemed constantly at death's door, lifted her skirts and set her feet flying through a jig. Afterward, she collapsed into a chair, laughing and blushing at the wild applause.

Through it all, Ruby was forced to dance with nearly every man in Hanging Tree. All except one. Quent Regan, she noticed, had danced with every woman in the room. But he had steadfastly managed to avoid coming near her.

Now, as another song ended and Arlo Spitz escorted her to a chair, he said, "How about some punch, Miss Ruby?"

"Yes, please. That would be nice."

She picked up her fan, but before she could use it, Adam caught her hand. "Come on. They're playing a reel. And Diamond says she'd rather sit this one out."

Ruby and her brother-in-law joined the other couples, clapping their hands, moving through the steps. But as the reel ended, the music began again, and Farley Duke announced that every man had to change partners and dance with the lady on his left. Adam turned to his left, Ruby turned to her right. And found herself face-to-face with Quent Regan.

For a moment neither of them moved. Quent scowled, looking as if he'd been caught in a trap. Then, stepping closer, he reluctantly opened his arms. Ruby hesitated, and thought about running from the room. But everyone would see. And she would be the topic of discussion for a very long time to come.

She could get through this, she told herself. It was, after all, just a dance. Lifting her hand to his shoulder, she began to move with him.

At first their movements were stiff and awkward. "Looks like you're having fun tonight." Quent had never before noticed how small her hand was. And how cold.

She lifted her head in that haughty way. "I am having a marvelous time. And you?"

"Great. Just great."

Someone bumped them, and Quent felt the quick press of her body against his before Ruby managed to pull back. Heat jolted through him. God in heaven. His body was on fire.

Ruby wished she had her fan. A moment ago she'd been cold. Cold and rigid with anger. Now she was far too warm.

She struggled to think of something simple to say. Something impersonal. "I saw Beau Baskin passing a jug earlier." The hand at her waist tightened. A barely perceptible move. But she felt it through every pore of her body. She could remember a time when that same hand had stroked, and aroused. *Mon Dieu,* she was nearly jumping out of her skin.

"Beau's probably lying in the street by now, dead drunk." Without meaning to, Quent pressed his lips to her temple.

Ruby's hand tightened at his shoulder as she absorbed the tremors that exploded through her.

"I'll take Beau over to the jail in a while. Lock him up till morning so he can sleep it off." With his lips in her hair, Quent could smell the sweet, earthy scent of her. It always did something to his brain. And his body. Right now his body was reacting in the worst possible way. The whole damned town could see him. And he couldn't stop himself. Now that he was finally touching her, he could feel himself slipping.

It had been so long. So damned long.

The music ended, but Quent continued holding her, standing so still he looked like a statue.

Arlo hurried up, holding out a cup. "I got that punch, Miss Ruby."

She seemed not to hear. She didn't even look at him. And when he tried again, Quent growled, "The lady doesn't want punch right now, Arlo."

"Well, yes. I can see...I guess..." The deputy gave them both a long, puzzled look, then drained the cup and hurried away for more.

The music started again. A slow waltz. But though the couples around them circled and twirled, Quent and Ruby stood, barely swaying, just holding on to each other.

"Ruby..."

"Quent..."

They spoke each other's name in unison. Each stopped, flustered, waiting for the other to finish.

Ruby's face colored.

Quent's jaw clenched.

He swallowed and tried again. "Would you like some air?"

"That…that would be nice. Some other time. But I don't think it would be proper to leave since Jade and Dan—"

"For God's sake, Ruby." The words were wrenched from him. "Won't you, just this once, take pity on me? I want you away from all these prying eyes. I want you alone. Now."

Her eyes widened. She looked up into his and could read a slow, simmering fury there. And something more. Something she hadn't recognized until this moment. Anguish. Torment. The same torment she'd been suffering all these long agonizing weeks.

She wanted to touch a hand to his cheek. But she dared not. One touch, and they'd both be lost. Instead, she lowered her head, avoiding his eyes.

"Oui."

It was all she said.

All he needed to hear.

Chapter Eighteen

They couldn't remember how they slipped out of the Golden Rule. How they walked past their family, friends, neighbors. Surely they smiled. They even spoke. But it was all a blur.

Once they were outside, Quent took Ruby's hand. It was no longer cold. In fact, it radiated heat like a bonfire.

They stepped over the prone figure they knew to be Beau Baskin. And without a word they headed toward Ruby's shop.

Along the way they saw men tending campfires, and women tucking their children into bed beneath wagons. The music from the dance drifted on the night air, and joined in the muted sounds of voices talking, laughter trilling clear as a bell.

When they reached the shop, Ruby opened the door and Quent followed.

She lifted a lantern down from a shelf. Before she could light it, Quent's arms closed around her, and his mouth found hers. The lantern fell from her nerveless fingers and clattered on the floor.

Neither of them noticed.

The taste of her lips had his blood pumping furiously. "I've been so hungry for you, Ruby. Starving," he muttered against her lips, then inside her mouth, as he feasted.

"Oh, Quent. It's been so long." She kissed him back with a fierceness that surprised them both. "So long."

His hands were at her shoulders, pressing, kneading, then moving along her back, igniting fires everywhere they touched. And they touched her everywhere. He couldn't seem to stop. He had this frantic need to fill himself with her. His hands, his mouth, his body and soul.

He breathed her in, feeding his starving lungs.

And he tasted. The softness of her lips. The delicate skin of her throat. He heard her little sigh of pleasure as she arched her neck for more of his open-mouthed kisses.

Oh, the press of his lips was the most exquisite feeling. How had she lived so long without it? With each movement, as his lips burned a trail of fire along her shoulder, she couldn't hold back the little sighs and moans that escaped.

He couldn't get enough of her. He tasted, nibbled, devoured. His mouth moved lower, to the soft swell of her breast. When his lips closed around her already erect nipple, the sound that issued from her throat was unlike any he'd heard before. A low, guttural groan of pleasure and pain and need.

Impatient with the satin fabric that acted as a barrier, he tore it aside, shredding it into tatters.

They were beyond caring.

His hands and mouth moved over her, suckling, feasting. Arousing. Igniting fires that smoldered and burned.

But still it wasn't enough.

She wrapped herself around him and kissed him until her lungs were aching. Instead of coming up for air, she took the kiss deeper.

He felt the madness taking over, sweeping him along. He lifted her and drove her back against the wall. And still their mouths mated.

Impatient, he pushed aside her skirt. His hand found her, hot and wet and ready as he drove her to the first peak.

She was rocked by tremors. Her whole body seemed to erupt. Dazed, she could only cling to him as he took her on a dizzying ride. But before she could clear her mind his mouth had found her breast again, and she was climbing, climbing.

In her eagerness to touch him, all of him, Ruby fumbled with the buttons of his shirt. In her frustration she ripped several loose, then slid it from his shoulders.

When she pressed her mouth to his chest he groaned with pleasure. The feel of her lips and fingertips on his flesh was driving him mad.

"I need to feel you, Ruby. All of you."

He tore away the last of her gown and petticoats, then unbuckled his gun belt and shed his clothes. They dropped to their knees, with only their discarded clothing as a cushion on the hard floor. And then they were lying together, and he was kissing her, touching her in ways she'd only dreamed of.

His mouth left hers to burn a trail of fire down her body.

"Quent." Her voice betrayed her shock and surprise. "What are...what are we doing?" she managed.

"Pleasuring ourselves. Oh, sweet heaven, I hope I'm giving you as much pleasure as you're giving me." He felt as if he'd entered the eye of a storm, and was being buffeted by wind and rain. The need was building, building, and he was helpless to hold it back any longer.

"I can't be gentle." His voice was thick with need. "I've wanted you for so long."

"I don't want you to be gentle," she whispered. She'd lost all attempt at control a long time ago. Now she felt wild and free. "I just want you."

"Oh, Ruby." His mouth fused with hers. His wonderful, clever hands moved over her, taking her beyond any place she'd ever been before.

"I've tried so hard not to want you," he muttered. "But I've been lying to myself. Look at me, Ruby. Look at me," he whispered hoarsely, gripping her face between both his hard, callused hands. "I want you to hear this and remember."

Her eyes, blurred by a red mist of passion, cleared, then focused.

"I'm sorry for anything I've ever done to hurt you. I'll do whatever I can to make it up to you. Do you understand?"

But she was beyond understanding. He could see

it in her eyes. And so he had to tell her. Precisely. Carefully.

"Nothing matters anymore. All I know is that I love you, Ruby. That's what matters. You're what matters to me. I love you. Only you."

Love. His declaration pierced her heart, leaving her shattered.

She clutched at his head and, to keep from weeping, covered his mouth with hers. "Then love me, Quent. Love me now."

He entered her then, and she rose up to meet him. In a frenzy they came together, clutching frantically, rocking. He plunged into her, deeper and deeper.

This was what he'd been craving, needing. Ruby. Only Ruby. Loving him. Letting him love her.

He cried out her name as the shudders racked her. Then he followed her, exploding until his body was limp and drained.

They lay in a tangled heap, their breathing still ragged, their heartbeats still unsettled.

"I've missed you so much."

"Not as much as I've missed you."

They were lying together on the chaise, where Quent had carried her after the storm inside him had subsided. He felt calm now. Pleasantly sated. And filled with so much love for this woman in his arms.

"So much has happened. To you. To us. To this." He swept a big hand to indicate the room. "I like your shop, Ruby. I like what you've done in here. You've turned this simple room into your home."

"*Oui.* It feels more like my home than Papa's big

ranch ever did. It is the first, the only thing that is completely mine.''

"The room smells like you. Sweet, dusky, wonderful. What is it?''

"In the bayou we call it potpourri. I keep it in a dish in each room.''

"Um. Sounds mysterious. What does it mean?''

She laughed, and he thought how much he'd missed the sexy, throaty sound of her laughter. "It sounds much better in the French than in the translation. It means rotten pot.''

He grinned. "You're right. I like the sound of potpourri better. What is it?''

"It is a mélange, *chéri*. A mixture of many things. Flowers, herbs, spices. But mostly roses. I love the fragrance of roses.''

"I never gave much thought to it. But now I love it, too.'' He breathed it in, then pressed a kiss to her hair. "It reminds me of you. It will always remind me of you.''

She moved, shifted, until her lips found his. Against his mouth she whispered, "We feel right together here in my room.''

"We are right together, Ruby. Not just here. Everywhere. I've had a long time to think things through. There's so much—''

His head came up at the sound of a gunshot. He swore softly as he sat up and swung his legs to the floor. "Probably nothing more than some damn fool rancher who can't hold his liquor. But I have to see to it.''

"Don't go, Quent. Let Arlo take care of it.''

He pulled on his pants and slipped into the shirt, idly noting the missing buttons. "Arlo couldn't shoot fish in a barrel." He sat down on the edge of the chaise and pulled on his boots, then strapped on his holsters and checked his pistols. "Want to walk back with me? The social should be winding down soon. Then all I'll have to do is pick Beau Baskin out of the dust and lock him up for the night."

She laughed and shook her head. "You go. I think I'd like to wash up and repair the damage to my gown."

"I'm sorry," he said, glancing at the heap of clothes that littered the floor.

"I'm not." She stepped naked from the chaise and walked to him, and had the satisfaction of seeing his eyes go dark with the quick flare of passion.

Quent felt his throat go dry, and wished he'd never heard that gunshot, especially when she wrapped her arms around his neck and kissed him with a thoroughness that had him straining against her.

"Are you sure you have to leave?" she whispered.

"Oh, God." He'd known there was an imp in her. He'd seen it in her eyes. Tasted it on her lips.

"I'll be right back. As soon as I…" He kissed her once, twice, three times before he managed to turn away and stagger to the door. "As soon as I can take care of a couple of obligations."

He pulled the door open and cautioned himself not to look back, or he'd be lost. Outside, he took several deep breaths, then started up the street.

With a satisfied smile, Boyd Barlow stood in the shadows and watched until the marshal disappeared.

It had been even easier than he'd expected. He'd seen Quent Regan leave the hall with the woman, had followed them here to this little shop. He'd seen their silhouettes in the darkened window, knew exactly what they were doing. That's when the idea had come to him. He had the perfect way to avenge his brother's murder. And it had been Quent Regan himself who'd given him the answer.

The damned fool marshal had gone soft on a woman. What better way to get to him than through her?

He'd waited until the lantern was shining inside the shop. Then he'd run to the end of the street, behind the livery, where he'd fired off a shot. He knew his quarry well. Knew that Quent Regan wouldn't neglect an obligation to the town, even if it meant sacrificing his own pleasure.

And Marshal Regan had done exactly as he'd expected, hurrying away within minutes of the gunshot.

The outlaw took the badge out of his pocket and pinned it to his shirt. Then, with a confident grin, he sauntered up to the shop and knocked on the door.

Ruby tied up her hair and washed in a basin. Then, humming a little tune, she slipped into a clean gown and brushed her hair long and loose before picking up the remnants of her clothing scattered around the floor.

"Oh, my," she said with shaky little laugh. She was still dazed at what had happened between her and Quent. It had been...magic. There was no other explanation for it. One minute they were ignoring each other, or trying desperately to. The next they were caught up in a wild dance of desire that had left her breathless.

"I'd better get these things mended before Patience sees them and asks for an explanation," she muttered aloud.

She padded barefoot into the shop and located her needle and thread. But before she could return to her sitting room, there was a knock on the door.

Her lips parted in a smile as she hurried to answer it. "That didn't take you as long—"

She arched a brow. The man standing there was a stranger.

"I'm sorry. I thought you were someone else," she said. "My shop is closed until morning."

"Yes, ma'am." Boyd gave her his best smile. "I hate to bother you. But I'm just in for the town social. I have to leave first thing in the morning. And since I'm an old friend of Quent Regan's, I thought maybe you'd make an exception."

"A friend of Quent's?" She stared at the badge pinned to his shirt. "I see you're a lawman, too."

"Yes, ma'am. Homer Johnson. And you are...?"

"Ruby Jewel."

"Yep. That's what Quent said." He glanced beyond her, his gaze sweeping the room. "Quent said you could probably help me with a—" he caught sight of the gowns hanging along one wall "—a dress for my wife."

"*Oui.* A dress." She stepped aside, permitting him entrance. "I suppose, since you are a friend and fellow lawman, it wouldn't be polite to turn you away."

She started toward the row of gowns. "Do you have an idea of size and color?"

When he didn't answer she turned. He was leaning against the closed door. In his hand was a very deadly looking gun.

"We won't worry about size and color," he said with a chilling smile.

"I don't under—"

"You just worry about doing what you're told. Come here."

Ruby began backing up until she felt the cool wall behind her.

"Damn you! I said come here."

He was across the room in quick strides. Using the butt of his gun, he hit her so hard she staggered to her knees and fought a wave of pain and nausea.

"Now you've learned that I won't tell you twice," he shouted as he hauled her to her feet. "If you know what's good for you, you'll do what you're told the first time."

"Who—" she felt a trickle of blood along her cheek "—are you?"

He caught sight of himself in the tall looking glasses. The twin images made him laugh. With his face clean shaven and his hair cut short and darkened with boot black, even his own mother wouldn't recognize him.

"An old friend of your lover boy. With an old score to settle."

Still laughing, he dragged her into the back room. Spying the rumpled quilt on the chaise, his lips curled in a sneer. "Well, isn't this cozy? The town marshal thought he'd keep his harlot all to himself."

He tossed her down onto the lounge, then stood over her, brandishing the gun.

It pleased him to see the fear in her eyes. They were all alike. When they saw that he meant business, they always started crying and wailing and begging for their lives.

It gave him a sense of power. He liked seeing how far he could push them.

And this time it was Marshal Quent Regan who would beg. If not for his own life, then for the life of his woman.

When the outer door was suddenly opened, he spun around, his gun at the ready.

"Miss Ruby. I hope you don't mind."

Ruby recognized the voice of Patience. But before she could call out a warning, Boyd dragged her to her feet and wrapped an arm around her throat. His other hand held a gun to her temple.

"We saw the light and—" Catching sight of Ruby in the grasp of the stranger, Patience swallowed back whatever else she was about to say.

Ruby's eyes were wide with terror when she saw both Patience and Neville Oakley, standing hand in hand, wearing identical looks of astonishment.

"Well, well. Looks like you just changed my plans a little," Boyd said.

"What...? Who...?" Patience couldn't find her voice.

Beside her, Neville glanced from Ruby to the man

holding her hostage. He seemed taken aback by the badge. "Are you a lawman?"

"A lawman?" Boyd threw back his head and gave a chilling laugh. "I make my own law. At the end of this gun."

"You let go of Miss Ruby," Neville said. "She's too fine a lady for you to hurt her."

"Would you like to be her hero?" Boyd taunted.

In one quick movement Neville shoved Patience out of the way and lumbered forward, unmindful of the danger to himself.

"Big dumb fool," Boyd shouted as he fired at point-blank range.

Ruby screamed. Patience let out a piercing cry.

Neville's face registered shock, then pain. But, though he staggered, he continued forward.

Boyd fired a second shot and Neville stiffened, before crumpling to the floor.

"Oh, dear God," Patience shouted as she dropped to her knees beside Neville. "You've killed him. You monster, you killed him."

The outlaw grabbed her by the hair and dragged her to her feet.

Tears streamed down her face, and hysteria bubbled dangerously close to the surface.

He slapped her hard, then snapped, "Now, you listen, girl. Listen good, 'cause I'm only going to tell you once. You know where the marshal is?"

In a state of shock, she nodded.

"You find him, you hear? And you tell him Boyd Barlow has his woman. And unless he comes here alone, unarmed, Ruby Jewel won't live to see the morning. You got all that?''

She sniffled and struggled to pull herself together. But all she could see was Neville's body, and the ever-widening pool of blood.

"Get going, girl."

Through the layers of pain and shock, Patience looked up to see Ruby in the clutches of this madman.

The fear was gone from Ruby's eyes now. In its place was a slow, simmering fury. Her teeth were clenched, her jaw set. And despite the blood that ran from the wound in her temple, she looked every inch a queen. It gave Patience the courage she needed to pull herself together.

Boyd brandished the gun.

With a final glance at Neville's still form, Patience fled.

Chapter Nineteen

"Lots of people heard that gunshot, Marshal." Arlo's face was flushed as he shuffled into the jail to make his report. "But nobody saw the shooter. Haven't found anybody hurt, so I have to believe it was just some drunken cowboy shooting at the moon."

"Maybe." Quent lowered the unconscious Beau Baskin onto a cot, where he'd sleep off his liquor until morning. "Still, I think we ought to take another turn around the town, just in case."

"Okay. Where would you like me to start?"

"Why don't you head on over to the Golden Rule, and work your way back. I'll take the other end of town and work my way toward you. Between us, we ought to cover everything."

Arlo nodded and checked his gun before heading out.

Quent did the same. But as he was leaving he nearly collided with Patience Carter.

"Marshal." Her breath was coming in short gasps.

She couldn't seem to find her voice. And it seemed that at any moment her legs would fail her.

"Take it easy. Are you hurt?"

"No. No."

Quent caught her in his arms and led her inside the jail. He helped her to the seat behind his desk, then knelt and took her hands in his. He'd had years to hone his skill in offering comfort, security, a sense of calm authority to the citizens of his town, and getting them to move beyond shock to reveal necessary details. "Now, what seems to be the problem, Patience?"

"It's Ruby." Her voice trembled, and the tears started again.

"Okay. Easy, Patience. What about Ruby?"

"There's a gunman in her shop."

He felt the first quick jolt of fear. The gunshot. A trick? God in heaven, why hadn't he stayed with her? What if...?

"He said he'll kill her unless you come to her shop alone and unarmed. Oh, Marshal, he means it. He's already shot Neville Oakley."

Another stab of fear, but he pushed it aside. "Is Neville dead?"

"I don't know. The gunman wouldn't let me go to him."

"And Ruby? Has he..." He couldn't seem to form the words. "Is she all right?"

"There's blood on her face."

He thought, for the space of a moment, his heart might stop.

"But it doesn't look too bad. Just a cut and bruise."

He clamped down on his feelings.

"All right now, Patience. You're going to have to hold yourself together. You've got to be brave. I need you to find my deputy and have him wait, with as many armed men as he can find, near the edge of town. Then you need to fetch Doc Prentice. Tell him to get close to Ruby's shop, but not to show himself. Think you can do that?"

She swallowed, then nodded.

"Good girl. Now think, Patience. Did this gunman tell you his name?"

She nodded again. "Boyd Barlow."

She saw the instant change in Quent's face. Shock. Anger. And then something so dark, so frightening, she shrank from him.

He stood and began unbuckling his gun belt. Alone and unarmed. That's how Barlow wanted it played out.

There was no room for fear now. Or for what-ifs. The only thing that mattered now was Ruby. He would do whatever he had to. And if it meant his life for hers, he'd give it gladly. His life wasn't worth a damn without her.

Ruby knelt beside the still form of Neville Oakley. There was a pulse. Feeble, thready, but a faint heartbeat. Enough to assure her that for the moment the gentle giant was still alive. She wrapped the quilt around him, then shot a hateful glance at the gunman who stood at the window, watching the street.

"Your lover boy will be here soon," he said with a shrill laugh.

Quent would come, she knew. And because of his feelings for her, he would do as this monster ordered. He would come alone. Unarmed. And risk his life for hers.

She blinked away the tears that threatened and touched a hand to the rope of gold at her throat. "Oh, Papa," she whispered. "What shall I do? Please help me. I can't bear the thought of Quent sacrificing his life for mine. What shall I do?"

Almost at once she remembered something her father had told her when she was young.

It was on one of his infrequent visits. She had confided, tearfully, about the cruel taunts of classmates and teachers.

"Then it's time I shared this secret with you, Ruby," her father had said. "In my dealings with ordinary people I try to be a gentleman. In my business dealings I try to be an honorable man. But in my dealings with bullies I have a secret weapon."

"What is it, Papa?" she'd asked, eager to hear the secret that would end these acts of cruelty.

Onyx Jewel had smiled. "I never let them see my fear. Because bullies are cowards who hide behind cruel words, or behind a stick, or a rock, or a gun. They prey on those who can be hurt by their words, or their weapons."

"But I am afraid, Papa. I don't know how not to be."

Seeing that she still didn't understand, he'd said gently, "It isn't that I have no fear. Every man is afraid of something. But fear must be put aside for the moment, so that energy can be put to better use. In your battle with a bully, you have to fight like the bully does. Whether with words or guns or even tricks. Never let him see your fear. That way, he'll never get the best of you, Ruby. That way, the bully can never win.''

Those words had kept her sane when Sister Clothilde had locked her in the box for over an hour. And through the years those words had kept her going, despite the cruel taunts of others. She'd learned that there would always be another bully. But she would never let him get the best of her.

And now, remembering her father's words, she experienced a strange sense of calm. *Thank you, Papa. I remember. I'll fight like he does. This bully won't win. I promise.*

This was not a time for tears or weakness. What was needed now was courage. Fearlessness. Defiance.

She would watch and wait. And if even a single moment's opportunity presented itself, she would seize it.

The sky was awash with stars. Clouds scudded across a full moon. The main street was deserted, except for a few lovers taking advantage of the night to linger in each other's arms. Most of the townspeople had made their way back home, or to their wagons. The lights were going off at Millie Potter's boardinghouse.

Quent walked alone.

He loved this town. He knew every person in it. Knew their history, their secrets, had shared many of their joys and sorrows.

He'd never questioned why he did what he did. Had never given much thought to the fact that he was willing to step forward and fight their fights, risk his life for theirs. Oh, he'd seen the respect in their eyes for his father. But he hadn't stepped into his father's role just out of a need for respect. It had gone much deeper. He'd realized, when his father was shot dead by an outlaw, that a shining light had been extinguished.

Tonight, another shining light was threatened. Another outlaw had a need for vengeance.

Not this time, he vowed. Not while he still had a breath left in him.

He strode up to Ruby's shop.

From inside came Boyd Barlow's voice. "That's close enough, lawman. Lift those hands."

Quent raised his hands, then waited until the door was thrown open. He stepped inside.

The room was in darkness. As he peered around, a match was struck, the flame held to the wick of the lantern. In the blaze of light he saw Boyd Barlow yank Ruby to her feet and wrap an arm around her throat while he pointed a gun at her temple.

Just seeing it, Quent felt something dark and ugly beginning to take life inside him.

"Come on in, Marshal. The fun's just about to begin." Boyd cackled.

Quent stepped closer, needing to see for himself that Ruby was unharmed.

There was an ugly swelling at her temple, and blood on the side of her face.

Seeing the fury that leapt to his eyes, Boyd said, "I had to teach your fancy woman here how to take orders. But she learns real good. Don't you?"

When Ruby didn't respond, he tightened his grasp on her throat until she nearly gagged. "You hear me, woman? You learn real good, don't you?"

"Y-yes."

"That's better." He looked over at Quent. "Now, I'm only going to tell you one time, just like I told her. Only, if you don't do what you're told, it won't be you who pays, it'll be your woman. You understand?"

Quent nodded. "I understand completely, Barlow."

"You hiding a weapon?" Boyd demanded.

Quent shook his head.

"Good." Boyd waved the gun. "You stand right there where you can see. And your woman and I are going to lie on this cozy thing here." He shoved her ahead of him toward the chaise. "I figure, since the two of you had such a good time here, you might enjoy seeing how much fun your woman will have with a real man."

Out of the corner of his eye Quent caught a glimpse of Neville Oakley's body, still as death, beneath the quilt. But he kept his gaze on Ruby as she was pushed down onto the chaise.

Boyd Barlow was enjoying himself. Revenge was sweet, indeed. He could see the hatred, the fury, etched on the marshal's face. To add to his enemy's misery, Boyd sat on the chaise and tugged at the hem of Ruby's gown, pulling it up so high it revealed a length of shapely thigh.

He chuckled at the strangled oath that escaped the marshal's lips. "Maybe by the time I'm done with your woman, she'll be good enough to get a job over at Buck's saloon."

He ran his hand along her leg and felt himself harden. This was going to be fun. And there wasn't a damned thing the lawman could do about it. Except get himself killed.

"All right, woman. I'd like to see more." He didn't bother looking at Ruby. He was having too much fun watching the marshal squirm. "Take off that dress and show me what you showed your lover boy."

He gave a smug grin when he felt Ruby shift, saw her hand lift to the buttons of her gown.

Oh, the look in Quent Regan's eyes was worth all these weeks of waiting and planning and scheming.

"I'm going to make you so sorry for killing Ward," he said.

"It might have been my bullet that killed him." Quent's tone was chillingly soft and deadly. "But his death is on your hands."

"What?" Boyd started to rise. His gun hand was actually shaking with anger.

"You heard me," Quent said between clenched teeth. "Your brother was just a wild kid. But he was no killer. He just wanted to be like you. You're the reason he died, Boyd. You and your big plan to make a name for yourself by killing a marshal. If you hadn't planned that ambush, your brother would still be alive. Drinking in some saloon. And maybe getting a chance to grow up, and love a woman, and make a life for himself.''

"Liar! You're a damned liar." Ruby was forgotten now. Tormented by guilt at Quent's words, Boyd felt his vision cloud with an uncontrollable fury. "You take that back. You hear me? I said you take that back. I didn't kill my own brother. You did, you..."

Ruby had waited. Now, calculating that he'd completely forgotten about her, she brought her arm up with all the force she could manage, sending Boyd's gun flying out of his hand and across the room.

There was no time to waste. Quent leapt the distance separating him from the outlaw. The impact sent both men sprawling.

Quent's hands were at Boyd's throat, pressing hard on his windpipe. But before he could succeed in choking the life out of him, the outlaw brought his knee up, shoving Quent backward.

As Quent shook his head to clear his vision, Boyd gave a vicious kick to his jaw. For the space of several seconds Quent was blinded by pain. Stars swam in front of his eyes.

Despite his pain he scrambled to his feet before Boyd could land a second blow, and caught the outlaw squarely on the nose with a punch that had blood streaming down his face.

In retaliation Boyd brought a knee to Quent's groin that had him nearly doubled over in pain. Before he could straighten, the outlaw picked up a bowl filled with potpourri and broke it over the marshal's head. Quent staggered, straightened, then began pummeling Boyd's face and head with blows that sent him reeling into a table, knocking it over and sending the lantern, books, knickknacks flying in all directions, until at last, bruised and bloodied, Boyd dropped to his knees.

Across the room Ruby snatched up the gun and moved in close to point it at the outlaw. "I'm not as good a shot as the marshal," she warned. "But at this distance, I can't possibly miss."

Boyd lifted his hands in surrender.

With a satisfied smile, Ruby handed the gun to Quent. But her smile faded when the marshal removed his badge and tossed it aside, before pointing the gun at Boyd's temple.

"What do you think you're doing?" the outlaw demanded.

"This is no longer between a lawman and a gunman." Quent's tone was laced with cold, deadly fury. Unlike anything Ruby had heard before. The sound of it sent a chill along her spine.

"When you touched my woman, you made it personal, Barlow. So now I'm going to kill you. Not as Marshal Quent Regan. As a plain, ordinary man, who's had enough of scum like you."

It took Ruby the space of several moments to realize the impact of Quent's words.

"You can't mean this, Quent." But she knew, by the murderous look in his eyes, that he did. "Stop and think about all the people in this town who depend on you."

"And what good did that do you?" he demanded. "I wasn't here when you needed me. Couldn't stop this madman from touching you." He saw the blood, still seeping from the cut on her head. His voice nearly broke. "From hurting you."

"But I'm fine now. Safe now. Because of you."

"Not because of me." His tone was filled with self-loathing. "You saved yourself. And none of this would have happened to you except for me. It's me he's wanted all along. To make a name for himself as the man who killed Marshal Quent Regan. Well, from now on there is no Marshal Regan. What good was he? All he could do was come here, alone and unarmed, as this piece of trash demanded. And all because of that damned badge."

"But if you hadn't done what he'd ordered, if you'd come here armed, with half the town behind you, he would have killed me, Quent."

"Do you think I don't know that?" He allowed himself to touch her. One touch. Just to assure himself that she was really all right. Then he swung back to the outlaw. "And that's why I'm going to kill you, Barlow. To make sure you never have the chance to hurt an innocent again."

He leveled the gun, his finger gripping the trigger.

The outlaw couldn't take his eyes off the gun. His gun. A gun that had so easily snuffed out the lives of people who'd gotten in his way.

He was sweating now, the sweat mingling with the blood, running in little rivers down his face, down the front of his shirt.

"You killed that young rancher and his wife, didn't you, Barlow?"

The gunman nodded.

"You used my badge to gain their trust."

Again he nodded, watching as Quent's finger tightened.

"But you weren't content to just kill them and help yourself to their meager belongings. You had to brutalize the young woman before you ended her life, didn't you?"

"Yes," Boyd whispered, his body beginning to shake.

Quent leaned closer, until the tip of his gun was pressed to the outlaw's temple. "Animals like you don't deserve to live, Barlow. You need to be put out of your misery."

Boyd Barlow began to sob uncontrollably. "Don't shoot me. I don't want to die, Marshal."

"I told you. The marshal is dead. I'm just Quent Regan now. And I don't care about anything except putting an end to your miserable life."

Ruby touched a hand to Quent's arm. She could feel the tension humming through him, could feel the quivering of his muscles. Thinking quickly, she said, "I know how you feel, *chéri*. Truly I do. For I, too, wanted this man dead. But I'm begging you. If you would honor your father. If you would be worthy of the trust my father once placed in you, you must find the courage to turn away from this thing you wish to do. Please, Quent. Don't sink to his level. If you do, he will have won. And Papa said..." Her voice caught in her throat. "Papa said that bullies must never be allowed to win."

She saw the look on Quent's face. Saw that her words had touched him. "Oh, my darling," she said, and now the tears came, catching her by surprise. She pressed her cheek to his shoulder, muffling her words. "After all you've been through, you can't let him win. You're so much better than this. Please, Quent. Don't let him win. He isn't worth it. You're a man of such tremendous courage. Find the courage now to do the right thing."

For long moments Quent studied the outlaw and struggled for the need to satisfy his blood lust.

Finally, keeping his gun trained on Boyd, he dragged Ruby hard against his chest.

"Just let me hold you," he muttered. "Just for a few minutes. Until I'm sure you're really safe. Really here in my arms."

"I am, *chéri*. I'm fine now. And so are you. Oh," she said, sobbing uncontrollably now, "so are you."

That was how Arlo and Patience and Doc Prentice found them a few minutes later. Still clutching each other fiercely. Boyd Barlow still cowering on the floor.

And then, suddenly, the little shop erupted into chaos as the Jewel sisters and their husbands arrived, along with Carmelita and Rosario.

"Can't leave you two alone for a minute," Diamond said, staring around at the debris. "You go and get yourselves into another mess. What was it this time?"

"An outlaw," Ruby said between sniffles. "But Quent took care of him."

"Of course Quent Regan took care of him. That's what Quent does best," Diamond said.

"An outlaw? You see?" Carmelita started to cry and rushed over to gather Ruby to her ample bosom. "You leave the safety of your ranch, and this is what happens to you. You belong at home, where I can cook for you, and the wranglers can take care of you."

Pearl and Jade gathered around Ruby, hugging her fiercely, while their husbands studied the marshal and his prisoner.

"Looks like you two had quite a fight," Adam said as Arlo tied Boyd's hands behind him. "Think you broke his nose, Quent."

Quent shook his hand, which was beginning to swell. "Good," he muttered. "That makes me feel better."

"You've been thinking all along that Barlow was still in the territory, haven't you?" Cal asked.

Quent nodded, then glanced at Ruby surrounded by her family. "But I let my guard down tonight."

"We all did." Dan clapped a hand on his shoulder. "But I'd say you more than made up for it."

Doc Prentice, kneeling beside Neville, finished probing and poking while Patience held Neville's cold hands in hers.

"Two bullets," Doc announced. "One went clear through his side. Missed anything vital. The other's lodged in his shoulder. It'll take half the town to carry him to my place. Would you mind if I did the surgery here, Miss Ruby?''

"Not at all.'' She managed to break free of the women fluttering like moths around her. "Use the chaise. If it hasn't been broken, along with everything else.''

"He's too heavy to lift. I'll just see to him right here on the floor.'' Doc opened his black bag.

"Is he…is he going to be all right?'' Patience asked timidly.

"Neville's as strong as an ox. He'll be just fine in a week or two.''

"He was so brave. So noble. He actually risked his life for Miss Ruby.'' Patience burst into a fresh fit of sobbing, and Doc found himself having to hand her over to the Jewel sisters to be consoled.

"Is that so, Ruby?'' he asked. "Was Neville a hero?''

Ruby nodded. "Even after the first bullet, he kept on coming, determined to stop the gunman.''

"Well, that beats all.'' Doc shook his head. "Before I start on Neville, let's have a look at your cut, Ruby.''

She gave a little hiss of pain as he dabbed at it with disinfectant.

"You'll be just fine,'' he assured her.

"But of course. Papa always said I had a very hard head. Like him.''

Doc chuckled. "That he did. Onyx Jewel was the hardest, toughest man in Texas. And you've inherited a little of him, I see. In fact, all his daughters have a little of Onyx in them.'' He glanced over at Quent

Regan, still standing alone, his face revealing a battle with his emotions. "You seem to have survived this thing better'n the marshal."

Ruby's heart went out to Quent. How she wished they could find a moment alone, so that she could comfort him.

Just then Diamond gave a yelp.

"What is it?" Adam rushed to her side and she clutched his arm while her face went pale.

"Pain," she managed, between gritted teeth.

"Is that your first?" Doc asked from his position beside Neville.

"No." She waited until the worst of the pain was gone, then took several shallow breaths. "I've been having them for a while now. Just figured it was from all the excitement. But this one was worse than the others."

"Maybe you'd better lie on the chaise, Diamond," the doctor said.

"You think...?" Her face went chalk white. "But I can't have this baby now."

"And why not?" Ruby asked.

"Because I want it to be born at the ranch. Pa's ranch. It's only right."

Carmelita's tears were suddenly forgotten. Now she was as efficient as the doctor. "A baby will be born whenever and wherever it pleases. Now do as Doc Prentice says and lie down." She turned to the men. "You will all have to go. Unless you wish to help with the delivery."

That cleared the room in minutes. The only men

who remained were Doc and the unconscious Neville.

As Quent and his deputy led the prisoner away to the jail, Ruby stood at the window and watched. As if aware of her there, Quent turned. For the space of a heartbeat their gazes met and held. Then he was gone.

And Ruby had no time to think as she was swept up in the madness and majesty and miracle of birth.

Chapter Twenty

It was a fresh, glorious morning. A cool breeze danced through the open door, giving a hint of the approaching autumn. The sun rose over Widow's Peak, touching the clouds with an artist's palette of pinks and purples.

Ruby stood in the doorway studying the crowd that had suddenly taken over her tiny back room. On one side lay Neville Oakley, resting comfortably under the ministrations of Patience Carter, who hadn't left his side since Doc had removed the bullet from his shoulder.

On the other side of the room Diamond lay on the chaise, holding her newborn son.

Adam sat beside her, looking at the two of them with a smile so dazzling, it rivaled the sun.

During the height of the chaos Rosario had been dispatched to the ranch to fetch quilts and pillows. The family had turned the back room into a bunkhouse. Pearl and Cal, Jade and Dan, and Carmelita and Rosario all lay sleeping wherever they could find room on the crowded floor.

Looking at them, Ruby had to swallow several times before she could dislodge the lump in her throat. As a family they had banded together, to comfort her and then to welcome the newest member into their ranks. It was something she wouldn't soon forget.

Family. Her family.

With a last look she turned, picked up her shawl and let herself out.

Most of the outlying ranchers and their families had packed up and left at dawn, in order to get back to their chores. With the social behind them, the town was returning to normal.

Except for a few lingering wagons and carts, there were few people out on the street at such an hour, since it was too early for the merchants to open their shops.

Ruby made her way to the jail in time to see Millie Potter just hurrying away. As she opened the door she could smell the coffee and biscuits.

Just thinking about sharing breakfast with Quent had her heart racing.

With a bright smile she started across the room, then stopped.

Arlo was seated in the chair, his feet propped on the desk. His mouth was so full that when he spotted Ruby, he had to hurriedly chew and swallow before he could speak.

"Morning, Miss Ruby." Arlo took a swig of coffee, swished it around, then took another. "Did your sister have her baby?"

"Yes. A beautiful little boy." Ruby glanced around. "I expected to see the marshal here."

"No, ma'am. He's already gone."

"Gone?"

"Marshal Regan decided to take the prisoner to Abilene. Said he didn't want to keep him here in jail waiting for the visiting judge, who won't be through these parts for another couple of months. Said he couldn't stand looking at him for that long. Might forget his good intentions and shoot him."

Her heart fell. "How long did Marshal Regan expect to be gone?"

Arlo buttered another biscuit. "Didn't say. And I didn't ask. Could be a couple of days. Could be a week or more. But don't you worry, Miss Ruby." Arlo patted the gun in his holster. "I'm here to see that the town's kept safe."

"*Oui.* Thank you."

She turned away, feeling bitterly disappointed.

Once again, it seemed, Quent's duties would keep them apart. Not that she had any right to complain, she supposed. He was only doing what was required of a good lawman. But she'd needed the comfort of his arms. Had spent the whole long night anticipating this.

She took a long, deep breath and returned to her shop. Where she lost herself in the backbreaking work of cleaning the debris and restoring the rooms to order.

"Good day, Ruby."

Ruby's mouth dropped open. She climbed down

from her perch on the chair, where she'd been arranging a variety of jars and bottles on a shelf.

"Hello, Lavinia. Gladys. Effie."

The three women crowded through the doorway and swiveled their heads, trying to see everything at once.

"What..." Ruby had to swallow twice before she could find her voice. "What brings you ladies to my shop?"

"We've been planning to come since the day you opened." Lavinia, clearly the leader of the gossip pack, made a slow turn around the shop as she spoke. "But you know how it is. With one thing and another, there just wasn't time until today."

Ruby could see through the lie. But she was so surprised, and so pleased to have three new customers, she kept her thoughts to herself.

"Arlo said you were quite the brave little hero when that nasty outlaw captured you." Effie fingered a lacy shawl draped over a table. "He said the marshal claims he'd be dead now if it hadn't been for you."

"I'm sure it was a dreadful experience." Gladys lowered her voice, touching Ruby's arm as she spoke. "Why don't you tell us all about it, dear?"

Dear? Ruby had to work hard to swallow her laughter. "There isn't much to tell. I was caught unawares."

"Yes. All alone here in your shop. And the rest of the town still at the social." Gladys caught Ruby's hand in both of hers, while the other two women gathered close as though sharing secrets. "How did he happen to find you?"

"I suppose he thought a woman alone was an easy target."

"Arlo says he was following the marshal." Lavinia's eyes were boring into Ruby's. "Were you and Quent Regan here? Alone? While everyone else was at the social?"

"I... Yes." Ruby was tempted to lie. For her it would be as easy as stealing. Instead, she opted for the truth. "The marshal walked me home from the dance. When he left, the outlaw could see that I was alone."

"Well, Arlo says he picked the wrong woman when he picked a Jewel." Effie's tone made it sound as though she were defending her best friend. "And he said that Neville Oakley was a hero, too. Walked right into that outlaw's bullets to save you."

"*Oui.* He was so fine and brave. The thought of his sacrifice brings a tear to my eye," Ruby said softly.

"The whole town's talking about him. It's comforting to know that we have such a big, brave man in our midst," Gladys said.

"Did I hear that Diamond's baby was brought on by all the excitement?" Lavinia hated to be outdone by Gladys or Effie.

"I don't know if the excitement had anything to do with it. But Diamond did indeed have her baby just after the outlaw was taken away to jail. She has a new little son."

"A son."

The three hens clucked approvingly.

"What'll she call him?" Lavinia was practically twitching with excitement. So much news. And right from the Jewel women themselves.

"I think she and Adam will name him for my father," Ruby said.

"Why, yes. Of course. Onyx Jewel Winter. A fine name."

"I think perhaps Onyx Adam Winter," Ruby corrected gently.

"A fine name. Fine. They're both well?" Lavinia pressed.

"Very well. And still recovering in my back room."

"You don't think...?" Lavinia stared hard at the closed door. "Could we have just a peek at the new mother and child?"

"Not today," Ruby said firmly. "But perhaps in a few days, when Diamond is feeling up to seeing folks."

"You'll be sure to tell her we'd like to come calling," Effie said.

"*Oui.* Of course." Ruby could just imagine the look on Diamond's face if she had to put up with this silly prattle.

"Oh, my," Lavinia cried, glancing around. "Look at the hats."

"And the gowns," her friend Gladys said with a sigh.

"Something smells wonderful." Effie breathed deeply. "What is so enticing?"

"Potpourri." Ruby pointed to the small dishes

filled with the sweet-smelling concoction. "Mostly dried flowers," she explained. "And the other lovely scents are coming from these vials and jars of my mother's skin balm. Would you care to try a sample?"

The three women gathered around as she opened a small vial and poured a bit into each outstretched hand.

"Rub it gently over any part of your body, and it will soften and soothe. It is especially good after a day in this Texas sun."

The women rubbed and patted and sniffed.

"Oh, my," Lavinia said. "If it feels this good on my hand, think what it will feel like on my face."

"*Oui.* I give you my promise. If you do not feel better, you may return the vial and I will refund your money."

"You will?" Gladys picked up a big jar. "What do you call it?"

"I am calling it Madeline's Balm," Ruby said with a trace of pride.

"Well, I have to have this." Gladys hugged it to her bosom. "I'll have the smoothest skin in Hanging Tree."

"Oh, no, you won't, Gladys Witherspoon." Lavinia Thurlong snatched a bigger jar from the shelf. "It won't be smoother than mine."

Not to be outdone, Effie Spitz helped herself to a jar, as well.

"I think I'll try on a gown while I'm here," Lavinia said.

"I was just thinking the same thing." Gladys beat

a path across the room to where the dresses were hung.

"And I need a bonnet." Effie made her way to the front window, where Ruby had set up a complete display of bonnets, feathers and pins.

The three women were still busy trying on every gown, shawl and bonnet in the shop when the door opened and Ruby looked up to see Quent standing in the doorway.

With his clothes and boots dust covered from the trail, and his guns and holsters at each hip, he looked completely out of place in this frilly shop. He removed his wide-brimmed hat and shook it against his thigh, sending a puff of dust around him.

A light came into Ruby's eyes that hadn't been there moments before. And her heart started doing strange things. Missing beats, then fluttering wildly.

"Marshal." With the three town gossips watching, she tried to appear calm and professional. But her palms were sweating. And she had to press them to the table in front of her to remain standing.

"Ruby." He knew she had customers, but they were a blur. All he could see was Ruby, standing there looking so beautiful it made his throat ache.

"I...thought you were still in Abilene."

"I turned over my prisoner to the sheriff in Oak Creek." He took several steps toward her, until the gun and holster at his hip bumped a small table, sending the display of fancy buttons flying in all directions.

At once he dropped to his knees and began picking them up. Ruby hurried over to kneel beside him.

When all the buttons had been retrieved, they emptied them into a dish, then got to their feet.

Before she could turn away, Quent caught her hands. "Ruby, I...need to talk to you."

"Oui?" She gave him a bright smile. "What about?"

"About...things." He became aware that the women in the shop had stopped chattering and were watching and listening.

"Things." Ruby, too, had noticed the change in her customers. "Can it not wait?"

"No, dammit." He gave a hiss of frustration. "I mean, no. It can't wait. Can we talk back there?" He nodded toward the back room.

"My family is there."

"Still?"

"Oui. They will probably be there for days, until Doc Prentice says Diamond can make the trip back to her ranch."

He ran a hand through his hair in a gesture of futility. "Then we'll have to talk here."

"No!" Nerves had her nearly shouting as she backed away until her hips were pressed to her desk. Couldn't he see who was in her shop? Didn't he realize that every word would be repeated? "I... don't think that's a good idea."

"Ruby." He wasn't about to be stopped now. He gripped her by the upper arms. "I've just spent the whole night on the trail, with nothing to do but think. I want this thing settled between us now."

"This...thing?"

"These feelings. I can't keep them bottled up inside me any longer. I know there are some who would say we're all wrong for each other. You have a wicked sense of justice. And you're wild and irreverent. All the things I can't be. But maybe that's why you touch me the way you do. You fill all the empty places in my life. Last night..." His hands tightened a moment, then gentled. He moved them up her arms, across her shoulders. His voice, too, gentled. "Last night was the best night and the worst night of my whole life."

Lavinia nearly choked.

Gladys cleared her throat.

Effie giggled.

He looked over, and for the first time realized that he was playing to a very attentive audience. His voice was a growl of anger. "Don't you ladies have someplace to go?"

"Why, no, Marshal. We're here to shop. But don't mind us," Lavinia said breezily. "You go right ahead with whatever you have to say."

Through gritted teeth he asked, "Where's Patience?"

"She's in the other room. Tending to Neville Oakley."

"You'd better call her out here." There was a fire in his eyes. "Right now."

"But—"

"Call her, Ruby." A little muscle was working in his jaw.

"Patience," Ruby shouted. "Could you come in here a moment?"

The young woman stuck her head out the door. "Do you need some help?"

"No…" Ruby began.

"Yes." Quent picked Ruby up and tossed her over his shoulder. "You'd better take care of the shop. Ruby's going to be busy for a while."

"Where are you taking her?" Patience demanded.

"To jail. It's the only place left in this whole damned town that isn't crowded." He stalked off, carrying Ruby like a sack of grain.

Lavinia Thurlong, Gladys Witherspoon and Effie Spitz nearly fell over each other to pay for their purchases, so they could follow along at a distance.

Arlo looked up as Quent stormed into the jail and set Ruby on her feet.

"Morning, Marshal. What's Miss Ruby done this time?"

"Go outside and sweep up, Arlo," Quent said.

"Already did."

"Then do it again." Quent handed him the broom and shoved him out the door, locking it behind him.

Ruby was so furious, she was practically breathing fire. "Do you realize what you just did?"

"I got rid of Arlo," he said smugly.

"I mean, by carrying me off to jail again. You heard your deputy. That's what the whole town will think. What has Ruby Jewel done this time?"

"I don't give a—" He bit back his oath and said, "I don't care what the town thinks, Ruby. All I care about is what you think."

"About what?"

"About us. About you and me. I've had plenty of time to think this through. I'll give up the law, if that's what you want."

"And why would I want that?"

"Because you can't stand my badge of authority. You said so yourself."

She shrugged. "Maybe I did say that. Maybe there was a time when I meant it. But not now. Besides, what else could you do? You said yourself you've been a lawman all your life."

"I don't know. I could try farming. Or ranching."

"And what would the town of Hanging Tree do for a marshal?"

"They'd find somebody else. Arlo, maybe." Even as he said it, he winced.

"Enough of this foolish talk. The town needs you. And you need this town. I won't hear of you giving up the law."

"You mean you'd be willing to be married to a lawman?"

"Marriage?" She drew herself up to her full height. "I haven't heard any talk of marriage."

"That's because I haven't gotten around to it yet. But I'm getting there. Now, there's the matter of where we'd live. Your ranch is too far from town. And my job doesn't allow for more than a room in the back of the jail."

"*If* you were to ask me to marry you, and *if* I were to accept," she said carefully, "there is a simple solution."

"What?"

"We could hire Farley Duke to add another story to my shop. We could live above it. Of course, it will be filled with frilly dresses and sweet-smelling jars and pots and vials and all manner of feminine frills."

"And with my luck I'd probably have six strapping sons who'd have to walk through their mother's prissy shop every day of their lives.''

Her eyes widened. ''Is that what you're hoping for? Six strapping sons?''

He shrugged. ''I'd settle for three. And maybe three girls for you.'' He was staring at her in a strange new way. ''Would you, Ruby? Like children, I mean?''

''At least half a dozen,'' she said on a sweet sigh. ''I was always so alone. It was my dream to be part of a big family. But I think you've forgotten something.''

''I have? What?''

''A proper proposal.''

''You mean…on my knees?''

She smiled. ''*Oui*. On your knees.''

''Ruby, I'd crawl over broken glass for you. Or through fire.'' He dropped to his knees and caught her hands. ''Ruby, please say you'll marry me.''

''That is not a very romantic proposal.''

''Dammit, I love you. I want to marry you. Do you love me? Will you marry me?'' He waited, feeling his heartbeat stop.

She made him suffer a moment longer. Then she could bear no more. ''*Oui*. Oh, I do love you, Quent. And I will marry you. On one condition.''

''Anything.''

''That you will never again offer to be a farmer or a rancher.''

He stood, then pulled her close. ''I give you my word,'' he murmured, covering her mouth with his.

''*Bon*. Now,'' she muttered against his lips, ''let's

go back to my shop and share our happy news with my family.''

Just then Arlo began pounding on the door. And through the window they could see Lavinia, Gladys, Effie and a crowd beginning to form. All were pointing at the jail and grinning like fools.

As Ruby started to pull away Quent gathered her close.

Against her temple he whispered, ''Oh, Ruby, have mercy. I've been wanting to hold you like this for so long.''

Giving in to the heat that surged through her veins, she wrapped her arms around his waist and pressed her lips to his throat. ''So have I.''

He took a long, deep breath. ''There's a cot in the back room. And the door is locked.''

''But my family…''

''Ruby, you said yourself they'll be there for days.''

''And the townspeople…''

''Have already figured out what it took us all this time to learn.'' He nibbled at the corner of her mouth. ''At least for the next hour, let's just forget about everyone except us.''

''Us.'' It was, Ruby thought as she followed him to his room and lost herself in his kisses, the sweetest word she'd ever heard.

And then there was no time to think, as with sighs and kisses and tender touches, he took her to that special place where only lovers can go.

Epilogue

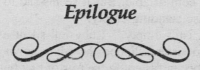

Carts and wagons clogged the main street. Throngs of ranchers and their families streamed into the Golden Rule. Everyone was wearing their Sunday best. And their best had become much better since they'd begun frequenting Miss Ruby Jewel's shop.

This day was the biggest in the town of Hanging Tree. Bigger even than the social. And all because two of its most popular citizens were being married.

Upstairs, in the brand-new suite of rooms above her shop, Ruby was surrounded by her sisters.

"Hold still," Pearl commanded as she laced the ribbons of Ruby's sheer white chemise. "I can't believe how much gossip you two have fueled. The whole town is talking about the fact that their marshal spent more nights here than he did at the jail."

"He can't stay away from me. I can't help it if he flaunts his love."

"If you don't let me finish lacing this, you'll be flaunting more than love." Pearl finished tying with a flourish, until Ruby's bosom was modestly covered.

"Now this," Jade said, helping her sister step into frothy white petticoats.

"Ruby," Diamond called from across the room where she sat nursing little Onyx. "I wish you'd reconsider. I love these rooms. They're big and spacious and comfortable. But it seems sad to see Pa's ranch house standing empty."

"But it isn't empty." Ruby fell silent a moment as her two sisters slipped the white gown over her head and began fastening the row of tiny buttons that ran from waist to neck. "You said yourself that you'll probably stay there a month or two, so that Carmelita can give you a hand with the baby."

"And then what?"

Ruby shrugged. "I don't know. I only know that my heart is here in town, with Quent."

Diamond fastened the front of her gown, then, with the baby at her shoulder, crossed the room and stared at her sister. "Oh, my. I think it's easy to see why Quent was smitten. Ruby Jewel, you're as pretty as a brand-new calf prancing in a pasture of clover." She gathered Ruby close for a hug. "I'm so happy for you. I know how happy Adam has made me. And now little Onyx. And I want the same kind of happiness for you and Quent."

"Thank you, *chérie*." Ruby's eyes sparkled. "Motherhood has changed you."

"In what way?" Diamond studied her reflection in the looking glass, while the others merely grinned.

"For one thing, you are wearing a gown without complaint."

Diamond chuckled. "You're right. I forgot to grumble. Well, the truth is, these gowns you made me—with the buttons down the front—have made my last few weeks very comfortable.''

"You see. There is something to be said for dressing like a lady.''

Diamond shook her head. "For a couple of months. Then it's back to buckskins for me. I'm a rancher, remember?''

Patience entered, carrying a bouquet of wildflowers. For a moment she could only stare at the three sisters in their pale pink, yellow and blue gowns. And at Ruby, in a white confection that would rival a queen's. Then, her eyes misty, she thrust the flowers into Ruby's hands. "Neville and I picked these. We wanted them to be as special as you are.''

"*Merci*. They are beautiful. Where is our town hero?''

Patience flushed, clearly pleased by the way the town had embraced Neville since his heroic actions. "My new husband...'' Oh, how she loved that word. Almost as much as she loved hearing him call her wife. "Is outside. He doesn't feel right coming into your shop. Says it's too fancy, and he's afraid he'll break something. But he's the same way in his big rooms behind the livery. Ever since I fixed them up with some pretty rugs and new chairs, he's been skittish.''

Ruby laughed. "It's the same with Quent. Even now, he feels clumsy and out of place in the shop.''

"Speaking of Quent,'' Patience said softly, "he's right outside the door. Pacing.''

"As he should be,'' Jade said in her lilting voice. "But he isn't alone. Our husbands are with him. And Gil and Daniel.'' She turned to Ruby. "It was sweet of you to ask Daniel to carry your ring. And Gil is bursting with pride over the fact that he's going to give away the bride."

"And why not? They're family. And this is a special day for our family."

When Patience took her leave, Quent grabbed the door before it could close and forced his way through.

"You mustn't see the bride, Quent. You have to leave." Pearl started toward him, but at the look in his eyes, she took a step back.

"You can't keep me out any longer," Quent said, daring them to argue. "I need to see Ruby."

Seeing the way he was sweating, Pearl turned to her sisters and whispered, "I think we ought to take pity on him. What do you say?"

Diamond and Jade nodded. With quick kisses on Ruby's cheek, they slipped from the room.

Quent couldn't stop staring at Ruby. She was a vision. Suddenly all his nerves were forgotten. This was why he'd dressed in a fancy suit. And why he'd permitted the entire town to watch him make a fool of himself in church. And why he'd allowed himself to be caught up in all the silly festivities of the past weeks. Dinner at the widow Purdy's. Cake and lemonade with gossips Lavinia, Gladys and Effie, who acted like fussy old aunts. And elderberry wine at Millie Potter's, who kept saying she'd known all along that he'd fallen for Ruby. When he hadn't even known it himself.

But here she was. Still taking his breath away. And the need for her just grew every day, until all he could think about was seeing Ruby, being with her, holding her.

"Nervous?" she asked.

He stepped closer and took her hand. "I was. But not now. What about you?"

She shook her head. "How could I be nervous, with my big, brave, strong lawman beside me?" She glanced at his lapel. "I didn't think you'd wear your badge today."

"Why not? I'm still a marshal. Even on my wedding day."

She lifted her hands to it and began to unpin it.

His eyes narrowed slightly. "I thought you said you didn't mind my badge?"

"I don't." She slipped it off and casually tossed it down. "But that isn't your badge."

He looked puzzled. "I don't understand."

"This is." She opened her palm to display an old, dented, badly worn badge that winked in the sunlight.

"My father's badge." He felt a lump in his throat. His voice was gruff. "I thought it had been lost in the scuffle with Boyd Barlow. How did you...? Where did you...?"

"Even though I am about to marry a man of the law, it is difficult to give up everything in my less-than-perfect past. I managed to slip it away from Boyd Barlow while he was...otherwise engaged. He, more than any other, deserved my petit vengeance, *chéri*."

"Remind me to never get on your bad side," he said with a laugh.

She pinned the badge to his lapel, then stood back to admire. "*Oui.* It looks right. Perfect."

He hauled her into his arms. Against her cheek he muttered, "Oh, Ruby. You're the one who's perfect. Promise me you'll never change."

"*Oui.* I promise. And I promise something else. I will love you, my beloved lawman, for all time."

"I remember when you called me a *cochon,*" he said with a laugh.

She returned the laughter. "You are a *cochon.* But you are my *cochon.* And a most loved one."

The kiss she gave him was long and slow and deep.

A knock sounded on the door, and Diamond's muffled voice could be heard calling them to hurry. "There's a churchful of people waiting for you two."

As they joined her family for the walk to the church, Ruby felt her heart nearly bursting with happiness.

"Merci, Papa," she whispered. "For giving me my heart's desire. The family I always dreamed of. A chance for a new life in Texas. And best of all, a man who loves me...just as I am."

The sun slipped from behind a cloud, bathing them in golden rays. And Ruby smiled, feeling the benediction of her father's love upon all of them. This was Onyx Jewel's finest gift to his daughters. The fulfillment of his promise to be with them always.

* * * * *

Take 4 bestselling love stories FREE

Plus get a FREE surprise gift!

Harlequin Historicals presents an exciting medieval collection

THE KNIGHTS OF CHRISTMAS

With bestselling authors

Suzanne BARCLAY

Margaret MOORE

Debborah SIMMONS

Available in October
wherever Harlequin Historicals are sold.

WANT WESTERNS?

Harlequin Historicals has got 'em!

In October, look for these two
exciting tales:

WILD CARD by Susan Amarillas
A lady gambler wanted for murder falls for a
handsome sheriff

THE UNTAMED HEART by Kit Gardner
A dashing earl succumbs to a reckless woman
in the American West

In November, watch for
two more stories:

CADE'S JUSTICE by Pat Tracy
A schoolteacher heals the soul of the wealthy
uncle of one of her students

TEMPLE'S PRIZE by Linda Castle
Two paleontologists battle each other on a dig,
and uncover their hearts

Four new Westerns from four terrific authors!
Look for them wherever Harlequin Historicals
are sold.

Harlequin® Historical

COMING NEXT MONTH FROM

HARLEQUIN HISTORICALS

- **THE KNIGHTS OF CHRISTMAS**
  by **Suzanne Barclay, Margaret Moore** and **Deborah Simmons**
  Three bestselling Harlequin Historical authors bring you this
  enchanting Christmas anthology filled with heartwarming tales
  of yuletide romance from bygone eras.
  HH #387 ISBN# 28987-1 $4.99 U.S./$5.99 CAN.

- **WILD CARD**
  by **Susan Amarillas**, author of WYOMING RENEGADE
  Lady fugitive Clair Travers finds there is no escaping the
  law when her heart is captured by handsome county sheriff
  Jake McConnell.
  HH #388 ISBN# 28988-X $4.99 U.S./$5.99 CAN.

- **THE ARRANGEMENT**
  by **Lyn Stone**, author of THE WICKED TRUTH
  A beautiful reporter who sets out to expose the scandals of
  mysterious composer Jonathan Chadwick finds her own soul
  laid bare by his passion.
  HH #389 ISBN# 28989-8 $4.99 U.S./$5.99 CAN.

- **THE UNTAMED HEART**
  by **Kit Gardner**, author of TWILIGHT
  In a Wild West town, a peace-loving earl and a fiery ranch
  hand battle against their love as they both become embroiled in
  a deadly mystery.
  HH #390 ISBN# 28990-1 $4.99 U.S./$5.99 CAN.

DON'T MISS THESE FOUR GREAT TITLES AVAILABLE NOW:

#383 THE LIEUTENANT'S LADY
Rae Muir

#384 RUBY
Ruth Langan

#385 THE FOREVER MAN
Carolyn Davidson

#386 TO TAME A WARRIOR'S HEART
Sharon Schulze

Free Gift Offer

As Seen on TV!

With a Free Gift proof-of-purchase
from any Harlequin® book, you can receive
a beautiful cubic zirconia pendant.

This stunning marquise-shaped stone is a genuine cubic
zirconia—accented by an 18" gold tone necklace.
(Approximate retail value $19.95)

Send for yours today...
compliments of ⬥HARLEQUIN®

To receive your free gift, a cubic zirconia pendant, send us one original proof-of-purchase, photocopies not accepted, from the back of any Harlequin Romance®, Harlequin Presents®, Harlequin Temptation®, Harlequin Superromance®, Harlequin Intrigue®, Harlequin American Romance®, or Harlequin Historicals® title available at your favorite retail outlet, together with the Free Gift Certificate, plus a check or money order for $1.65 U.S./$2.15 CAN. (do not send cash) to cover postage and handling, payable to Harlequin Free Gift Offer. We will send you the specified gift. Allow 6 to 8 weeks for delivery. Offer good until December 31, 1997, or while quantities last. Offer valid in the U.S. and Canada only.

Free Gift Certificate

Name: _____

Address: _____

City: _____ State/Province: _____ Zip/Postal Code: _____

Mail this certificate, one proof-of-purchase and a check or money order for postage and handling to: HARLEQUIN FREE GIFT OFFER 1997. In the U.S.: 3010 Walden Avenue, P.O. Box 9071, Buffalo NY 14269-9057. In Canada: P.O. Box 604, Fort Erie, Ontario L2Z 5X3.

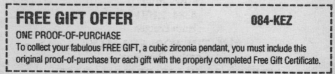

FREE GIFT OFFER   084-KEZ

ONE PROOF-OF-PURCHASE
To collect your fabulous FREE GIFT, a cubic zirconia pendant, you must include this original proof-of-purchase for each gift with the properly completed Free Gift Certificate.

084-KEZR